BEYOND THE SETUP

NIKKI WITT

Copyright © 2026 by Nikki Witt

All rights reserved.

No part of this book may be reproduced in any form or by any electronic or mechanical means, including information storage and retrieval systems, without written permission from the author, except for the use of brief quotations in a book review.

Developmental Editing: Memos in the Margins

Proofreading & Formatting: Kristen's Red Pen

Cover Designer: Aubrey Labitigan

To my real-life Peter.
Thanks for showing us exactly how we deserve to be treated.
This story wouldn't exist without you.

AUTHOR'S NOTE ON CONTENT

This book contains themes related to domestic violence and emotional abuse. While the story centers on healing, growth, and finding safe love after trauma, some scenes may be difficult for readers with similar lived experiences. Please take care of yourself and read at your own pace.

CHAPTER ONE

NESSA

My phone buzzes under my pillow for the millionth time in the last thirty minutes. Nora is probably worried about me, and I know I should answer the phone. Instead, I roll over and let out an obnoxiously loud huff. I haven't slept this late in years, but I'm just not ready to face this day yet.

"Mrrrow." The sound startles me out of my pity party as Lorelai jumps up onto the bed and walks directly onto my chest.

I know she's probably just hungry—she's used to eating much earlier—but her continued meows are starting to sound a little judgmental.

"I know. I know. I'm getting up." She's right. *Get it together, Vanessa!*

Okay, my name isn't actually Vanessa. It's just Nessa, but if Lore could talk, I know she'd be using my 'full' name right now just like my dad would. My mom wanted to name me Vanessa, but my dad convinced her to stick with the name they'd actually be calling me. Despite that, he loved to yell 'Vanessa!' anytime I got into trouble, and the tradition stuck. This definitely feels like a full not-name situation.

I force myself into a seated position and shake myself awake.

I'm mid yawn when my phone buzzes again. This time, I reach for it and immediately see a string of text messages and three missed calls—all from Nora.

> **NORA**
> Let's get coffee. Daily Grind at 9?
>
> **NORA**
> I know this is hard. Talk to me.
>
> **NORA**
> Nessa. Please answer me.
>
> **NORA**
> It's 10:15. I'm busting your door down in 10 minutes if I don't hear from you.

I chuckle knowing she isn't kidding. I'll have a Kool-Aid man sized hole in my door if I don't put her out of her misery soon. I do feel bad for making her worry, but once I finally cried myself to sleep last night, I was out like a light.

> **NESSA**
> I'm alive.
>
> **NESSA**
> Just woke up. Be there in 15!

Three little dots pop up before I even send the second message. I don't want to keep her waiting any more than I already have, so I grab a sweatshirt, throw on the same leggings I wore yesterday, and race out the door.

"Large brown sugar espresso with..." the barista begins, obvious annoyance in her tone. I quickly grab my drink before she has to recite every last ingredient and flash her my biggest smile. Maybe she'll remember that I'm kind—not crazy—the next time she makes my drink. I do get it, though. My order is a bit obnoxious, but it's so good. I toss a couple dollars into the tip jar, thank the barista again, and join Nora in the oversized chairs at the back of the coffee shop.

"How'd you snag these?" I ask as I plop down beside her. These chairs—gigantic, faux leather armchairs that are squishy in all the right places from overuse—are almost always taken. That's how comfortable they are, and even though they're hideous, Nora and I have spent many mornings here plotting how we could smuggle them into our cars.

"Someone was leaving right when I walked in. I damn near tackled that old lady to save your spot." She laughs, and I quickly scan the coffee shop to see if she's kidding.

"Oh my god. Nora! She's like ninety."

"Not my fault I'm faster than her." My eyes widen in horror, and she lets out a loud belly laugh. "I'm kidding, Nessa. She probably does wish she was faster than me though. These chairs are like clouds."

"I thought I was going to have to pay for her order or something. Your sense of humor worries me sometimes."

"I know." She tosses her blonde hair over her shoulders and shrugs, completely unfazed, before completely changing the subject. "It's time to get yourself back out there. It's been a year! I know you're worried about Emma, but you can't use that excuse forever. Now that you've got some free time, let me set you up. Please."

She's giving me her best puppy dog eyes with her bottom lip pushed out, but I'm not falling for it. "It's not *free time*. It's forced," I counter.

"I know it is, but this is the perfect way to keep your mind busy while she's gone."

She's got a point. Emma is only one, still a baby if you ask me, and every second that she's visiting her dad is pure torture. I *do* need a distraction. I'm just not sure I need this kind of distraction.

"Fine. I'll think about it." It comes out harsher than I mean for it to, but I don't know if I'm ready. Nora, of all people, should know that. We became inseparable in the fifth grade, even though we'd known each other from the playground for years. By the third week of school, the teacher moved us to opposite sides of the classroom in hopes that we'd actually get our work done in a timely manner. It worked, but every other moment—recess, lunch, after school, weekends—we spent together.

When my high school boyfriend broke my heart, she was there. When she got pregnant our senior year, I was there. Even when I went off to college three hours away, our bond was impenetrable. We spent the majority of every university break together and talked on the phone every single day, despite the physical distance between us. She knows everything about me and there's nothing I can't be honest about with her, which is precisely why she already knows I plan to be celibate for the rest of my life.

"Oh my god. This muffin is so good," I say with a moan in a half-hearted attempt to change the subject.

"Let me try it! What kind is it?"

"Blueberry cheesecake," I respond as Nora takes a monstrous bite out of the cream cheese-filled center. "Dude, that was the best part! You owe me a muffin next time."

"Deal," she says, her mouth still full of muffin. "Don't think for one second that I don't see what you're trying to do."

"Okay, fine! Tell me about him." I let the words out in one big huff of air like it pains me to give in. "It has to be better than some Tinder creep, right?"

Nora has been trying to convince me to get back out there for months now. I have steadfastly refused, and apparently, she's decided to take matters into her own hands. She's moved on from the idea of me getting a Bumble date or even just a hookup. In her eyes, anything is better than spending every other weekend shut in and feeling sorry for myself. Last month, she stole my phone and created three different dating profiles for me, but I haven't opened any of the apps. I have enough going on without adding dating randos to the mix. She's promptly moved on to the idea of a blind date instead, which I guess is better... ever so slightly.

"Finally!" she half screeches in exasperation. "His name is Peter. He's been Rob's best friend since they were in diapers. Literally, they've been friends since they were like two. He's funny and not weird and *not* Matthew."

"Not weird?" I chortle. "Now I'm convinced he is weird. Like *40 Year Old Virgin collectable figurines covering his house* weird or something."

"Only *still likes Pokémon* weird," she giggles. "I promise he's not that weird."

I'm worried about many things when it comes to dating again but how weird he is isn't one of them. Well, at least it wasn't.

"Do you *actually* know him? Does he know about me? Did he agree to a blind date? Does—" Nora interrupts me before I can spiral any further.

"Woah. Slow your roll, lady. He's been in my life since I met Rob, so yes, I really do know him pretty well. I mentioned it to Rob, and he thinks he'll be up for it. I didn't want Rob to mention it to him until I'd convinced you. So... can I ask him now?"

"Fine. Just know I will resent you forever if this ends badly. Like forever, forever." Despite my attempts to keep my voice and breathing calm, it's becoming quite apparent that this conversation is getting my anxiety going.

"Nessa. It's okay. I know him. Rob vouches for him. He's not Matthew," Nora reassures me, though Rob's vouching for Peter is not the reassurance she hopes it to be.

Nora had Daisy a few weeks before we graduated high school, and Rob came into their lives when she was about the same age that Emma is now. At first, Rob stepped up and helped Nora raise Daisy like she was his own. He provided things that a struggling teen mom just couldn't and even got up in the middle of the night when Daisy did.

Gradually, though, he stopped being quite so awesome. He stopped spending time with them, instead opting to play video games every waking hour. He doesn't help cook or clean, and Daisy spends more time with Nora's dad than at home with Rob while Nora is working. He is twenty times better than Daisy's biological father but still has a lot of room for improvement, if you ask me.

I trust Nora's judgment and know she wouldn't suggest this if she thought Peter would hurt me or Emma in any way, but being friends with Rob is not a good start for him. Despite my reservations, she's not wrong about my need for a distraction.

"Rob can ask him as long as we double. I don't know if I can ever see myself getting serious again, though. I refuse to overlook any red flags. I will show Emma what a real man looks like, or I'll show her how badass her mom is for doing it all on her own. Settling is not an option." The tremble in my voice is evident. Saying it outloud feels so empowering yet so daunting. My list of green flags that any potential partner would have to check off is a mile long, but I'm determined not to repeat my previous mistakes.

"Yasss! I am texting him right now." Nora squeals with the delight of a five-year-old who's just been handed an ice cream cone. "It doesn't have to be serious. He can be a friend with benefits for all I care. Let's face it, it's been so long you're starting to get cobwebs down there. It's a serious problem that we must remedy immediately."

I can feel my face redden as soon as the words are out of her mouth. Nora and I are very open about our sex lives, and even though I am very much regretting that right now, she is not wrong. I haven't gotten laid since before Emma was born. It is long overdue, but did she really have to announce it to the entire coffee shop? "Shh! I'm well aware that it's been too long." I laugh and jab my thumb towards the table next to us. "But that guy over there did not need to visualize cobwebs on my lady bits!"

"Maybe if more people knew, you wouldn't be in this predicament." Nora smirks as she pulls out her phone.

I swear I see her green eyes sparkle as she announces, "Peter said he's in!"

"He said yes, already? That was fast."

"I'm already planning our double date in my head."

I don't even know what to think about how quickly he agreed to this whole setup. I know I told her she could ask him, but I was not expecting him to be quite so eager.

As we head to our cars, I fiddle with the best way to tell her I've changed my mind. My life is an absolute mess right now. A serious relationship is the last thing I need. Oh my god. What if Rob knows about my cobwebs and told Peter? No. Nope. Can't do this. But before I can roll my window down and tell her to cancel, she's gone.

CHAPTER TWO

NESSA

"Aghhh!" I half scream with frustration as I slam my phone down onto the couch. This is the third time tonight that I've tried FaceTiming Matthew with no luck. I just want to talk to Emma and tell her good night. She's never gone to bed without Mama's kisses and a softly whispered 'good night.' I know the kisses aren't plausible, but I can at least tell her I love her before she goes to sleep if Matthew would answer the damn phone. This is the very first time in her little life that she's been away from me for more than a couple hours, and it's all I can do to distract myself out of worst case scenario mode.

Almost a year ago to the day, I loaded Emma and as many of our belongings as I could into the car while Matthew was at work... or with one of his mistresses. Actually, I really don't know where he was, but I saw the opportunity and knew I had to take it. For my sake and for hers. She deserves to grow up in a happy, stable home, and not in the middle of fighting and chaos.

Without warning, I'm instantly transported back to our bedroom the morning we finally left.

Emma and I are snuggled together on the bed, still half asleep, when Matt comes stomping down the hall.

I jolt awake, instinctively tightening my hold on my baby, as the bedroom door slams into the wall. "Where the hell are my socks, Nessa? I'm late and sick of my stuff not being where it should be. How are you not smart enough to put laundry away properly?"

"Um," I stammer, rubbing sleep from my eyes. Somehow, Emma hasn't budged. She is in her favorite snuggle spot—nestled right up next to my breast. Fireworks could have been going off inside the house, and she'd sleep right through it as long as she was snuggled up with me, which is good news because I can already tell this is going to escalate quickly. "I finished folding and putting away all the laundry last night after I got Emma to sleep. By myself, might I add. You'd know that if you'd been home before 3:00 a.m. Did you check your drawer?"

"What time I get home is none of your business. Of course I checked my drawer. I'm not an idiot!"

I wiggle myself free from Emma's squishy embrace to help find his socks. I just want him to leave us in peace for the rest of the day, and if that means finding a grown man's socks for him, so be it. Days spent with just Emma and me are my favorite. Though she is just a few months old and can't do much, we fill our days with fun regardless: walking to the little pond near our house to watch the geese and ducks frolic or reading book after book with her curled in my lap. I just need to get him on his way.

"Here they are. I accidentally put them in my drawer instead of yours. My bad. It was late and—"

"Yeah. That is definitely 'your bad.' You—" Matt blurts without even letting me finish.

"Bye now. Have a day," I cut him off right back. I can't be bothered to even suggest he have a great day like I usually would. 'Have a day' is the best he's going to get from me after that little temper tantrum.

Cutting him off might not have been my wisest choice, though, given his mood this morning. Before I can even consider back tracking, the steaming cup of coffee he'd been holding smashes against the wall mere inches from my head. The hot, brown liquid splashes the side of my face, stinging instantly, and puddles all over the bed right next to where

Emma sleeps. The loud smash jolts her awake causing her to wail with all her little might.

The shards of glass and coffee mess can wait until we are alone and our nerves are settled. I gently scoop her into my arms and snuggle back into bed next to her. My face burns where the coffee landed, a chunk of coffee mug sliced the heel of my foot in my rush to grab Emma, and my heart pounds a mile a minute. But finally, I hear Matt's truck pulling out of the driveway and breathe a sigh of relief. Emma is back in her happy place and everything is okay for now. I've put up with this long enough. Even if Emma is oblivious, she won't be for long. I have to get us out of here before it is too late.

Lorelai's insistent meows pull me from my memory. "We're safe now. We're safe now. We're safe now," I whisper to myself while gently scratching Lorelai under her chin.

Matthew actually got Lorelai for me in the early days of our relationship—before he let his true colors shine through. Despite the hell he put me through, two great things came from those three horrible years: Lorelai and Emma.

Lore's purring and nuzzling at my cheek is exactly what I need to get my rugged breathing back under control. I chose her name after my all time favorite character, Lorelai Gilmore. Cat Lorelai prefers carbs to cardio, talks a mile a minute, and is quirky and fun just like her namesake. I don't know if the name just fits her perfectly or if the seven times we've watched the show from start to finish since she was a tiny kitten have taught her how a Lorelai ought to behave. Either way, Lorelai fits her to a tee, and she's my soulmate.

"Alright, Lore. Tell me to get up off my ass. I've moped around enough today. I need fresh air, sunshine, and movement. Water wouldn't be a bad idea either." After the large coffee I had with Nora, I brewed myself another cup as soon as I got home. My body is begging me to give it some water, but coffee is my emotional support drink of choice, so it will have to do.

"Mrrrow," Lorelai responds.

"Okay. Okay. I'm getting up. Do you know where my headphones are? I think I'll go for a run," I tell her as I wipe a small tear from my eyes.

Prying myself off the couch, I pull my hair into a haphazardly high ponytail and slip on neon-yellow running shoes, leggings, and a bright purple cropped tank top with the words 'Running late is my cardio' across the front. Despite the fact that it will be dark soon, my colorful outfit should keep me visible as the sun sets. As I quickly stretch my legs, I slide one headphone into my ear. Running with only my thoughts is a recipe for disaster, but so is me—a woman in my mid-twenties—drowning out my entire surroundings while running alone. So, one headphone will have to do.

Even though everyone told me my entire life would change as soon as I became a mother, I never really understood what they meant. Everything, literally everything, changed, including my ability to read whenever I want. When she was really little, we often snuggled together on the couch while she napped and I read my newest library find, but my reading days abruptly ended as soon as she became mobile. Until I discovered audiobooks which are the perfect solution for moms with loud, needy toddlers. Instead of reading physical books, I now listen to audiobooks on our daily walks or when I go for a run.

Today, however, I'm too agitated and worried to focus. Not to mention, someone else's happily ever after is the last thing I want to read about right now. So instead, I turn on the *I'm All In* podcast and set off in a brisk jog. Luke Danes, well Scott Paterson but he'll always just be Luke to me, recounting one of my favorite episodes is exactly what I need to end this day on a higher note.

A mile and a half into my run, my podcast stops as my phone vibrates in my pocket. I stop in the middle of the sidewalk, wipe my sweaty palms on my pants, and try to slow my heart rate and breathing enough to talk on the phone.

"Emmy!" I shriek as her face fills my screen, pure joy evident in my voice. "Mommy misses you so much. I hope you're having the best time with Daddy."

"Mama!" Emma yells with just as much enthusiasm. Her face is so close to the screen that I can only see her nose and one of her eyes like if she gets close enough she might be able to reach me.

Mama was her first word, and the sound of it now immediately melts my heart. She's only fifteen months old, so I know this phone conversation is going to be extremely one-sided, but I couldn't care less. Seeing her two little golden brown pigtails sticking straight out from the top of her head, those squishy little cheeks, and an ear-to-ear smile is really all I need. I need confirmation that she's doing okay without me. Her sweet face, lit up at the sight of me, instantly perks my sullen mood.

Seeing Emma in the house we fled floods me with sadness, guilt, and resentment. As soon as I told my dad that Emma and I were leaving, he offered to let us stay with him until I could find a place of our own. We'd made it to his house, three hours away, by the time Matthew realized we were gone and began calling my phone repeatedly. He called seventeen times in an hour despite my refusal to answer and the letter I left on the kitchen counter. On the eighteenth call, I finally answered.

"*Get your ass home, right now,*" his voice bellowed through the phone before I could even say 'hello.'

"We're at my dad's. Feel free to visit Emma anytime you want." My index finger hovered over the red button, ready to end the call, when he began yelling.

"*My daughter will not grow up living with your dad. Bring her home right now, or I'll never see either of you again.*"

Ha! What a dream that would be! With nothing productive left to say, I ended the call and powered down my phone, breathing a sigh of relief at the physical distance between us. With my phone now off and hundreds of miles between us, I could finally relax.

Though I'd contemplated leaving Matthew for years, realizing my baby deserves better is all it took to ensure I never went back. Matt, true to his word, had nothing to do with her for the better part of a year. Until he was forced to provide for her. Last month, with my dad's help, I finally had the money saved up to file for divorce and full custody, automatically setting him up for court-ordered child support. After nearly a year of no contact, I was hopeful that our divorce and custody could be settled quickly and in my favor. But as soon as the first child support payment was taken from his check, he called in an outrage.

"Why the hell would you do this to me, Nessa?" he barked.

"You're her father. Whether you want to be in her life or not, you have a responsibility to take care of her."

"You took away that responsibility when you decided to leave. You can do it on your own until you decide to come home."

"I am home," I said as I hung up the phone.

About a week later, his lawyer filed a request with the court for him to start getting weekends with Emma. I tried desperately to show my lawyer that he isn't safe, describing yelling matches that startled Emma from sleep, bruises he'd left on my arms, and all the threats he'd made to my safety. Despite my tearful begging, I finally conceded defeat to Dylan, my lawyer, who was adamant that a judge would not rule in my favor if I withheld contact from her father, even with his history of aggression towards me. He explained that, legally speaking, Matt's behavior would not be viewed as unsafe for Emma unless something happened directly to her.

Though the legal system disagrees, Emma not being around violence of any kind matters to me, and I will do everything in my power to make damn sure she is safe and thriving. Tempting a judge to give Matt full custody because I kept him from her is not something I am willing to risk. Thus, my so-called *free time*.

I will play by the rules, no matter how backwards they sound to me. I've never gone down quietly in my entire life, and I won't start now, but I will do anything for my precious baby girl. Right now, that means giving up every other weekend so she can develop a relationship with her father. Maybe he'll step up and be a decent dad. Maybe he'll give me something to use against him in court to prove that my concerns were valid. Either way, I am doing what I have to to get us through this despite the constant screaming in my head begging me not to let her out of my sight.

The sound of Emma's wet smooch to the phone screen pulls me from my thoughts, reminding me exactly why I'm doing this. "Doodle, look!" My silly nickname for her instantly draws her attention to me. "Mama sees a puppy." I turn the camera around so she can see the giant yellow labradoodle headed my way. It's definitely not a puppy, but all dogs are puppies to her.

"Pu!" she bellows and giggles as he wags his tail back and forth. "Pu!"

Knowing her attention is certain to wane any second now, I ready myself to end the call that I've longed for all day. "Mama loves you, doodle butt. Sweet dreams," I coo as I blow her a kiss through the phone. Maybe I'm hearing what I want to hear, but I'm pretty sure she just tried saying 'bye' as I hung up the phone. Each milestone feels monumental, and this one is no different. Hearing her newest word gives me the push I need to make it through the rest of the weekend.

"You got this," I chant to myself as I pick back up to a jog. "We got this."

CHAPTER THREE

PETER

I drop my keys on the kitchen counter with a thunk and take the three steps required to get across my tiny kitchen. The entirety of my apartment, minus the bedroom and bathroom, is visible from just about any vantage point. Despite its size and minimal decor, it has everything I need: a couch, bed, and computer equipment. As I grab a can of Mountain Dew from the fridge, my phone buzzes in my pocket. After a long day of coding and finally making headway on a new video game, I'm ready to order some takeout, lay back in my recliner, and fall asleep to whatever new action movie I can find. My phone buzzes again before I can even grab the remote and sit down.

ROB
What's up?

ROB
I want to run something by you

PETER
Oh, boy

I chuckle as I hit send. There's no telling what he's going to say after an introduction like that.

> **ROB**
> Nora wants to set you up with her best friend...

> **PETER**
> Again? Who this time?

I add a playful shrug emoji before hitting send.

Nora loves playing matchmaker, but I thought by now she'd be running out of single friends to set me up with. I don't mind it, but I also don't mind bachelor life. I like the life I've built for myself, but honestly, it's probably about time for me to find someone I can settle down with. At twenty-seven, I really haven't had what I'd call a 'serious' relationship, and I'm not a fan of one-night stands. I've dated a little, but my relationships tend to fizzle out pretty quickly. If the right person came along, I'd be down to trade in this one-room bachelor pad for something more conducive to starting a life together. I just haven't found the right woman yet, despite Nora's efforts.

Over the last couple years, Nora has set me up on two blind dates. Lindsey was sweet but boring, and the conversation stalled before it ever really began. At my aunt's recommendation, I took her out for dinner at a lovely Italian restaurant with plans to extend our date if it went well. I'm not saying I'm the life of the party because I'm definitely not. I actually prefer a chill night in to loud, crowded events, but the silence across the table made for one of the longest dinners of my life. It was obvious she wasn't having a good time, either, so I opted out of suggesting we get ice cream after. I drove her home, hugged her good night, and never heard from her again.

A year or so after that, Rob and I planned to go see a remake of a movie we loved as kids. The original came out in the late '90s, and Rob and I watched it together nearly every weekend.

We'd camp out in my living room with spicy chicken wings and endless cans of Mountain Dew. When I showed up at the movie theater ready to nerd out with my best friend, Nora was there with a mischievous grin and a newly single friend from work.

Jennifer talked non-stop throughout the movie, leaning over to whisper in my ear about various patients at the dental office they work at, what was happening in the movie, and her favorite places to eat. I avoid confrontation at all costs, so I took it in stride and humored her with whispered responses throughout the movie. We had some decent conversations, but missed the entire movie. Afterwards, the four of us walked next door to a sandwich shop for a quick bite. Nora quickly took the seat next to Rob, ensuring Jennifer and I sat as close as possible. Conversation flowed just fine, but this time the sparks just weren't there. In case you were wondering, I rented the movie a few weeks later. Turns out, it was actually pretty good for a remake.

> **ROB**
> Her name's Nessa. Hold on. I'll find her Facebook pic or something.

His response takes less than a minute as if he's holding our conversation open waiting for each of my replies.

> **PETER**
> I'll agree to it as long as you and Nora will be there, and we all agree to not go see a movie.

> **ROB**
> Pretty sure Nora already has it planned. We'll be there.

> **ROB**
> Also, I will never tell Nora what movie we're seeing ever again.

Honestly, this is the perfect excuse to make a trip to see Rob soon anyways. After he started dating Nora, he moved away from our hometown. He's only about two hours from me, but it means we hang out about once a month instead of several times a week like we used to.

Nora means well, and she's become a good friend of mine these past six years. Maybe the third time's the charm. Perhaps, she'll keep suggesting friends for me until the end of time. I guess we'll find out in a couple weeks.

I type out a response agreeing to visit whenever Nora has my newest blind date planned and hit send just as a picture of Nessa pops onto my screen. If I wasn't fully on board two minutes ago, I am now.

Her long, brown hair flows in loose curls around her face. Her ivory skin glistens in the sun with a smile that fully reaches her eyes. She's squeezing a giggling little girl who's clutching a stuffed white unicorn with rainbow hair in her lap. She's breathtakingly beautiful. Something about her pale blue, almost gray, eyes keeps me locked in, unable to look away. I'm about to text Rob about the young girl in the picture, the foil "1" balloon suggesting she recently celebrated her first birthday, when a knock at the door alerts me that my dinner is here.

I grab a paper plate and fill it with my favorite pizza—sausage and black olives with extra cheese. Settling back into my recliner, I kick the foot rest up and begin searching for a movie. Thirty minutes ago, I was feeling something action packed, but for whatever reason, I'm in a rom-com mood now. I'm not too manly to admit I like a good romantic comedy every now and then.

Let's not tell Rob, though. The poking fun will never end. He's strictly an action or fantasy movie guy despite my attempts at trying to sway him. I blame my mom. She loved a good romance movie, and I'd often end up sharing her bowl of popcorn equally sucked into whatever movie she was watching.

The deadline for my newest video game is at the end of the week. Yes, that's right. I get to create and play video games for a living. It's a nerdy kid's dream, but I've been working fourteen-hour days for the last ten days straight, which is exactly why I fully expected to finish my pizza and fall asleep with my movie playing in the background and my plate still in my lap. The last three nights have played out exactly like that until I wake up at two in the morning and force myself to move to my bed. I'm exhausted and have to be back at it by six tomorrow morning, but I just cannot get my mind to settle.

This is the first time Rob has shown me my blind date in advance. Hell, last time I didn't know she was coming until she got there. I don't know if seeing her in advance is making my upcoming date more real or if it's just her. Nessa. I like the sound of her name on my tongue and she seems so genuine in her picture. Can you deduce someone's genuine-ness from one photo? I don't know, but I'm beginning to think so.

Maybe it really is time for me to settle down. I know my Aunt Deedee would be elated. She's been badgering my brother and me about bringing a woman home to meet her for years now. The closer I get to thirty, the more insistent she becomes.

Nora's blind dates have never been something I overly look forward to, though I don't dread them either. This time, however, I find myself eager to see how it goes. I'm tempted to ask Rob all about her. Something tells me Nora would immediately tell Nessa my every word if I were to pepper him with questions, and if I've learned anything from these setups, it's that keeping expectations low is paramount. Removing the temptation, I set my phone down and return my attention to the TV. I don't want to get anyone's hopes up, including my own, especially if this date pans out the way the first two did.

CHAPTER FOUR

NESSA

Despite the fact that it's February, the weather is surprisingly nice. Missouri weather can be quite unpredictable. Last week, it snowed so much my graduate classes were canceled for two days straight. I've always loved school and that hasn't changed, but any excuse to stay home with Emma, especially a few days after her first visit with Matthew, was completely welcome. Despite last week's snow, today is nearly 60°F. The sun is shining making it the perfect day to squeeze in some outside time after being cooped inside for most of the winter. Since Emma is home with me this weekend, I intend to make the most of it.

Nora and I are following the girls around the park while simultaneously trying not to hover. We stay a short distance from them, allowing them to play and Nora and I the chance to chat. Daisy is seven and, despite their age difference, shrieks with excitement every time she sees Emma. Nora and I always fantasized about raising our kids together, and now that our dream has come true, I'm unbelievably grateful that Emma will always have a built-in best friend.

Daisy's light blonde hair is split into two perfect French

braids, though I highly doubt they will last long with the way she's darting across the playground. Despite the slight chill in the air, she threw her jacket off as soon as she started running with Emma in her arms. Emma has only been walking for a few months now, hence my need to be a tiny bit of a helicopter mom. She's mastered walking on flat surfaces like our living room carpet, but the stairs on the playground equipment and wood chips covering the ground are a totally different ball game.

There are two different play areas here; one for toddlers and a bigger set for older kids along with a row of swings. Emma refuses to play on the smaller playset no matter how many times I try to persuade her. She's stubborn like her mom—preferring the challenge of keeping up with Daisy on the big kid equipment to playing with me in the baby area. We've only been here twenty minutes, and she's landed flat on her bottom three times already. After the third wipe out, Daisy resorted to carrying her up to the slide instead of holding her hand as they walked up several flights of stairs to the tallest slide this park has to offer.

"When is Daisy's school play?" I ask as I sip my espresso—yes, that crazy sweet espresso—and wait for the girls to appear at the bottom of the twirly slide.

"This Tuesday at six. Are you coming?" Nora responds, handing me one of the muffins she brought as payback for her stealing mine last week.

"We'll be there! I'm definitely going to need help keeping Emma off the stage. She's going to bolt for Daisy as soon as she sees her."

"Girl, you know I'll hold her the whole time. Don't you worry. Plus, Rob has gotten attached to her too. Daisy was her age when we met, and I think he misses it."

"Do you think you'll have another baby? Does he want that?" I ask gently, knowing that being a full-time working mom to a first grader as well as handling all the domestic responsibilities already weighs on Nora.

"I don't think I'm ready, but he's been dropping hints for several months now. I just can't get through to him how much work adding a newborn to our family would be. He's never had to care for a newborn before, and I'm worried all of it will fall on me. Raising Daisy on my own was so hard. I can't do that again. My plate is full taking care of the people who already live under our roof. I can't add another unless he's willing to pitch in."

"I get that," I say reassuringly. "Being a single mom isn't for the weak. Even just having an extra pair of hands so I can cook dinner would be so helpful."

"Yes, it would be." Nora nudges me playfully with her elbow. "That's exactly why you need to go on that date next weekend."

"I've given it a lot of thought. I'm not going to think of it as a date. I'm going to have a good time with my best friend. If Peter and I hit it off, sweet. If not, we can all still be friends. I'd like to make more friends around here anyway, and I've been meaning to get to know Rob better." Up until Emma and I moved in with my dad last year, I lived three hours away from Nora. We texted constantly and visited as often as we could, but most of the time that didn't include Rob. I'm trying so hard to give him the benefit of the doubt now that Nora and I live five minutes apart and can see each other as much as we want. "Are you ever going to tell me what we're doing for our not-date?"

"Nope! I'm going to come over next Saturday after my dad picks Daisy up. I'll help you pick your outfit and get ready with you. Then we'll go pick the guys up and head out. Peter is driving to our house on Friday and staying the night. So, we can go any time on Saturday," Nora explains.

I'm not even sure which part of that statement I should address first. "I think I can manage getting myself dressed. It's not a date, remember?"

"Uh-huh. Sure," she replies with palpable sarcasm. "I'll just come to supervise then."

"You know what? Actually, I only have three outfits that still look cute on me. I might need your help after all, especially since I don't even know where we're going."

It's not an exaggeration in the slightest. Most of my pre-mom clothes don't fit quite right anymore, and I can't bring myself to go shopping. If Emma needs something, I go get it without a moment's hesitation. But, clothes for me don't feel like a necessity anymore, so I'm stuck trying to make my old outfits work. "What do you mean he's driving in on Friday?"

"Oh. Well, um," Nora stumbles over her words. "Uh, he doesn't live here." She forces the words out nearly in a whisper. It's clear she didn't fully know the best way to drop this bomb.

"Why on earth would you set me up with someone who doesn't even live here?" It doesn't come out quite the way I'd hoped. I'm not annoyed, exactly, more so confused. "Where does he live?"

"In Jeff City. He grew up right next door to Rob, and I think he still lives pretty close to there. It's only a two hour drive; it's not that big of a deal. He comes here about once a month and stays the weekend with us. You could drive to him when Emma is with Matthew." She almost growls his name with a snarl. "You're worth it. He'll come here more often for you. I'm willing to bet on it. That's how sure I am."

"Good thing it's not a date," I say, unsure which one of us I'm trying to convince.

After almost an hour on the playground, Daisy's braids are sticking out in every direction, exactly as I predicted. Emma's pigtails are drooping and her face is red from exertion as she climbs into my lap to rest her head gingerly on my shoulder. One handed, I grab the blanket we brought and try to wave it in the air, hoping it will land somewhat flat.

Emma and I love to lay in the backyard under our giant oak tree and read, blow bubbles, or color. This king-size, sun-faded pink blanket gets plenty of use at home and is perfect for a picnic at the park. It's big enough for all four of us to sit on without being squished and is surprisingly comfortable, even with leaves embedded into its fabric. Nora grabs it from me to properly spread it out in a big patch of grass next to the playground. There's plenty of sunshine in this spot, perfect for a quick lunch on this cool day.

Emma will need her nap soon before it's too late to lay her down. Though it's only happened a few times, I've learned my lesson the hard way. Nap time is the two hours a day I get to myself, and I cherish every second of it. It's my time to clean up from the morning's activities, prep dinner, and knock out as much homework as possible. If she gets down for a nap after three o'clock, she's up until midnight. If she skips her nap entirely, she's a total bear until she falls asleep at 6:30 p.m. and then wakes up before the sun. Neither of those are fun for anyone, so we will enjoy our picnic quickly and head home for her regularly scheduled nap time.

As I finish unpacking our lunch, Daisy tickles Emma's belly and softly kisses her forehead. "I hope she's not scared of me at my play. I'm a wolf, but I won't eat her. Just the little pigs. I swear." She's looking at Emma as she says it who then makes a loud snort sound like a pig, completely oblivious to anything else Daisy said.

Daisy's genuine concern about scaring her makes a huge smile appear on my face. Emma doesn't have an intact family, but she is, without a doubt, surrounded by people who love her.

Our drive home from the park is only six minutes long, but Emma manages to fall asleep anyway, completely exhausted from her afternoon of play. This presents a whole new challenge—transferring her to her crib without waking her. If I can get her laid down and sneak out of the room, I'll have two uninterrupted hours to unwind and get a few things done. If I'm not ninja-level stealthy, she'll wake with a false sense of rejuvenation from her short snooze that'll turn into meltdown city by dinner time. As soon as I'm in the door, zonked out toddler in tow, Lorelai wraps herself around my feet. She's purring and meowing loudly, like I've been gone for weeks instead of hours.

"Shhh. I'm evicting you if you wake her," I joke in my quietest whisper, "but, for real, no cat nip tonight if you trip me." She meows much quieter this time, and I know she gets me in all my quirky glory.

Once Emma is tucked into her crib with Lore nestled at her feet, I tiptoe as quietly as possible to the couch with my laptop tucked beneath my arm. There are only two seating options in our living room: an unsightly, brown couch or an uncomfortable (and somehow even uglier) light blue loveseat. After six weeks of living with my dad, I gathered up as many necessities as I could with the little money I had and moved into this place.

Though I love my dad dearly, it was time for Emma and me to branch out on our own. This meant scouring Facebook Marketplace for everything I wasn't able to fit in my car when we fled. Matthew couldn't even be bothered to contribute to his daughter's wellbeing, there was no way I'd be able to convince him to let me have a couch or bed.

Nora gave me Daisy's crib she had stored in the attic along with a few other baby items. My mom let me have my lumpy, spring-loaded bed from my teenage years, and I found my couches for free on Marketplace. Our house already had a fridge, and for now, we're making due without a microwave. I bought a kitchen table for twenty dollars and surrounded it with five mismatched chairs.

All of Emma's and my clothes fit into my car along with the coffee maker and a few toddler essentials, so we have everything we truly *need*. Our house is far from aesthetically pleasing and the loveseat is so firm it's hardly even usable. But I'm determined to make this little house a home, and little by little, it's getting there.

If I had stayed with Matt, Emma would have her own room, a dedicated playroom filled with toys, and a big backyard to run in. My dad and Nora keep reminding me that none of those things really matter, and deep down I know they're right, but the guilt I feel for pulling her away from all the things I now struggle to provide for her is endless. Regardless, we've made due with what we have. I'm much happier in our little two-bedroom duplex and its small fenced-in backyard than I ever was in a house double its size with Matt by our sides.

Choosing the only viable seating—not the rock hard loveseat, obviously—I grab a fuzzy blanket and prop my laptop open on the arm of the couch, my little makeshift table. I login to all three of my courses every day to make absolutely sure I do not fall behind. I'm already well into next week's assignments, always worried that in the daily grind of momhood I'll fall behind. This isn't my first semester of grad school, but it is my first semester after becoming a mom. I know life with a toddler is going to make meeting all my deadlines even harder, so getting a jump start and staying ahead of schedule is key.

I started working on my graduate degree to become a counselor while I was pregnant with Emma. My very first class discussed domestic violence and was the first time I realized that what Matt was doing to me had a name. Dr. White talked endlessly about red and green flags, domestic violence often going unreported, and the challenges women face trying to get free. Because of this class, I learned that I was not the problem in our relationship, despite Matt twisting stories and gaslighting me into doubting myself. I also learned that many people in my shoes never leave, and if they do, they're likely to find another abusive partner.

I refuse to become a statistic. I'm free, and I'll never be trapped again. I have Dr. White, and Emma, to thank for that. College with a toddler is no easy feat, but I'm determined to get through this and build a better life for me and my girl.

CHAPTER FIVE

PETER

As I walk up the front steps, I immediately register Daisy's nose smushed into the front window pane, her breath fogging the glass. She beams as soon as I step through the door, kicking off my shoes, and dropping my overnight bag with a soft thud on the entry rug.

"Petey!" Daisy shrills as she nearly face-plants in an attempt to untangle herself from the curtains.

I scoop her up and spin her above my head. She's almost too big for me to lift this high anymore, but it's our thing, and I have no plans of stopping anytime soon. She instantly lets loose a high pitched giggle bringing an ear-to-ear grin to my face.

"Miss me?" I chuckle, setting her gently back on solid ground.

"You know it. Mommy! Petey's here."

Nora and Rob's house is pretty compact so it's likely Nora already knew I was here before Daisy's announcement. I waltz into the kitchen, Daisy right at my side, to find Nora leaning against the kitchen counter as she chops. The kitchen is Nora's favorite room in the house, and it shows. Despite its size, it looks like the kitchen of a five-star chef with at least three appliances I've never even heard of.

"Something smells delicious." I make a dramatic sniffing gesture as I give Nora a small side hug. I know where Rob will be, and it's not the kitchen, but I want to say hi to Nora before heading back to his gaming room.

"That's because *I'm* making it, Petey." Nora smirks as she playfully uses Daisy's long-time nickname for me. She's cocky about her cooking ability, but she has every right to be. Most nights, I order takeout or pop something frozen into the oven. Today, however, I haven't eaten since breakfast in preparation for whatever Nora will be serving for dinner. I don't even know what she's making but it smells garlicky and delicious. My stomach audibly growls from the scent alone.

I lean in close to Nora and drop my voice to a whisper. "Someone in the office brought cookies today. I hid some in the pantry so Daisy wouldn't see them until after dinner."

"I heard that!" Daisy laughs as she runs towards the pantry.

"Not until after dinner, young lady," her mom calls back. "Thanks, Pete. Maybe a little more subtle next time." Though she's scolding me, she wears a smile with a hint of an eye-roll.

"Oops." I shrug, pretending not to see the chocolate chip cookie in Daisy's hand as she passes through to the living room. A small smile touches my lips as I watch her disappear.

My almost non-existent experience with kids, outside of Daisy, has made me indifferent to the idea of having kids of my own. After Rob and Nora moved in together and I met Daisy, it was clear I just hadn't known what I was missing out on. Daisy is my little partner in crime, and she looks forward to my visits just as much as Rob does. I can only hope my kids are as cool as her one day.

Nora tosses me a piece of garlic bread and nods to my bag. "Go on. Rob has been waiting for you to unleash your newest masterpiece."

"Thanks," I mumble with a mouthful of bread as I grab my bag and make my way down the hall.

"Hey, man! Look what I have," I declare, holding up a copy of my newest video game. As usual, the black out curtains have cloaked the room in darkness. Rob, in his gaming chair, is only visible by the glow of the TV screen. Having been in here more times than I can count, I expertly make my way around the end table covered in empty soda cans and plop down into an oversized bean bag chair, the only other seat in his gaming room.

"Ooo! Which game is this?" His voice is full of genuine curiosity as he peels his eyes from the screen and turns towards me.

Every time my design partner, Alex, and I finish creating a game, I bring it to Rob's to test out together. Alex and I have already worked out all the bugs, but if something about the game's premise and design is inefficient, Rob will be the first to let me know—usually with a steady stream of colorful expletives. I pop the disk in as I start to explain.

"It's called *Echoes of Aethel*. Our characters explore the ruins of this ancient city uncovering crystals, magic, and challenges to complete. It's one of my favorite games I've created so far."

"Hell yeah! Let's do it," Rob declares while fumbling through the desk drawers for a second controller. "How's Aunt Deedee?"

"Bull-headed and sassy as ever," I laugh. "I still go see her once a week. She finally let me take down her Christmas lights yesterday."

"You know she's never ready to give up the festive cheer. It was your mom's favorite time of year."

"I know. That's why it's mid-February, and I just now convinced her to let me take them down."

Aunt Deedee, my mom's oldest sister, took me in when I was sixteen. Without her and Mom's other sister, Kathy, Rob and I likely would have dropped out of high school. By junior year, Rob was staying with us more often than not. Deedee would make sure we got out of bed on time, and Aunt Kathy would drive us to school, despite us being old enough to drive ourselves.

Their assumption that we'd drive anywhere but school was spot on.

Aunt Kathy passed away late last year. With Deedee the only sister left, I make sure to see her as often as possible and pitch in any way I can. Anytime Rob comes to town, he drops in for a visit with her too. At her age, I know the visits and help are appreciated. Even though she thinks she can still handle everything on her own, there was no way I was letting her up on the roof to take down the last of her Christmas decor. At nearly seventy, she's getting around very well for her age, but it's obvious she's a little lonely and household projects just aren't as easy for her anymore.

"Fuck me." Rob groans as he drops his controller to the ground. "Let's go see if dinner's ready before this dragon kicks my ass again."

"It's only the first Echo. The challenges get so much harder. You've clearly lost your touch," I chide as we make our way to the kitchen.

After piling my plate to the brim with the most delectable looking chicken carbonara, I slide into my seat next to Daisy. Stouffer's has nothing on Nora.

"You ready to meet Nessa?" Nora asks, wasting no time.

"Yeah, it should be fun," I mumble with a mouthful of creamy noodles.

"Nessa is coming over? I have to get the picture I drew for Emma finished before she gets here!" Her fork bounces off of her plate with a clang as she pushes her chair back.

"Sorry, sweetheart. She's coming tomorrow after Papa picks you up."

"Ugh, they better still be here when I get home." She flops back into her seat, her face an exaggerated pout.

"I'm assuming Emma is the little girl in the picture you sent?" I'm looking at Rob as I ask but still catch sight of Nora whipping her head in our direction.

"You sent him a picture?" She gasps in frustration. "I purposely didn't show Nessa one or tell her anything about him. It's supposed to be a *blind* date. Blind."

"Showing him her picture has got to be better than just showing up at the movies without any warning," Rob tries, and fails, to sound lighthearted.

"Agh. I know. That was not my best move." Nora takes Rob's jab in stride. "I was afraid you'd both say no to us coming along. To be fair, I'd only known Jennifer for like two weeks. She was new at work and wouldn't stop talking about how lonely she was. I just thought a date might help. This one is different, though, Petey. I swear."

"Third time's the charm, Nor. You really told her nothing about me?"

"Basically. I mean, obviously, she knows your name."

Rob and I both stare at her in unison. My name? That's it?

"She also knows you're Rob's best friend," she blurts out as if this clearly is all the information Nessa should need.

"For all she knows, I could be an ax murderer."

"Hush," she teases with a light swat to my arm. "She's refusing to call it a date anyway. This might be strike three for my matchmaking business."

"I'm not letting you hold your friend hostage to score me a date." My voice is playful, but I'm serious.

"She just doesn't know how cool you are yet. She'll come around."

"Emma must be her daughter. Is that why she's hesitant? Or she truly doesn't want to date?"

"Emma is definitely part of it. It's complicated. She really is great. I know you'll love her. Don't let him discourage you from having a good time tomorrow." She looks pointedly at Rob as she begins to clear the table.

Rising to help clear the plates, I catch Rob's eye as he gives a 'what can you do?' shrug. Nora can be a force of nature when she sets her mind on something. I know she means well and just wants me, and Nessa, to be happy. This whole blind date setup is already messier than usual, and I don't know what to make of it. Knowing Aunt Kathy would roll in her grave if I sat idly by while Nora cooked and then cleaned up after all of us, I scooch in next to her at the sink.

"I can be cool, calm, and collected. If she really doesn't want this to be a date, it doesn't have to be." I move the figurine of a chicken wearing an apron—yes, the entire kitchen is covered in them—so as not to knock it over while I rinse.

"I know you can, Mr. Cool as a Cucumber." Nora giggles. "I'll blink twice really fast in your direction if I think she needs space, deal?"

"Deal." Once the dishes are finished, I dry my hands on my pant leg and head to my room.

Once I'm tucked into bed, my mind once again refuses to settle after the mention of Nessa at dinner tonight. 'My room' is actually the playroom with an air mattress blown up. It's about as comfortable as you'd imagine an air mattress to be. The cheerful, bright decor and walls covered in rainbows helps, but even rainbows and unicorns can't calm the buzz in my head.

The air mattress groans a little as I shift, seeking comfort that isn't here. Usually after a long work week, I'd pass out within minutes. Tonight, though, Nessa's face from her photo keeps replaying like a perfect loop in my mind. The way she holds her little girl, the smile that lights up her face, and the determination in her eyes. And the way Nora shut down my inquiries about her hinting at... what exactly? My previous blind dates fizzled out quickly, and I fully expected this one to be the same. But something about this just feels... different. More... weighty. More real.

I have no idea if I should have this much anticipation. So, I decide Nessa is right; it's not a date. I'm meeting a new friend tomorrow. That's it. I just wish my brain would get the memo and let me get some sleep first.

CHAPTER SIX

NESSA

Hangers hit with a clink as I rifle through the closet for what feels like hours, though I know it's only been a few minutes. I cannot, for the life of me, decide on a top. I've pulled on my favorite pair of jeans with just the right amount of distressing down each leg. They hug my ankles leaving my shoe choices wide open. Technically, they're maternity jeans with a stretchy cotton band where the usual button would be, but once I find a shirt to wear, no one will be able to tell.

"I come bearing gifts," Nora calls as she bursts into my bedroom. She's wearing a pair of black leggings with a dark blue oversized hoodie and carrying two large iced coffees; it's exactly what I need right now.

"Oh my god. Bless you! You know normal people knock, right?"

"I'm not *normal people*."

"Truer words have never been spoken." I laugh. "I could have been naked, you know?"

"You are literally not wearing a shirt right now."

I look down and remember why I'm still in the closet. "Oh, yeah. I don't know what shirt to choose. It would help if I knew where we're going. Is that what you're wearing today? Should I go more casual?"

"Oh, goodness no. I brought clothes to change into. Let me look at what you've got." She shoves past me into the closet and instantly pulls out a bright red, form fitting top with lace lining the cleavage area. "Wear this."

"This is a little much. It's very… boob-y."

"Even better. Put it on."

I groan as I set my coffee down and slip the top over my head. It actually looks pretty good with the ripped jeans and *definitely* accentuates my chest.

"Yep! That's the winner. It's perfect."

"It doesn't look like I'm trying too hard?"

"It's the perfect amount of effort, I think. You look cute but you're also comfortable and ready for whatever the day brings. Don't think about it for another second," Nora reassures me as she slips into her own pair of skinny jeans and a stylish oversized sweater that hangs off one shoulder. "Matthew picked Emma up last night, right? How did it go?"

"Ugh. It was fine. He didn't say a single word to me, which honestly is preferable. Emma cried for me as he strapped her into his truck, and I cried for a good hour after she left. I almost called you this morning to cancel, but I seriously need to get out of the house today." Needing to get out of the house is the understatement of the century. I've wallowed in self-pity since the minute Emma toddled out the door last night. Date or not, I need a distraction, stat.

After letting Nora add a few beachy waves to my hair, we're ready to head out the door. She insisted I let her do my makeup, but I wouldn't budge. I don't even own makeup, which is why she brought her own, but it still felt unnatural for me. I don't ever have the time to do my makeup anymore, and I refuse to try to look like someone I'm not. Matt tried to mold—force—me to be exactly who he thought I should be, and in the process, I lost sight of who I really am. Makeup or no makeup may sound like such a trivial decision, but for me, it holds so much more weight than that.

I come with baggage, a past, and a bare face. If Peter, or anyone else for that matter, doesn't like it, so be it. Nora is used to my face, but I don't think she really understands why I care so much. She let it go easily enough, though.

"Hop in the backseat," Nora directs as we pull up in front of her house. She throws the car into park and runs towards the front door. A minute later, Nora, Rob, and a lean, slightly scruffy man with thick dark hair walk out the front door. Rob hops in the driver's seat as Nora bolts past the man, who must be Peter, to the passenger door.

"Subtle," I joke, with an eyebrow raised, before Peter slides into the seat beside me.

Nora's car isn't necessarily small, but it's small enough that Peter's leg lightly brushes mine as he settles into the backseat, sending an unexpected tingle through me.

I've literally never *not* known what to say in my entire life, but if someone doesn't speak soon, there's no telling what will burst from my lips. We've only been in the car for a few minutes, but it feels like an eternity. The silence isn't awkward, per se, but… okay it's a little bit awkward. How do people even act on a blind date? Do I introduce myself? Nora hasn't shut up since she barged into my house earlier, yet she chooses now to take a vow of silence? And, Rob? Hello? Your bestie is right here. Someone say something. Anything.

"I'm Nessa," the words jump from my lips before I can think anymore about it. "I come with a toddler, trauma, and a whole lot of baggage." Oh. My. God. What the fuck is wrong with me? Pull the car over. Let me out, right now. I did *not* just say that out loud.

Nora's laugh bursts from her with a snort as Rob, helpfully, adds, "oh, boy."

Peter genuinely chuckles before responding. "I'm Peter. I come with video games, an insane amount of computer gear, and nerdy commentary at the ready."

I can feel my cheeks begin to cool as soon as he responds. He took that word-vomit surprisingly well, but I'm caught on one thing he said. Video games, just like Rob. He's funny, I like that, but is he going to be unable to pull himself from his games just like Rob?

"Hmm, video games. What kind?" I'm genuinely curious but also hoping to see if he locks himself in his room for days on end like his friend or if he has a better game/life balance.

"Honestly, all of them. It depends on my mood. I tend to get sucked into whatever genre I'm currently designing."

"Designing?" My eyebrows knit together. I thought he meant he likes playing video games, not creating them.

"I forgot Nora told you absolutely nothing about me. I design video games for a living. Oh, and I'm not an ax murderer, in case you were wondering."

"As a matter of fact, I was wondering. That's good to know." A small smile touches my lips. I did not expect to get off to such a good start after my ridiculous introduction, but I'm feeling more comfortable by the minute. "I know pretty much nothing about video games, but my sister and I could kick some ass at Mario on our Gameboys back in the day. Do you make anything like that?"

"I haven't gotten to create any big name games like that. Though I would absolutely die at the chance. I'll have to show you some of my stuff. Well, it's not really *my* stuff. I'm half of a two-man team that creates, builds, and then fixes new video games. I'm mostly the second half of that team; I test them and then fix any bugs I find."

"Zzzzz." Nora fakes snores with a rasp. "You're boring us to death, Petey."

"It wasn't *that* boring," I protest with a grin.

"His work is actually really badass," Rob chimes in. "I own all of his games."

"Thank you. Someone here gets me. In an attempt to keep everyone awake for the rest of our drive, what do you do, Nessa?"

"I'm actually a full-time student right now," I answer with obvious pride in my voice. "I'm studying to be a counselor… wait, did you just call him Petey?"

"That's not embarrassing at all," Rob laughs.

"It's Daisy's name for him, and it's sweet not embarrassing," Nora chides as she turns up the radio and turns to Rob. "Alright, let's give them some privacy."

With the attention effectively taken off of us as Rob and Nora start softly singing along to the music, I finally stop fidgeting long enough to take Peter in. I know most women want a tall man, but even though he can't be more than a few inches taller than me, I'm really not hating it. He has short, slightly wavy, brown hair that he's purposefully made messy and golden brown eyes to match. Regardless of his gamer vibes and the fact that he codes for a living, his skin is surprisingly tanned and his muscles are slightly visible through his shirt. A sign that he must get outside every once and a while and do more than game, right? His dark wash jeans and navy blue pocket-tee hug him in all the right places. In the midst of me very clearly checking him out, he turns to me, a smile pulling at his lips.

"So tell me about school. Counseling is grad school, right?"

"Uh," I clear my voice and try to focus. He definitely just caught me ogling him. I'm on a roll today. "Yeah, it's grad school. I have about a year and half left. I transferred to a new university after leaving Emma's dad, so it's taking a little longer than it normally would. I also work part-time in the counseling center's office."

"Ah," he adds, seeming genuinely interested. "You're diagnosing us all right now, aren't you?"

"Oh, absolutely." I let out a small laugh and work to tamper the smile I can't remove from my lips.

"I knew it."

"Honestly, I just want to help people. I know that's so cliché, but it's true. If I can make people's lives better... then my life is better, too, you know?"

His eyes are locked on mine like this is the most interesting thing he's heard in weeks. He's really, truly listening to what I have to say. Something about his gaze and the way he's soaking up my every last word makes butterflies take flight in my stomach.

"Okay, you little lovebirds. We're here." Nora's announcement breaks into the moment.

"We're... where?" I ask, a bit confused, as Rob parks the car. "Isn't this the convention center?"

"Yes! Don't you remember going to the chili cook-off with me and my dad?"

"Well, of course I do."

Nora's dad raised her alone, so he took her, and by default, me, everywhere he wanted to go. We went to the chili cook-off pretty much every year starting in middle school. He'd buy us wristbands for all the activities and send us off with enough money for ice cream while he drank a few beers with his buddies. Truthfully, it was always a good time, and the memories I have of it are fond ones, but I'm not really sure this is the best place to get to know someone new.

Nora's face starts to drop as she takes in that she may be the only one who is excited for this. She's been looking forward to this day for weeks, and I refuse to let her feel like she let anybody down.

"And now I see why you told me to choose the flats. I'd have died in those wedges. Let's do this." Pasting an encouraging smile on my face, I swing open the car door.

CHAPTER SEVEN

PETER

This is my version of hell.

The quiet car ride turned out to be pretty perfect. Despite Nora saying Nessa doesn't want this to be a date, our connection felt immediate and real. She's funny, not afraid to say what she's thinking, and obviously has a big heart for others. And, now we're smack in the middle of an introvert's nightmare.

Nessa walked with her arm lightly brushing mine as we entered the convention center and got our wristbands. The attendant at the entrance provided us with sample cups, spoons, and a map of which businesses occupy each booth and the type of chili each one is serving. There are rows and rows of booths in the main room with a live band at the front. To the side, there's a beer garden and a room full of carnival style games.

I like chili as much as the next guy, but it is unbearably loud and crowded in here. There are so many people that we're all shoulder to shoulder. I've dropped two spoons after being hit with a rogue elbow, and a drunk guy nearly dumped his bowl down the front of Nessa's shirt.

"Holy shit. I can breathe fire after that one." Nessa pants as she fans her mouth with her free hand.

"Not a spicy fan, huh?" I pretty much have to yell to be heard.

"Not even a little bit. I can't tell you how many times I've told Emma something is spicy when I just don't want to share it with her. It won't be long before she knows that Oreos aren't spicy and Mama is just full of shit. There's literally nothing spicy in our house."

"Bummer." I laugh. "I love spicy food. I thought that last one was pretty good."

"And when he says 'spicy,' he means he loves *spicy*, spicy. Like *burns the whole way down* spicy," Rob adds.

"Hey, Ness! I need something to drink. Come help me." Nora grabs her by the elbow as she turns back towards us. "You guys want anything?"

After giving them our soda requests, the ladies trot across the room towards the drinks booth. "Did you know we were coming here?"

"Nope. Nora and I have been here several times, and I think she just saw an opportunity to get us all together especially since it reminds her of her childhood with Nessa. It's loud as fuck, though. Don't worry. I have a plan."

"What's that?" I bring the next sample to my mouth as I wait to hear his plan. This one is sweet and chunky, and is going straight in the trash.

"Just take Nessa to play a game or something when they get back. I'll talk to Nora."

As if on cue, Nora and Nessa rejoin us, their hands outstretched to hand us our drinks.

"Come with me," I say, leading Nessa out of the crowded, main room. I'm not wasting any time. The sooner we're out of here, the better. Quiet night in, please.

"This is the part where you ax murder me, isn't it?" she chortles.

"Now what fun would it be if I told you beforehand?"

There's no line at the ring toss booth, so I pay the attendant and hand Nessa three of the six rings I bought. "Every ring you land earns you a question. It can be anything, and we have to answer honestly. Go!"

"I'm nothing if not honest." A determined look crosses her face as she begins tossing her rings towards the bottles.

"Wow, you suck at this. Now I'm worried about trying your video games," she teases after expertly landing all three of her rings. "Want me to go first so you don't waste your one and only question so soon?"

"Oh, my question will not be a waste, but you should definitely kick us off."

It's much quieter in this side room, and I can physically feel myself relax. There are carnival style games lining each wall, think Plinko and tossing darts at balloons, and a ticket booth in the center of the room. Most of the game booths have small lines, but it's far quieter and less crowded than the main room. I can once again hear myself think, and am ready to get to know her a little better.

"Hmm, okay..." She rubs her palms together as she thinks. "Did Nora bully you into coming on this... coming out with us today?"

"Not even a little. I actually didn't talk to her about it until last night," I reassure. "Rob asked, sent me your picture, and told me you're Nora's best friend. It didn't really take much convinc—"

"He sent you my picture? That is so unfair. Nora wouldn't show me a picture of you no matter how much I begged. I was starting to think you had two heads or something."

"Begged, huh? I thought this wasn't a date. 'Begged' sounds pretty eager to me." I regret the words as soon as they leave my mouth despite the playfulness in my tone.

"She told you that too? What else did she say? I did not get equal blind date etiquette here! I feel cheated." It comes out matter-of-factly, but she's still wearing a playful smirk.

"That's it; I promise. If it helps, she was not happy when she found out Rob sent me a picture. He's never done that for Nora's setups in the past—"

Nessa interjects before I can finish my thought. "She's set you up before?"

Despite the calm way she asks it, she looks taken aback. "Um, yeah she has. They were all flops though. She, like everyone else in my life, is ready to see me settle down, I guess."

"Hmm," is all she utters in response.

"Alright, question two. I'm ready. Let's hear it," I offer in an attempt to bring back the smile that's now faded.

She rebounds quickly. "Have you ever dated someone with kids before?"

Straight to the point. I see why she and Nora are so close.

"Once, yeah. Her kids were older, though, and our relationship didn't really last long enough for me to get to know them." I'm a few years shy of thirty, and I'm not naive to the fact that a lot of women my age will likely already have kids. Nessa seems genuinely concerned that kids might be a deal breaker, so I try to reassure her without pushing the issue too much. "You can't scare me away that easily."

Her sweet, ear-to-ear grin returns to her face. "That's a miniscule part of the baggage I come with. Buckle up," she chuckles. "Your turn."

"Hmm," I say in mock concentration. "What's the last thing that made you laugh? Other than me, obviously."

"*That* is the burning question you've been holding on to? What happened to not wasting your one and only shot?"

"Your answer will be far from a waste. I can already tell." Undeniably, there are so many questions I'd like to know the answer to, but I'm certain Nora will waltz in here and immediately blink twice if I dig too deep too quickly.

She twirls a lock of hair around her finger as she contemplates her answer. "This is going to sound so silly. Last night after Emma left, I was laying in bed cr… I was laying in bed watching videos, and this random cat video popped up. They moved the camera underneath a glass table to show what their fluffy, fat cat looked like curled up on the table from the bottom." She snorts. "Oh my god, this is so stupid. Have you ever seen what a cat nap looks like from underneath? It's fucking hilarious. I cry-laughed for a good ten minutes. Here, wait. I'll show you."

She hands me her phone with the video pulled up. She's right, it makes no sense until you see it. As soon as the camera darts underneath the table, revealing the cat's paws smooshed up to its chin, I let out a howl of laughter.

"See! Comedic gold, I tell you."

As predicted, my question was 110 percent *not* a waste. Did I learn about her relationship with Emma's dad or why she's hesitant to call this a date? Nope. But did I get a glimpse into her glowing personality, and successfully lighten the mood. Yep. That's a win in my book.

"There you are!" Nora gasps in mock frustration. "We've been looking everywhere for you. Let's blow this popsicle stand."

"We've barely been here an hour, Nor. We can stay." Nessa's using the exact tone she had when we first pulled in here.

"Honestly, I'm full already, and Rob has a better idea. Let's go."

Nessa flashes her phone screen back towards me with tears of laughter in her eyes as the four of us make our way towards the exit. She took a screenshot of the chonky cat and made it her background picture. Two hours ago, you couldn't have paid me enough money to go to an event like this, but I might have just had the most memorable first not-date of my life.

Once we reach the car, I slip into my seat next to Nessa. I had every intention of sitting beside her when we left Rob's house earlier, but Nora's dart to the front seat so I couldn't have it was delightful to watch. This time, though, our bodies brushing together is no accident.

The car drive to our new destination is short, and I'm not quite ready to give up the light touch of Nessa's knee against my own. Seeing that Rob's idea of a fun first not-date location is much more up my alley, literally, I force my leg off of hers and step out of the car.

"I didn't bring socks," Nessa says with disappointment as we walk towards the bowling alley.

"It's fine," Nora assures. "I'm sure they have socks here."

"I don't even want to think about how crusty bowling alley socks are," Nessa adds with a cringe.

"Eww. Good point. Hold on." Nora returns to the car and rifles through the trunk. "Here you go."

Nessa effortlessly catches the mismatched, blue and yellow socks covered in daisies that Nora launches in her direction.

"Nice catch," I compliment as I hold open the alley's front doors.

"Thank you," she replies with a curtsey.

As soon as we're inside, memories of many afternoons spent bowling with my dad flood me as I take in the familiar smells of floor polish, rented shoes, and popcorn. It's still loud in here but a different kind of loud; the rhythmic clanging of balls and pins is comforting rather than overstimulating like the chili cook-off.

Rob adds our names onto the screen in front of our bowling lane as the ladies skip off to pick their balls. "This is so much better, right?"

"A million times better. Thank you," I say with a small sigh of relief. "I hate events like that, but honestly, I have a feeling Nessa could make a colonoscopy fun."

"Gross," he chortles. "Third time's the charm, then, it would seem."

"It's definitely a step up from the last two, but I don't know if she's quite ready to admit this is a date just yet."

"Admit? So it's a date to you even if it's not to her?"

"There's chemistry for sure, and I think she's having just as good of a time as I am. Time will tell, I guess. What size ball do you want?" I turn to look at the wall lined with various bowling ball options.

"We got balls for everyone," Nora announces as she and Nessa set four balls on the machine in front of us. "I'll go first."

The first game ends with me squarely in the lead, Nora trailing far behind, and Nessa just barely ahead of her.

"This bowling alley has fried pickles that are to die for. I need something to help me feel better about how much I suck at this," Nessa groans.

"I'll come with you and get us all some drinks," Nora says as she jumps up from her seat.

I don't even try to hide the fact that I watch Nessa walk the entire way to the counter. The way she takes her defeat in stride and is clearly enjoying herself despite her reservations has me entranced. *She just wants to be friends*, I silently scold myself. *Get it together, man.*

CHAPTER EIGHT

NESSA

"Get me a side of fries too," Nora calls to me from the bar. I'm in line to order my fried pickles with the obligatory side of ranch dressing. Despite the line for food being merely five feet from the bar's line, we still have to speak in a slight shout to hear one another. It's not overly crowded or loud, exactly, but music is playing from an old jukebox and the bar area is popular. Once I put our order in, buzzer in hand, I join Nora in line.

"What are you getting?"

"I'm getting both of us a Sex on the Beach, a beer for Rob, and probably a Pepsi for Peter," she rattles as we inch closer to the bartender. "How are you feeling so far?"

"Surprisingly, pretty good. I legit typed out three different messages telling you not to come get me this morning but couldn't bring myself to hit send. I thought I'd be miserable and it would be awkward, but so far it's actually been kind of fun. I think I like him... as a friend," I quickly add that last part in so Nora will stop waggling her eyebrows at me. "I haven't had to fight the urge to cry a single time; that right there is a win. Set me up again in two weeks please; this turned out to be a welcome distraction."

"No." Her voice is firm and matter-of-fact. Definitely not the response I was expecting. I thought she'd be delighted by that admission. "I really think this is a good match up. You'll like Peter. He's a genuinely good guy."

"That must be why you've set him up with all your other friends before this," I chide. "Plus he doesn't even live here, so going out with him again in two weeks when Emma is gone again isn't going to happen."

"He deserves to settle down and be happy. Plus, you were married, remember?" She responds with a sigh, knowing full well that I only filed for divorce six weeks ago, and it's nowhere near official, yet. Though I've been separated for more than a year and my marriage was over long before that, I'm far from legally divorced. "Just give it a chance, Ness. He's clearly having a good time too. You don't know that he won't come see you again in two weeks."

Before I can remind her that my marital status hasn't changed, she hands me a tall, skinny glass filled to the brim with bright blue liquid and topped with a cherry and cute little umbrella. After a few steps towards our lane, she turns and hands me Peter's large styrofoam cup. I see what she's doing here, but I, surprisingly, don't mind.

"I'm far enough behind. You should be the one with a stiff drink, not me. Maybe it would give the rest of us a fighting chance," I quip, handing Peter his drink. He bowled just under 200 our first round, while I barely broke 100. Nora's score was even lower than that, and judging by the amount of liquid left in her glass, round two is not going to go any better for her.

"What, and risk looking like an amateur? Not a chance," he quips right back. "I don't drink, though my game tends to go downhill as the night goes on all on its own." Well, that's good news because this drink is the perfect amount of sweet and strong. I can feel my very limited bowling abilities leaving my body as I sip.

"You create video games *and* bowl on the regular. And you're single, why?"

"Just be glad I didn't bring my own bowling ball this time. I'd have the ladies lining up." A slow smirk slides across his lips, and I'm unsure if he's kidding. He definitely has a hot, nerdy vibe going, and it's all I can do not to let him know how much it's working for me.

Exactly as predicted, his second game is not as good as his first, though only by a few points. Since I haven't had any alcohol in a couple of years, I fully expected this drink to do me in. Instead of the expected gutter balls, I'm actually doing better than last round and even bowled two strikes. I can feel my cheeks beginning to heat and my arms turning a tad jello-y, despite still having a quarter of my drink left. Finishing it may not help me through round three, but it's delicious so I chug on.

"One of those better not be for me," I lightheartedly chastise Nora as she once again returns from the bar. "I can't handle it."

"Peter is always our designated driver, so one for me, one for you, and one for Rob," Nora explains as she hands out the shots. The tiny glasses are filled with a creamy reddish brown liquid and topped with whip cream. I stick my tongue out to lick some whipped cream off the top as Nora adds, "But first, you have to guess what it's called."

I give the drink a sniff before wagering my guess. "It smells cinnamon-y, so maybe something Christmas related. Ooo, I know! It's based on Taco Bell's cinnamon twists. I do like those."

Rob chortles. "I know what it's called and you're way off base."

"Fine, I give up. What's it called?"

Nora beams with an ear-to-ear smile that fully reaches her eyes. "It's called a cum shot."

Peter chokes on his soda and my jaw drops open. "Excuse me. What, now?'

She's not even trying to hide her enjoyment right now. She's full on belly laughing as she explains. "It's Fireball and some sort of coffee creamer. It's my favorite. Ready? One, two, three!"

She didn't give me enough time to think this through before the three of us tip our heads back in unison. "Good god. I'd rather take a real cum shot than whatever the hell that was. Gross," I choke out with a grimace.

"Oh, really?" Peter raises his eyebrows in my direction as my face turns a deep crimson red.

"Oh. Oh my god. I just meant that shot was really gross." Where the fuck is my filter today?

Clearly delighted with her own antics, Nora grabs her ball and steps up to bowl. She rolls two gutter balls and sits beside me with a thud.

"There's something seriously wrong with you."

"Just trying to help a girl out," she hollers as I grab my ball and take my next turn. I turn around to flip her the bird just in time to see her wink at Peter.

By the end of our third game, Nora has taken another shot and downed two more drinks. I tapped out after that horrendous shot but have been sneaking sips of her cocktail as we play. It's been so long since I've consumed any alcohol that I'm closer to drunk than tipsy at this point, despite having way less than Nora or Rob.

She did this on purpose. She knows I can't handle my booze and would let my guard down. Part of me is mad at her for putting me in this position, but the other part of me is lightly swaying to the music, having the most fun I've had in years.

Nora and I stumble our way to the car as Peter and Rob hold open our doors. He places his hand on the small of my back, guiding me into the passenger seat before rounding the car and climbing into the driver seat. The warmth of his touch lingers on my lower back as he pulls the car out of the parking lot.

Peter's hand finds my knee as he drives, sending sparks

straight to my lady bits. I quickly decide I am *not* mad at Nora after all. It's time I let my hair down and have some fun—starting with finding out if he was pulling my leg or not. "Do you really own your own bowling ball?"

"At the risk of bumping myself up to a new level of nerdy, yes I do. My dad bowled a lot when I was a kid. As I got older, we were on the same bowling team. We bowled together every week, so he got me my own ball for Christmas when I was about twelve. It's the one I still use."

"Well, when you put it that way, it's harder to poke fun. That's really sweet, actually."

"Ah, sorry to disappoint. I'm certain the opportunity will present itself again soon enough," he chuckles. His golden brown eyes lock with mine as he adds, "I had a really good time today."

"I've been low-key dreading this all week, but I'm really glad Nora set this up. I had a fabulous time." I let the words spill from me with alcohol induced courage. "You did not look like you were having a good time earlier."

"I've been having a good time since Nora stole the seat beside Rob from me. Crowds and overly loud events are overwhelming for me. You made it worth it though."

You made it worth it though. My cheeks instantly turn the color of a plump, ripe tomato. Thank God he's focused on the road. I've said enough embarrassing things today; I don't need him to see how much his statement is affecting me. He hands me his phone with the Maps app pulled up as he directs, "Put your address in. I'm going to drop you off at home before helping Rob get Nora in bed."

I do as I'm told despite the disappointment coursing through my veins. I'm not sure if it's the drinks talking or if I'm truly just enjoying his company. But I do know I'm not quite ready for the night to end.

A few minutes later, Peter carefully pulls into my driveway and walks around to help me out of the car. With my purse slung over my shoulder, nothing but Nora's socks on my feet, and my flats in my hand, I steady myself with the car door. Peter takes my hand, guiding me along the walkway. Emma and I blew bubbles while we waited for Matthew to pick her up yesterday, and I nearly trip over the half empty bottle on our way up the stairs. He effortlessly wraps his arms around my waist to steady me. His touch sends an electric jolt through me, making it even harder to regain my balance.

"I'm ready for question three," I whisper, our faces mere inches apart and his hands still gripping my waist.

"Let's hear it."

"Kiss me."

"That's not a question."

"Oh, right. Do you want to ki—" My question is cut off by the rough embrace of his lips on mine. My heart rate instantly begins to pick up as I take in the sweet smell of his aftershave and the way his plump lips feel as they linger on mine. The hardness against my lower belly suggests he's enjoying this moment as much as I am. "Come inside," I whisper against his lips.

"Nessa." The tortured way he says my name instantly sends need throughout my body. "I can't. You've had too much to drink, and I've got to get them home. God, I want to, though."

I groan as I softly caress his cheek with my hand, my head resting on his chest.

"Good night, Nessa." He plants a soft smooch to my forehead and turns back towards the car.

I let myself fall against the door as soon as I'm inside, its cold surface on my back pulling me from the moment. What did I just do? That was not supposed to be a date. We are supposed to be friends. Friends only. I just couldn't help it. The feel of his hand gently rubbing my back as we approached my front door. The way he looked into my eyes as if he's trying to see directly into my soul. And the way he said my name. Fuck. The way he growled out my name like he's never wanted anything more.

"Mrrrow." I'm immediately sucked out of my daydream as Lorelai paws at my feet.

"Did you see that?" I ask her.

"Meeeow," she scolds.

"I knew you were watching. Creep." Lorelai loves to watch for me in the windowsill anytime I'm gone. "I need to lay down," I add as she continues to chastise me as we walk down the hall.

The room slowly spins around me as I try to get some shut-eye. Instead, all I can think about is that kiss. *Friends. Friends, you lunatic. You have too much at stake. You're just friends.*

CHAPTER NINE
PETER

I've purposefully taken two wrong turns on the way back to Rob and Nora's. The drive between their house and Nessa's just isn't quite long enough after forcing myself not to go inside with her. I just need a few extra minutes for the desire pressing against my jeans to calm down before I have to get out of this car again.

I know I did the right thing by turning Nessa's offer down. She's been hesitant about even meeting me all week, taking advantage of her lapse in judgment while she's tipsy is completely out of the question. If and when I sleep with Nessa, it'll be when she's 100 percent ready. But damn, the right thing fucking sucks sometimes.

"Where we going?" Rob's unexpected laughter startles me from my thoughts.

"Oh. Uhh... missed my turn." I've been to their house a million times. There's no way that excuse is going to work, but it's all I can come up with.

"Uh huh. I'm sure you did."

Nora is nearly asleep, leaning against Rob, when we finally pull up in front of their house. He lightly shakes her shoulders and helps her out of the car. Despite being so near sleep she was drooling, she instantly perks up. "Told you she's perfect," she says through a yawn.

"She's... definitely something." How do you even describe Nessa? She's not afraid to say exactly what she's thinking but somehow is still a bit reserved. She's not quite ready to lay all of her baggage out there for me, and why would she be? Despite her holding back a bit, she's funny, and I have a pretty good feeling she's smart too. Not to mention the way that kiss made me feel. Nora's right. She's absolutely perfect.

The sun is peeking through the rainbow curtains the next morning as I try to remember where I am. My mattress lost half its air overnight, and I'm drooping dangerously close to the ground. I crawled into bed as soon as we got back last night, but it took me an hour to fall asleep, daydreams about what might have happened had I said yes to Nessa's offer playing on repeat in my head.

The last few weeks have been exhausting, and per usual, I relish the opportunity to sleep in like I'm still a teenager. Like everything else in my life right now, my sleep schedule is that of the ultimate bachelor. I stay up way too late, regret it the entire work week, and then catch up on all the shut-eye I missed over the weekend. With a yawn, I rub the sleep from my eyes and prepare to face Nora. I know she'll have plenty she didn't get to say last night. As I roll out of bed, a neon green sticky note catches my eye.

I programmed Nessa's number into your phone.
You're welcome.
XOXO Nor

This is not the handwriting of someone who swayed down the hall to bed like Nora did last night. She must have snuck in here this morning while I was still sleeping. She's well aware that I sleep like the dead, and frankly, it's got me feeling refreshed and ready for whatever she's going to throw at me today.

I pull on a pair of shorts and my shirt from last night, then make my way to the living room while I contemplate what I should do about the newest contact in my phone. The house is silent and completely empty, and there's no doubt in my mind it's by design.

"Fuck it," I mutter to no one as I pull my phone from my pocket and begin to type.

> PETER
>
> Good morning. I have a feeling you could use some coffee after last night. Care to join me?

A few minutes later, my heart nearly skips a beat at the vibration in my hand.

> NESSA
>
> A godsend. That's what you are. I can be ready in 10.

The fact that she didn't even bother to ask 'who's this?' is oddly comforting. I have a feeling Nora gave me Nessa's number instead of the other way around for a reason. She has no problem pushing both of us toward a relationship, but she also knows us both well. Nessa's reservation may have kept her from using my number even if she wanted to. Nora knew I'd use it the first chance I got, hence her making sure there were no distractions here when I woke up. She's clever, and I'm not mad about it.

After several taps on her front door, Nessa swings it open, her hair in a messy bun on the top of her head. She's wearing tight, black leggings that hug her curves perfectly and a red sweatshirt that reads 'Football. My second favorite F word.' A chubby calico cat brushes against my legs with a series of high pitched meows as I take her in. "Ha. I like your shirt."

"Thanks! It's accurate. Football is fabulous, but 'fuck' just has so much versatility. She likes you, by the way." She nods toward the cat. "That's one point for you."

"If I had known she held my fate in her hands, I'd have stopped for catnip." I make a mental note to buy some next time I'm at the store and crouch to scratch her chin. "You ready?"

"I know I don't *look* ready, but until I get some caffeine in me this is the best I can do."

It's all I can do not to tell her she's still absolutely breathtaking. She is, but I don't want to come on too strong just yet. "That is not what I meant, and you know it," I say instead.

She smiles as she slides into the passenger seat of my car. "You are never allowed in my car. I just want to put that out there now."

"Why's that?" I ask with genuine curiosity. I drive a Mazda Hatchback. It fits my computer gear perfectly and has just the right amount of that luxury feel without drawing attention to itself. It's the car version of Peter, if you will.

"For starters, there's not a rogue Cheerio in sight."

"There are a couple loose water bottles back there, I think." I thrust a thumb towards the back seat.

"My car's not messy, per se, but I am a tiny tyrant's chauffeur. There's extra shoes strewn about, snacks for days, and a small spot of melted crayon on the backseat. I can't let you in it after… this." She makes a sweeping gesture with her hands.

"I don't have a tiny tyrant helping me out. It's not a fair comparison." We pull into The Daily Grind, which, according to Nora, is Nessa's favorite coffee spot. Apparently, the rest of the town agrees judging by the fact that we just took the only spot left in the parking lot. "Let's get you some caffeine."

"You're not getting anything?" She eyes me cautiously as I hand the barista my card.

"I'm not a coffee fan. It even smells weird, honestly."

"This proves it. You are definitely going to murder me. How do you function without coffee? It's my life support."

"Caffeine comes in tastier forms than... *that*." I grimace, pointing at her drink.

"That's not possible. Wait. You invited me out to get something you don't even like?" She takes an exaggerated slurp through her straw before adding, "I was surprised you texted me and now I find out you aren't even getting anything."

"You were surprised?" I ask, clearly befuddled. "I thought we had a great time, and you knew it was me without even asking." I know I'm not misreading signals *that* badly.

"Oh, I had a great time too," she adds quickly. "I'm just a mess and those drinks hit me hard. I haven't had a drink since before Emma was born. I was sure I'd scared you off."

"You're not a mess, and I've already told you I don't scare easily," I assure her. "I had a really good time. Let the record show that saying 'no' to your invite last night was the most torturous decision I've ever had to make."

Her eyes go wide as her face instantly becomes a deep shade of scarlet. "Oh. My. God. I threw myself at you. I forgot about that."

"Not exactly how I would describe it." I laugh.

"When do you leave?" I'm surprised she didn't get whiplash with how abruptly she changed the subject.

"As soon as I take you home. But I'd like to call you, if you're still interested." A smile is plastered across my face as I gently touch her fingers with mine.

"Uh, yeah," she mumbles tentatively. "That sounds good. Do you mind if we move outside? It's not too chilly, and this place isn't great for my headache."

Once we're settled in the wicker chairs outside, I decide to quit beating around the bush. It's obvious we have a connection, and I'm dying to get some clarity. "Do you mind telling me what made you so hesitant to agree to go on a date?"

She audibly sighs. "Taking a page from my book, I see. Cutting straight to the chase. I told you, I'm a lot. My life is… just a lot. I come with baggage, remember?"

"Baggage is easier to carry with help."

"Where did you even come from? You're nothing like Rob. I've literally never met another guy quite like you."

"I'm one of a kind. What do you mean 'like Rob?'"

"You're friends. I assumed you were similar, which honestly, was one of the reasons I was hesitant. Plus, my relationship with Emma's dad isn't great. Frankly, he's a piece of shit. Agreeing to a date affects more than just me, you know? And who wants to date a hot mess single mom with a toddler, anyway?" She answers my previous question and the one about Rob all in one big burst.

"I think I do." At that, I can physically see the tension leave her body.

An hour later, I reluctantly leave Nessa at her door, once again. Though this time, I'd have gladly come in if she'd asked. Nessa's hesitation and insistence on yesterday not being a date becomes completely understandable after our conversation. She didn't go into great detail, but Matthew not treating her well and, as she later divulged, only recently reappearing in Emma's life does make dating tricky for her.

Dating is far less complicated for me, but barely a third into my drive home, I can't help but wonder how we'll make this work with the distance between us. I don't think I could move away from Aunt Deedee any time soon or my dream job for that matter. I am sure about one thing, though, the third time is indeed the charm. I make a mental note to bring Nora some daisies, her favorite flower, the next time I see her. She's earned them.

CHAPTER TEN

NESSA

The back corner of the university library is unnaturally cold, even for winter, and has a faint smell of old books that I find surprisingly comforting. My two project partners and I have been here for an hour with absolutely nothing to show for it. Our books lay closed, and our papers sit empty beside them.

"Are you even listening to me?" Jahara snaps her fingers in front of my eyes to get my attention as she adjusts her hijab.

One of my favorite things about this counseling program is their dedication to diversity. I grew up in a small-ish town in southwest Missouri where nearly everyone around me looks just like me. This program is opening my eyes to everything I didn't see growing up and instilling a passion for social justice that I hope to pass down to Emma.

My other favorite thing, and simultaneously one of my least favorite things, about this program is the amount of introspection required to make it through. Every class, no matter the subject, forces us to take a look directly at ourselves whether it be our upbringing, past trauma, personal goals, or even just how to be authentic in ourselves. This introspection happens to be the reason Jahara is having to yank me back to the present.

"Uh... no. Sorry. I am now." I force myself to focus and let the thoughts about my childhood go, for now.

Nothing about my childhood was particularly noteworthy. I'd say it was a mostly happy, normal upbringing. Both of my parents were present, I had a strong bond with my sister from the moment they brought her home from the hospital, and no one harmed me in any way. Today's lecture, the one the three of us are supposed to be completing a project on, just has me thinking about my relationship with my mom.

I was an outspoken and strong-willed child—shocking, I know. My mom never really understood me or attempted to build a relationship with me. This was made ten times worse when I was twelve and chose to live with my dad full-time after my parents split up. Emma is so young; she didn't get to choose which one of her parents to live with. The mere thought of her choosing to live with Matthew instead of me is a gut punch that has me sympathizing with my mom in a way I never have before.

"I've written down the pieces we each need to focus on," Scott, the third member of our project trio, says as he hands Jahara and me our respective duties. "I'm ready to get out of here. I'll email my portion as soon as it's done."

"Same," Jahara and I respond in unison.

As soon as I reach my car, my phone begins to buzz. "Fuck," I mutter as I slide the answer button and immediately drop my phone and empty coffee cup to the ground. Tossing my backpack, cup, and empty snack wrappers into the passenger seat, I raise the phone back to my ear ready to let my dad know I'm on my way home to relieve him from Emma duty.

"Hey. Sorry, I dropped my phone and the three hundred other things I had in my hands."

"Hey. How was class?" A gravelly voice I recognize immediately comes through my car speaker, and it is definitely not my dad's.

"Oh. Peter. Hi." We've been talking on the phone every night after Emma goes to sleep and texting randomly throughout the day too. I was not expecting him to call for a few more hours but the surprise brings a smile to my lips. "I can't believe you remembered. It was pretty good. I worked for a few hours before class then had a meeting with some other students about a project afterward. I'm headed home now."

"Of course I remember. I want to run an idea past you."

"Okay..." I say hesitantly. "What's up?"

"I really want to come see you. You said Emma is with her dad this weekend right?"

"Yeah, she is." One of the first things Peter and I talked about after he left two weeks ago was the fact that meeting Emma is off the table until I'm absolutely sure it's worth introducing them. He didn't press me any further on it, and I've been secretly hoping he'd want to see me this weekend as much as I want to see him. "You really want to make the drive again so soon?"

"I'd have made the trek last weekend too. I can stay at Rob's. I just need to see you again."

"Emma leaves at five on Friday. When can you be here?" There's no way my eagerness isn't coming through in my voice despite my trying to tamper it down.

"I should be there by six. Rob already said he'd blow my bed up for me." He chuckles.

"I can't wait, but I can't believe you want to sleep on an air mattress for me."

"There's not much I wouldn't do to see you again."

How am I supposed to respond to that? Verbally, I don't know, but my body responds immediately. My nipples stand at attention and the butterflies return to my stomach. *There's not much I wouldn't do to see you again.* Holy fucking swoon.

As I pull into my driveway, we say our goodbyes with promises to talk again in a few hours. I sling my backpack over my shoulder and jog up the steps ready to envelop Emma in my arms. Despite my eagerness to see Emma, I stop in the doorway as soon as I see the two of them nestled together on the couch. Emma is sprawled out on her tummy, half on the couch, half on my dad's lap as he reads her my favorite story: 'Dogs Don't Wear Sneakers.' He read it to me nearly every night growing up until I had memorized it word for word, and even then, he read it more often than not. When he came to visit Emma and me in the hospital the day she was born, he brought the same copy I'd had as a kid, now with fading and small rips from overuse.

Once he finishes the last page, he nudges Emma and points in my direction. "Mama!" she bellows as I drop my backpack to the floor and scoop her up.

"How was class, sweetheart?" My parents had me in their mid-twenties, so he's not quite fifty yet, but the effort it takes for him to rise from the couch reminds me that he's aging. The thought brings me back to my earlier thoughts about my childhood and our relationship. Papa, as he's more affectionately known around here, comes over every week to spend time with Emma while I work and go to class. He loves her even more deeply than he loves me, and she gets excited every time he walks through our door. I don't know what we'd do without him.

"It was good, Dad. Thanks for watching Emma. How was she?"

She squeals at the sound of her name.

"Perfect, as usual. She ate really well at dinner tonight, and we've read our favorite book at least a dozen times. There's a plate for you in the fridge. How was your"—he drops his voice to a whisper—"date the other day?"

Emma is still too young to have any idea what we're talking about, but we talk in hushed whispers nonetheless. I don't want to confuse her any more than her short life already has.

"Did I not tell you?"

"You did not, but I was trying not to pry. I want to know though, so fuck it." I learned my colorful language from my dad, but every time I introduce him to someone new, they're shocked when a curse word leaves his lips. He's not even old, but a grandpa with a potty mouth is intriguing, I guess. "So, how'd it go?"

"Honestly. It went really well. We've been talking every day since then, and I think he's coming down again after Emma leaves on Friday. He's thoughtful and funny. I really think you will like him."

His voice cracks as he says, "Please tell me if he's not good to you, Nessa. I still beat myself up every day for not noticing that you needed me sooner. I should have known he was—"

I cut him off as his voice breaks again. "Dad, look at me. It was not your fault. I didn't tell anyone. I didn't know how to. I promise I won't ever let it happen again. Emma deserves better."

"You deserve better, too, sweetheart. You both deserve better." He wipes at his eyes with one hand while balancing his granddaughter in the other. "I always hated him. I wish you would have listened to me."

"I know. You just say the word this time. If you hate Peter, I'll end it immediately. I'll trust your judgment from now on. I promise."

My dad has always been vocal about his opinion of my boyfriends, and I've ignored him every time. Now that I'm a parent, I realize he was trying to save me from getting hurt, but at the time, I took it as meddling. I wholeheartedly mean it when I say I will stop talking to Peter, or anyone for that matter, if my dad doesn't think he is right for me. As it turns out, he really does know what he's talking about. I can only hope that Emma doesn't have to learn that the hard way like I did.

"Dad knows best, and you know I will make it known if he isn't right for you, for both of you," he adds with a big squeeze hug. "I'll see you next week. I love you."

"I love you too."

After giving Emma a big kiss on her cheek and handing her

back to me, he adds, "I love you, too, Emmy," before walking out the door.

My dad's words replay in my head on a loop as I rock Emma to sleep that night. 'You deserve better too, sweetheart. You both deserve better.' Those are the words I'll hold with me long after he's gone. I intend to make him, and myself, proud this time.

CHAPTER ELEVEN

PETER

The smell of cinnamon and vanilla instantly envelops me as soon as I enter Aunt Deedee's house. Her house has had this sweet, comforting smell for as long as I can remember, and it always transports me right back to my childhood. Christmases spent here with Mom, Dad, my brother Andrew, and all our cousins. Easter egg hunts in the backyard. Countless summertime sleepovers. Aunt Deedee's house is, and has always been, the house our extended family gathers at. Her door is always open, and she's always prepared for visitors with fresh baked cookies, homemade lemonade, and hugs that can fix almost anything.

"Deedee, it's Peter. Where are you?" I call out as I set my toolbox on the kitchen counter. Her house was built in the '70s and still has the original hardwood floors and wallpaper to prove it. I've always loved Deedee's house—it's homey and eclectic—but it seems that something needs to be fixed nearly every week. This week, it's her kitchen sink. Though I'm much more technically savvy than I am a handyman, I try to help her as much as I can. Crawling under her kitchen sink to clear the blockage is the least I can do to remind her how much she means to me.

She doesn't respond, so I decide to get started on my project in case she's napping. As soon as I'm situated beneath the sink, she waltzes into the kitchen, her footsteps so light she makes no sound. "Oh, Peter. I'm glad you're here. I made cookies."

The unexpected greeting startles me with a jolt, and I crash my forehead into the pipes above me. "Son of a..." I start before remembering where I am and shut my mouth.

"Now, Peter, watch your language. You'll never find yourself a nice woman with a mouth like that." I can't help but chuckle at the thought. I think Nessa would quite understand the expletive that almost left my lips, but I don't dare tell Deedee that.

"Sorry, Aunt Deedee. If it helps, I think I can get this unclogged for you." I nod toward the sink that got me in trouble. "What kind of cookies did you make?"

Deedee loves to bake, so I know this question will distract her from my slip-up and her push for me to settle down as soon as possible.

"Chocolate chip and oatmeal raisin. Here you go." She hands me a gooey chocolate chip cookie, still warm from the oven, and a Tupperware container with several of each kind of cookie inside.

"Thanks! You know I won't eat these raisin ones, though. Yuck."

Remembering all of her children, grandchildren, nieces, nephews, and now great nieces and nephew's favorite foods is her superpower. So, I know she knows I wouldn't eat a raisin for a million dollars.

"Those aren't for you, dear."

"They're not? Then... who are they for?" There's no one else here, and I live alone. Though, I have been known to bring my boss Deedee's cookies from time to time.

Aunt Deedee is the oldest of three sisters—the youngest of which was my mom. My parents didn't have me until their mid-thirties, so although I don't know how old she is exactly, she has to be pushing seventy. Though she's dainty, she seems to be in good health and was a nurse for forty years. Her short hair is neatly combed to frame her face, and she's wearing a knitted sweater and freshly ironed jeans, like always. I trust that she's taking good care of herself, but giving me cookies she knows I loathe and suggesting I give them to... I don't even know who... has me worried her mind is slipping without me even realizing it. I make a mental note to keep an eye on her memory on my next few visits.

"They're for your lady friend."

I nearly choke on my cookie. I haven't mentioned Nessa to anyone. I know Deedee is eager for me to fall in love and settle down, which is exactly why I wanted to see how things go before mentioning anything to her.

"My what?" The words come out in a cough.

"I have my way of finding things out even when you can't be bothered to tell me," she scolds. "Rob called to see how I was doing this morning and told me all about her. I thought you might want to bring her some cookies. You can't show up empty handed, you know."

"Oh. Um. Thanks." I'm stammering. I should have known she'd find out anyway.

"Relax, Peter. I'm not upset. I do wish you'd have told me, though."

"I'm sorry, Deedee. I didn't want to get anyone's hopes up. I promise to come over Monday and tell you all about my weekend."

"Perfect. I'll make cinnamon rolls." And just like that, I know she's already gotten her hopes up. She's mentally planning my wedding as we speak.

Cinnamon rolls are my absolute favorite, and Deedee always makes them for me when something big happens—my birthday, high school and college graduation, and every single morning for the first month that I lived with her. She's always been able to read me like a book, and the thought that she's anticipating me having good news to share by Monday makes me smile.

"Can't wait! Well since you already know I'll be gone this weekend, you won't be surprised when I tell you I won't be able to make this week's shopping date." Since Aunt Kathy passed last year, I've gone with Aunt Deedee to the grocery store twice a month every month. She's more than capable of making the trip on her own, but I know she enjoys the company. Plus, I like knowing she won't have to carry in and put away everything on her own. If I had known before yesterday that I was going to visit Nessa this weekend, I'd have planned to take her tonight instead. Since I didn't plan this well enough, I add, "But, I have an idea."

"I think I can handle one trip on my own, dear."

"I'm sure you can, but what if I show you how to order it on your phone? It's about time you learned how, and it'll be handy for times we can't go together or the weather makes it difficult for you to drive. Then when I'm here Monday, I can help you get any heavy stuff put away while we visit."

Aunt Deedee is surprisingly good with technology, given her age. Her learning how to order anything she needs online will put me at ease while I'm gone, especially if these trips become a regular occurrence like I hope they will. Everything she needs being delivered directly to her doorstep, ensuring she only has to carry them a short distance, is nice too.

"That sounds fine. Stay for dinner and you can show me how to do it while we cook."

I don't cook often anymore, outside of frozen meals that require zero prep, but Deedee made sure I had all the skills necessary when I lived here. We often cooked dinner together after school and breakfast on weekends. It feels unnecessary to cook for just myself, which is why I rarely do it anymore, but she makes me put my rusty skills to good use anytime I'm here for a meal.

As I chop the veggies, I walk her through how to schedule a

grocery order to be delivered this Sunday and save all of her information into the app for future use. While dinner is in the oven, she scrolls and adds items to her cart like a seasoned pro.

Nearly two hours later, her sink is back in working order, I'm stuffed beyond belief, and am finally home to pack for tomorrow's trip. I don't need much, and normally I'd throw a couple pairs of pants and a few T-shirts into a bag and call it a day. But tonight, I find myself choosing things I specifically think Nessa might like.

After she wore her second favorite F word sweatshirt to the coffee shop, we bonded over our shared love for football. Knowing we both have the same favorite team, I fold my Kansas City Chiefs polo—the one that accentuates my pecs just right, making them look more prominent than they really are—and pack it neatly into my suitcase.

If I had my way, we wouldn't leave Nessa's house the entire weekend. With this in mind, I pack a couple comfier options to lounge in. Knowing Nessa is probably cooped up in her house more than she'd like and that she may need to be distracted from missing Emma this weekend, I also pack some casual date type attire. I throw in a couple hoodies and a few shoe options for good measure.

Aunt Deedee's *'you can't show up empty handed, you know'* keeps playing in my head as I pack. I pull my phone out and decide to make a delivery order of my own then head to put my packed bag into my car. I plan to head straight to Nessa's as soon as I leave the office tomorrow and do not want to have to take a detour home to grab my things. It would only add twenty extra minutes to my drive, but I'm eager to be there already, so every minute counts.

It's nearly 10:00 p.m. now, and the anticipation of our nightly phone call has me checking my phone every few minutes. Despite the distance and the fact that we haven't seen each other in two weeks, we've fallen into a solid routine. Every morning on my way to work, I send her a *'good morning'* text. Without fail, she responds immediately having already gotten up with Emma for the day.

We message back and forth throughout the day, chat for a few minutes on my lunch break, and end every night with a video call that often lasts an hour or more. It's not the same as being with her, but it makes me hopeful that maybe we can make this long distance thing work for the time being.

I'm instantly pulled from my worries about how we could possibly remedy the distance between us as soon as I see my phone light up with a FaceTime call.

"Hey there, beautiful." A smile spreads across my face as I answer the call and her face fills the screen.

"Emma took forever to fall asleep tonight. I know it sounds silly, but I think she can sense my trepidation about her leaving again tomorrow. It's only her third visit with him, so she can't possibly know it's coming. I haven't been able to stop worrying about it all night, and I swear she can tell."

"That doesn't sound silly. I'm sure she can feel your unease. Everything will be okay though, and I'll be there. I'm a good distraction."

"Oh, I bet you are." She winks, wearing a mischievous grin. She has definitely let her guard down over these last two weeks and seems genuinely excited for my visit. I promised not to push her, and I won't, but just the thought of her in my arms does unspeakable things to me.

After nearly two hours of effortless conversation, she forces me to hang up so I can get some sleep before an early day tomorrow. She's got a project due next week, and I know our late night calls have to be putting her behind. I don't want to be *that* kind of a distraction. But after weeks of talking with her every single night, I couldn't possibly stop now, even if I wanted to.

CHAPTER TWELVE

NESSA

Today's the day I've not so patiently been waiting for. Though our almost constant communication since I last saw Peter has definitely helped, my nerves are still getting the best of me. So far, he is everything I didn't know I was looking for. He's thoughtful, he really, truly listens when I speak, and it seems that nothing ruffles his feathers. Despite every part of me noting how polar opposite he is from Matthew, the last little wall around my heart refuses to budge.

Matthew was sweet at first, too, but my time in grad school has opened my eyes to the red flags that I missed because I hadn't known to look for them. At twenty-one, I interpreted his anger as passion. *He's only doing this because he loves me*, I'd reassure myself. *I'll be better, and then he won't act like this anymore.* I initially thought a friendship with someone like Rob was going to be Peter's first red flag, yet I still haven't found any. However, I'm no longer naive to the fact that it's still far too soon to be sure.

Though trepidation sits firmly in the back of my mind, I've been counting down the hours all day. I had just finished my project and all of next week's homework when Emma emerged from my room after her nap. I've successfully shoved the pile of clean clothes just waiting to be folded into a closet—out of sight out of mind—and am now planning what I'll order for dinner as Emma and I wait for Matt to arrive any minute.

She is nestled on my lap, sippy cup in one hand and a granola bar in the other, when the obnoxious rev of Matthew's engine pierces my ears. She startles and clings to me as I carry her to the front door. Before I can reach for the handle, the front door flies open slamming into the wall with a loud thud.

Lorelai lunges towards him with a hiss and swipes at his ankles, claws out and ready. She's never liked Matt, typically preferring to cower out of sight when he was home. Now that we've escaped, she's apparently ready to let him know how she feels. Her impeccable judge of character is apparent now more than ever.

"Go on. It's okay. I'll be right back," I soothe as I shut the door behind me.

"Let me have her," Matt practically barks as he yanks the Minnie Mouse backpack full of Emma's things from my grasp.

He can't be bothered to supply the things she needs in his own home, so I meticulously pack her a bag every other Friday, filled with everything she could possibly need while she's gone. It has an ample supply of diapers, wipes, and diaper rash cream, just in case, as well as snacks I know she'll eat, plenty of clothes, and even Band-Aids.

The first time he picked her up, I added baby Tylenol to the bag in case she needed a dose to soothe her teething gums. After remembering the many so-called jokes he's made about giving her an extra dose so she wouldn't wake him in the middle of the night, I promptly removed it from her bag. I then spent the entire weekend convinced she was in pain without me there to soothe her, but that was better than the alternative.

I'm abruptly pulled from my thoughts when he hisses, "I said give her to me," and pries her from my arms.

"Excuse me, young man." My overly nosy neighbor, Ms.

Garcia, calls out as she approaches. I've never been more thankful for her meddling than I am right now. Every encounter with Matt puts me on the brink of a panic attack, but with a witness, I know he'll put his nice guy mask back in place.

"Good evening, ma'am." He tips his ball cap in her direction.

"You best watch the way you speak to her. Do you hear me, young man?" I've never been so pleased by a grown man being reprimanded in my entire life.

"Of course, ma'am. My apologies." He glares at me as he turns to load Emma into his truck.

"I love you, sweet girl," I call over his shoulder as he slams the door, preventing me from telling her goodbye.

I slump against the hard brick exterior of the home I've so desperately created for Emma as I watch her disappear from my view. Before I can force myself back inside, Nora pulls into my driveway.

"I really hope he saw me flip him off." She grabs a tote bag from the passenger seat before walking over to me.

I snort as she grabs me by the hand to pull me up from my slumped, almost seated, position. "Ms. Garcia put him in his place too. Though I have no doubt he's already convinced himself she bought into his facade."

"Go old lady Garcia. I knew I liked her." With her arms around my shoulders, she guides me back into the house. Lorelai stands on the windowsill, her back arched like the black cat in every Halloween movie, until I'm safely back inside and Nora shuts the door behind us.

"What are you doing here?"

"I knew you needed moral support today. Plus, I brought you something." She slides the tote bag off her shoulder and opens it, revealing its contents.

"What is this?" I ask, knowing full well what it is.

She proudly holds up a lilac purple, lacy thong and an industrial size box of condoms. "Ribbed for your pleasure," she guffaws.

I want to protest, to tell her she's got our relationship all wrong, but instead, I howl with laughter. "You're right. I definitely needed moral support." I choose to simply ignore the gifts now sitting on the coffee table being investigated by my cat.

"These are just in case," she adds. "You can never be too prepared. I just hope you shaved your legs."

"Just in case I suddenly develop the stamina of a mythical sex goddess?" I chortle "And no, it's winter. No one has seen my legs in months."

"Unacceptable. Let's go." With a firm grasp on my arm, she drags me down the hall to my bathroom and begins to fill the tub. "Just in case," she says again. "Armpits too."

"Yes, mother," I reply with an overly exasperated sigh. "Peter owes you big time." I purposely didn't shave my legs in the shower last night as my own little insurance policy. I'm far less likely to take off my pants with grizzly bear level hairy legs.

"Okay, now that we can put the chainsaw away and use a normal razor"—she laughs at her own bad, and scarily accurate, joke—"I have to go. Have fun tonight. Don't do anything I wouldn't do." She winks as she turns to leave.

Now that I'm silky smooth, I climb out of the bath, grab a towel, and slip my headphones into my ears. Time to listen to a good book, get ready, and order some dinner before Peter gets here. The altercation with Matt still has me on high alert; focusing on the book I've been listening to should help calm me back down.

Thirty minutes later, I'm jolted from my book by the sound of my doorbell. I know it's just a doorbell; normal people ring the doorbell. But I was expecting the three light raps at my door that he did the morning after our… our not-date. The doorbell sound just has a harsher tone than the light knocks I associate with

Peter. I shake the odd thoughts from my brain as I open the front door, but it's not Peter I see.

Confusion floods my features as I take in my front porch. There are several grocery bags placed neatly in the corner. I did not order these. Honestly, the fee for grocery delivery is not something I can justify right now. My meager earnings from the job my professors very likely created just for me, coupled with WIC and SNAP benefits, are just enough to get us by while I earn my degree. If it's possible to order something with free delivery, I jump at the chance to avoid the store with a toddler, but grocery delivery doesn't fall into that category. So Emma and I get our groceries the old fashioned way. Before I can decide what to do with the groceries, Peter's car glides into view.

"Let me help you with those," he calls as he jumps from the car. "Perfect timing."

"Oh, thanks, but they're not mine. I didn't order these."

"I know. I did. I'll carry these in then come back out for my things."

"Oh, okay. Thanks." His comment has me even more confused. He told me he's staying at Rob's this weekend. Why does he have stuff to bring in?

"I brought a few of the games I've created for us to play together. I figured you didn't have a gaming system to play them on, so I brought that too. Be right back." He hands me a colorful bouquet of flowers that he pulled from one of the bags along with a container of catnip before going back out to his car.

My unease instantly fades. Not that I don't like the idea of him staying here tonight—I do more than I care to admit—but him not pushing the issue gives me much needed comfort. I'm sure he'd gladly stay if I ask, but it's important to me that I make the decision all on my own. The flowers don't hurt either. It's been years since someone has bought me flowers, and the thoughtful gesture makes me smile.

Once he's back inside, he sets his arm full of stuff to the ground and grabs the catnip container. "Where's Lorelai?"

"You really bought her catnip?"

"Sure did. She holds the key to your heart, and I'm not above bribing." Not only did he actually bring catnip for her, he remembered her name and the comment I made about her liking him. One more point for Peter!

As he hooks the gaming system up to my TV, I start to lay out the Chinese takeout I ordered. "I hope you like Chinese food. The restaurants in your area have nothing on Springfield style Chinese."

"It's one of my favorites, actually. How do you know the restaurants near me aren't better?" His eyes widen as he takes in the spread of food on my coffee table. Rory and human Lorelai Gilmore would be proud, if I do say so myself.

"I went to Mizzou. I tried every Asian style restaurant in the area. Trust me when I say, this knocks it all out of the park." Columbia, where the University of Missouri—more affectionately called Mizzou—is located, is only about thirty minutes from Jeff City, so I'm sure he's tried many of the places that I did.

"I'm a takeout connoisseur. I'll be the judge of that," he says as he piles noodles, rice, and chicken onto his plate. "You never mentioned you went to college at Mizzou. So did I. Maybe we met there and didn't even know it."

I can't help but imagine how differently my life could have been if we really had met there, years earlier. Emma could have him to look up to instead of the mess she's stuck with.

After we finish dinner, he helps clear the table and puts the remaining containers in the fridge before handing me a controller. "What should we play first?"

"Hmm. I haven't played one of these in years. What did you bring?"

He lays three games out on the couch. I've never heard of any of them, but that's to be expected. "This one's the closest I have to Mario Kart."

"Let's try that one." Him remembering my favorite game after only mentioning it once, solidifies something in my mind: he's different.

I've never been a big fan of video games, aside from the few I played with my sister growing up, so I'm pleasantly surprised to realize that I'm having a fantastic time. And that I don't completely suck. I won several rounds of the racing game, eventually got to the point of not dying instantly in the shooting game, and didn't completely hate the dragons in the fantasy game.

Our conversations have flowed naturally from the other games he's created and the cookies his aunt sent with him, to the reason behind my beloved cat's name. We've been playing for a while now, when he sets his controller down, pulls my legs across his, and wraps his arm around my shoulder.

"Is this okay?"

"It's perfect." The tender way he's looking into my eyes leaves me speechless. After a beat, I add, "I need to call to tell Emma goodnight."

"No problem. I can head to Rob's now so you can talk with her."

"I'm not ready for you to leave. It'll only take a minute. She can only say four words," I chuckle. "Stay right where you are, just be quiet please."

He mimes zipping his lips closed then resumes lightly rubbing his thumb over my thigh. It's a small gesture, but it provides the comfort I need to press Matthew's contact in my phone and brace myself for his answer. The call only lasts a few minutes, but Matthew doesn't say a word and Emma appears to have settled in. The ease of this phone call after the drama when he picked Emma up, brightens my mood even more.

"I want to try one of those cookies you brought."

He hops up from the couch, the comfy one of course, and snatches the container of cookies off the counter. "I want to kiss you again," he blurts as he hands me the container.

I can't say no to that, now can I? Cookies can wait.

When I don't say anything right away, he grabs at the cookie container in an attempt to back track. Before he can reach it, I take his hand in mine and gently press my lips to his.

He lets out a soft moan before pulling back. "Are you sure? I don't want to over—"

Before he can finish his sentence, I part his lips with mine. "I'm sure," I whisper against his soft, full lips. At my assurance, his hand immediately rakes through my hair, and I reposition myself into his lap, one leg on either side of him.

His kisses grow more frantic as his hands gently explore down my back and cup my ass. The slight tug of my hips forward makes his need evident against me. I throw my head back with a gasp as he begins to kiss and lick down my neck and across my collarbone. I begin to circle my hips, rubbing lightly against his erection, and let out a soft groan of pleasure.

"Fuck. Nessa. Fuck."

"Mmm," is all I can get out in reply.

He stands, my legs wrapped around his waist, and turns to lay me on the couch, stepping between my legs as he does it. He leans down, pressing his chest to mine, and gently nibbles my ear and neck. "I better go," he whispers in my ear.

"No. Wait. What?" I'm panting, my back arched off the couch toward him. "Why?"

"I have to stop while I still can, Ness. I want you so fucking bad, but not yet." He drops a soft kiss to my shoulder before adding, "Good night, beautiful."

I can't move from this spot even once he's gone. I know he's right. I need a little more time, but god damn. I've never wanted someone so badly in my life. My body's still pulsing with desire when I finally force myself off the couch and into bed. I'll be ready soon enough, and I can already tell it will be 110 percent worth the wait.

CHAPTER THIRTEEN

PETER

A series of buzzes and chimes jolts me from my dream. I've been replaying yesterday evening in my head all night, even while asleep. I know Nessa gets up early with a toddler everyday, while I like to start my weekend days as close to noon as possible. I don't want to show up to Nessa's too early, in case she decided to catch up on lost sleep as well this morning, but I also don't want to waste any of the time we have left this weekend. Thus, my alarm telling me it's time to get going. I pull on my most comfortable pair of jeans and a T-shirt then top it with my favorite KC Chiefs hoodie; it's faded and worn in all the right places.

As I walk into the kitchen, the smell of bacon and eggs hits me as Nora hands me a plate. "Breakfast is almost ready. Though, I must admit I was disappointed to see your car in the driveway this morning."

I got to Rob and Nora's late enough last night that everyone was in their rooms with the lights turned out, so I showered and went straight to bed. "It smells phenomenal, but I think I'll go have breakfast with Ness. I thought Rob told you I was staying here this weekend?"

"A girl can hope, you know? I was manifesting it going so well you'd decide to stay there instead."

"Coming back here was the last thing I wanted to do, but I'm not going to push her. You're doing that enough for the both of us." It comes out as playfully as intended. I know Nora's pushes are helping my case, allowing me to take things at Nessa's pace. Nessa has opened up about Matthew a lot during our daily conversation, and I fully support her need to take things slow. I refuse to give her any reason to believe my intentions aren't pure. Nora's meddling is the perfect amount of nudging for the both of us. "Here, these are for you."

"You got me flowers? These should be for Nessa, not me."

"Woah, man. You're making me look bad." Rob looks at the bouquet of white and yellow daisies that Nora is now preparing for a vase. I'm sure he meant it to sound like a joke, but it comes out accusatory.

"They're just a thank you for meddling in all the right ways. I genuinely enjoy spending time with Nessa, and it wouldn't have happened without you. For the record, I got her flowers too. I'm out of here; see you tonight."

"I really hope I don't see you tonight," Nora calls as I leave the kitchen.

I really hope she doesn't see me tonight either. Nessa's comfort level with me grows every time we talk, but actually being able to see each other face to face seems to have pushed our relationship, or whatever you want to call it, to another level entirely.

After saying hi to Daisy, I grab my phone, wallet, and keys then head to my car. Nessa opens the door before I can even finish knocking, as if she's been waiting for me to arrive.

"Good morning, beautiful." I plant a soft kiss on her forehead as she snatches the coffee I grabbed on the way from my hands.

"Good morning, my knight in shining armor. You know me so well." Her surprise and delight are evident as she takes her first sip. "Wait, is this *my* coffee order? There's no way you remembered everything that goes into my signature drink after hearing me order it *one* time. My order is on par with that of a sociopath."

"Yes it is. That's why I had the barista type it into the notes app on my phone after you ordered it. There's absolutely no way I was remembering all of that," I chuckle.

"Holy shit. You're perfect." Her eyes widen as soon as the words are out of her mouth. She might not have meant to say that out loud, but hearing it makes my heart warm.

"I know." I shrug my shoulder and give her a 'what can you do' look before adding, "Ready to make some breakfast with me?"

"Sure! What did you have in mind?"

"I thought I'd teach you to make Aunt Deedee's famous cinnamon rolls. They're my favorite." Though Deedee's version is far superior to mine, I've made them with her so many times that mine are a close second.

"Let's do it." She washes her hands as I grab the grocery bags from the fridge.

As I slide in beside her to wash my hands, too, I notice the flowers I brought her sitting perched in the windowsill above her kitchen sink in an intricate glass vase. I chose daisies for Nora, because I know they're her favorite—hell, she named her daughter after them—but Nessa's bouquet is much more colorful and eclectic with several different flowers bundled throughout. They fit her personality perfectly.

Now that the dough has risen and is ready to be rolled out, I press myself lightly against her back and wrap my arms on either side of her. She lets out a low sigh at my touch, and I can feel her heartbeat quicken against my chest. With the rolling pin grasped in her hands, I take her hands in mine, and we roll it out together.

Cinnamon cream cheese filling sticks to my fingers as we spread it across the top. She spins around to face me. Now pressed chest to chest, she stares directly into my eyes as she licks the sweet filling off my finger with a small moan of pleasure. Damn, that was sexy. I never thought baking cinnamon rolls would turn me on, but here we are.

I slide the rolls into the oven and return to Nessa, lifting her up onto the counter. Her cheeks and hair are dusted with flour, but her hands are completely covered in it. She places them on my cheeks as she pulls me in for a deep, lingering kiss, leaving flour handprints and a lust-filled grin on my face. I've never made these with anyone but Deedee, and I have no doubt she'd be appalled at how sensual we just made the whole process.

Actually, I don't know. Maybe she'd be proud to know her recipe is helping me win Nessa over. Either way, I never want to make these with anyone else ever again.

"What do you want to do today?" After smashing three rolls each, I rinsed while she loaded the dishes. Since I had my perfect night in yesterday, it's Nessa's turn to pick what to do.

"There's this trail I really like that has farm animals and a creek. I love taking Emma there to see the baby sheep and splash in the creek after we walk the trail. I'd love to show it to you. It's beautiful."

"Sounds perfect." Any chance to get a glimpse into her world sounds perfect to me.

The trail is only a short drive from her house, and we're briskly walking, hand in hand, in no time. "So tell me about Aunt Deedee. She's clearly important to you, not to mention, she makes a mean cinnamon roll."

"She really is, and hers are even better than mine. She's the closest thing to a mother figure that I have left." I haven't told her much about my childhood yet, and the gravity of my statement is evident in her eyes.

"What do you mean?" I'm used to receiving pitied looks when I talk about my parents, but Nessa's features suggest only curiosity and care, not pity.

"Both of my parents passed away when I was a teenager. Well, my mom died from cancer just before I became a teenager. I was twelve. My dad didn't pass away until I was sixteen, but Deedee stepped in to fill her shoes as best she could after Mom left us. She's Mom's older sister and always felt a responsibility to us. She'd come over for dinner, make sure my grades didn't fall, and take my brother and I shopping anytime she noticed we needed something. My dad did not handle the grief as well as she did, and neither Andrew or I would have been able to thrive without her."

"Oh, Peter. I'm so sorry to hear that. She sounds like an amazing person."

I lost my parents more than a decade ago, and them not being around eventually just became normal to me. But the way Nessa leans her head against my bicep in comfort has me realizing that there are still reasons to feel their loss deeply despite the fact that they've been gone nearly half of my life.

They'll never get to meet Nessa or see the joy she brings to me. They won't be there on my wedding day. They'll never hold my kids in their arms. The realization is enough for my long buried grief to resurface and bring a sting to my eyes.

"I know I'm not a real counselor yet, but I'm a good listener."

"I know you are. You're going to make a fantastic counselor one day." I put my arm around her shoulders and squeeze her to me as we continue our walk. "What do you think about coming to visit me in two weeks when Emma is at her dad's again?"

"I'd like that."

"You can stay with me, if you want, or we can get you a hotel room. Either is perfectly okay with me. While you're there, we could visit Aunt Deedee. I know she'd jump at the chance to meet you. You'll like her. She's just as outspoken as you are."

"It's a date."

I'm not sure if she means it's a *date*-date, but that's how I'm choosing to interpret it anyway. It's a date, indeed.

"I'm getting a little chilly; ready to go?" she adds with a small shiver.

"I'm ready when you are." Though it's now March, spring has yet to make an appearance. It's not cold, necessarily, but the wind does carry a small bite with it. At the feel of the goosebumps on her arms, I slip my hoodie over my head and start to place it over hers.

"You're going to freeze without this. I'll be okay," she protests as I get the hoodie settled and she slides her arms into the sleeves.

"We'll walk fast. I'm fine." Despite the instant chill I feel now that my arms are bare, the sight of her in my hoodie makes my body instantly heat.

"You brought a Chiefs hoodie just for me, didn't you? I'm never taking this off. It smells like you."

"It smells like me, huh?"

She playfully swats at my arm. "You know what I mean."

Yes I do, and I quickly make a mental note to wear the same cologne next time I see her. It's my favorite hoodie, but I'll gladly let her wear it as much as she wants. She wears it so much better than I do.

"You like the way I smell. That's what you mean." I playfully nudge her with my elbow and give her a wink.

We spent over an hour walking the trail, and even though Nessa seems unfazed, I am far from used to moving this much. Being a video game creator means I spend most of my days in front of a screen. My feet are screaming at me to let them free. As soon as I'm inside, I immediately kick my shoes off and plop down onto the loveseat.

"Oh, boy. That couch is not for sitting. It's just decoration. Ugly decoration, but it fills the room up." She laughs. "Do your butt a favor and come over to this one."

She is not wrong. Oof. That couch, if you can even call it that, has no business being used as seating. I quickly take her advice and take the spot next to her on the actual couch.

"Want to watch a movie?"

I've fallen back into my usual movie selections despite my movie choice the night Rob sent Nessa's picture. Tonight, however, a rom-com while snuggled up next to Nessa sounds just right.

"Sure!" She hands me the remote and pushes herself up off the couch. "I'll be right back. A movie requires popcorn and comfy pants. Pick whatever movie you want."

I find the perfect movie then head to the kitchen in search of popcorn. "Where do you keep the popcorn?" I holler as I hear her footsteps approaching.

She enters the kitchen, and I immediately take in her change in attire. She's gotten rid of the leggings and form fitting top she was wearing earlier and traded it in for… my hoodie. I know she was wearing it at the trail, but this is different. Damn. She looks fine as hell, and I have no doubt that my face is showing exactly what I'm thinking.

"You're trying to guess what I'm wearing underneath this, aren't you?" She smirks and slides past me into the kitchen. Well, *now* that's exactly what I'm thinking about. The fabric lands just below her ass. It's entirely possible that there's nothing underneath, and I can't bring myself to think about anything else.

"Bowls are down there." She points, pulling my eyes back up to hers.

Giant bowl of popcorn in hand, we make our way back to the couch. She snuggles up against me and balances the bowl on both of our laps. "What are we watching?"

I point to the screen. "You've never seen this?"

"Nope. Looks like something my grandma would watch."

I gasp in exaggerated horror and clutch at my chest. "It's *When Harry Met Sally*. It's a classic. How have you never seen this?"

"I'm pretty sure it's older than I am. I'm surprised it's in color."

"Okay, fair point. It *is* older than you are, but it was one of my mom's favorite movies. I must have watched it with her a hundred times."

I'm instantly flooded with memories of laying in my mom's bed, curled up beside her while this movie played in her hospital room. I could quote it nearly word for word, but Mom was too weak by then to quote it with me. So, we watched it in silence instead. She passed away two weeks later, and I haven't seen this movie since then.

"She did a pretty good job with you, so I'm going to have to trust her judgment on this one."

She places one hand on my cheek and wipes at the lone tear that snuck from my eye before pressing play. Despite my solid stance on talking during movies, the few times she interjected to crack a joke or comment on something she noticed felt natural and unintrusive.

By the end of the movie, Nessa has her head in my lap, her feet curled beneath her, and is gently snoring. That's my cue to go, so I scoop her into my arms, gently laying her head on my chest, and carry her to bed.

This is my first time in her bedroom, and I worry she wasn't ready for me to see it when I notice the Costco size box of condoms on her bedside table. I'm regretting my decision to bring her in here; it feels like an invasion of privacy, but the couch is not comfortable enough to sleep on all night long. She begins to stir from her slumber when I place her on the mattress and pull the covers up to her chin.

"Good night, Ness. See you tomorrow." I gently kiss her cheek and turn towards the door.

"Stay." Her voice is raspy with sleep, but she's looking intently into my eyes.

"What?" My mind must be playing tricks on me.

"Stay."

"Are you sure?"

"One hundred percent. Don't overthink it. Just come cuddle me, please."

At that, I slip in beside her, wrap my arms around her waist, and tenderly pull her towards me. With her head on my arm and body fully pressed against mine, I quickly fall into a deep, contented sleep.

CHAPTER FOURTEEN

NESSA

I slept better last night than I have in years, an undeniable sense of peace enveloping me. When I lived with Matt, I was constantly on edge, never sure when he'd have his next outburst. Though I haven't lived with him in over a year, the residual fear still lives deep inside of me. Not to mention, he knows where I live and is not above coming here simply to make a scene.

As I blink the sleep from my eyes, the memories of last night flood me. I fell asleep in Peter's lap, and he carried me to bed. He carried me to bed! At the memory, I realize why I am so damn comfortable right now. Peter's arm is delicately draped over my waist, my back and ass are pressed firmly against his chest and groin, and our legs are intertwined.

Is this why I slept so deeply last night? Even when Emma isn't here to wake me up with the sun, I usually wake up on my own at the same time, like clockwork. A quick glance at my phone tells me that I slept an extra two hours this morning. Peter's warm embrace clearly provided the comfort and safety I needed to fully relax and get a good night's rest.

I gradually roll to my other side, bringing my chest to his and slinging my leg over his hip. He doesn't even budge. My face mere inches from his, I take in his long black eyelashes, slightly messy hair, and the way his steady breathing feels against my chest. I could stay tucked up next to him like this for hours, but my urgent need to pee wins out. Not wanting to wake him, I gently slide out from under his arm, slowly placing it back onto the mattress, then tiptoe to my dresser. I quickly find a pair of athletic leggings and top then begin my stealthy escape to the door when the world's largest box of condoms catches my eye.

Was Nora expecting some kind of orgy? There's literally 200 condoms in there. I cross my fingers in hopes that Peter did not notice them when he carried me in here last night. I'm mortified, but I know Nora will absolutely crack up when she finds out her truckload of condoms now sits there mocking us. Peter has been unbelievably sweet and understanding about my need to feel completely comfortable with him before taking things to that level, but I've probably given him blue balls twice now. Thanks for the reminder, Nor.

I didn't used to be a morning person, but nearly a year and half of early morning wake ups with Emma has changed me. When the weather is nice enough—like it is today—we often go on a walk around the neighborhood after breakfast. With no one here demanding to be fed, I skip straight to the outside portion of my morning routine. I shove a single headphone into place, stretch, and start to jog. A good book and some cardio is all it takes to completely free my mind.

Peter is still in bed when I return, so I take the opportunity for a solo shower. Being the only adult in the home means Emma is by my side nearly every second of the day, including when I shower. I hate losing every other weekend with her and am beyond ready for her to be home, but a shower with both arms free is a luxury I'm prepared to revel in. Once the water runs cold, I force myself out of the shower and into a towel. I can hear Peter moving about the bedroom, so I throw on some clothes and make my way out of the bathroom.

"Good morning, beautiful. How long have you been up?"

"A bit. I went for a run and showered while you slept the day away."

"You should have woken me. Waking up with you in my arms is quickly becoming a dream of mine."

"I have to say, you're definitely missing out. It was not a bad way to start the day."

"See, now I have FOMO. Definitely wake me next time. I need to see what it's like for myself."

'Next time.' The thought of waking up in his arms again sends warm, fuzzy feelings throughout my body. It really was the best way to start my day, but now, I could really use some caffeine. "Follow me," I say as I head toward the kitchen. "What should we do today?"

"I only have a few hours before I need to head out. I promised Rob I'd help figure out what's wrong with his new controller before I make the drive home. Do you mind if we just hang out here until then?"

"Sure!" I plop down on the couch, cinnamon roll in one hand and an oversized 'Luke's' mug in the other. After setting my coffee on the table, I reach for the game controllers. "I'm definitely going to kick your ass this time."

"Not a chance."

I lost the first three games but am now on a two game winning streak when he blurts, "How many people did Nora think you'd be having sex with this weekend?"

I spit my coffee clear across the room even though I'm certain he just said that to distract me. It worked—I drove straight off a cliff and am now in last place.

"Clearly she expected us to build a condom fortress," I quip as I tug at the joystick on his controller, evening the playing field. "I was hoping you somehow didn't see those. Nora thinks she's funny."

"They came with a neon arrow pointing straight to them. Hard to miss, but I have to agree with her. She's a little funny."

I hold my thumb and forefinger mere centimeters apart. "Just a tad, and now we have a lifetime supply. Jokes on her."

"Hmm. 'Lifetime?' I don't know about that." He nudges my arm with his, never taking his eyes off the screen, but I don't miss the way his cheeks color when he says it.

Our remaining time together flies by in what feels like seconds. Peter has gathered his gear and treated Lore to a handful of catnip before he notices the dent in the wall behind the door. "What happened here?"

"Oh. Um." I hesitate, though I'm not sure why. "Matt threw the door open when he came to get Emma on Friday."

Anger instantly covers Peter's face. "He did what?" It comes out on a loud growl, and I involuntarily flinch and step backwards. He notices immediately and pulls me into his arms. "I'm so sorry, Ness. I did not mean to scare you. I just didn't know it was possible to hate someone I've never even met."

"It's okay," I choke out in a barely audible whisper. The way he's holding me is slowly bringing my heart rate back to a normal pace. I know he wasn't raising his voice at me, and the regret is plastered across his features. But a man raising his voice in my vicinity will likely never be *not* scary again.

"It's not okay. I never want you to be scared to tell me things. I'm so sorry. Did he hurt you or Emma?"

"Just the wall." My voice is still small and hesitant.

"I'll fix it next time I'm here. I'm so sorry, Nessa." He holds me in a tight embrace for several more minutes then gingerly kisses my hair before leaving. I've heard plenty of apologies before, but none ever felt quite like that one. It was full of tenderness and remorse like I've never experienced before. His raised voice was a setback in terms of trust, though something tells me I'll never hear that tone from him again.

After Peter is gone, I curl up on the couch with Lorelai and open up my laptop. I've got a couple hours before Emma will be home, and after putting my responsibilities on the back burner all weekend, I have work to do.

Halfway through my reading, my phone buzzes against the table.

> **PETER**
> I had the best weekend. I'm so sorry I scared you.

> **NESSA**
> I'm okay, really. He pisses me off too. It was just unexpected.

> **PETER**
> I've been beating myself up about it since I left. I did not want to have to leave after that. I will literally never raise my voice again, not even if the Chiefs make it to the next Super Bowl. That's how bad I feel.

I've known him less than a month, but somehow I don't doubt what he's saying for a second. I'm always going to be on the lookout for red flags, but my gut is telling me I can trust Peter.

The weeks that followed were business as usual. Matthew dropped Emma off without incident, and we've spent the days since like we always do: filled with walks, playing, reading, and endless snacks. Every morning starts with a text from Peter and ends with our nightly phone call. Despite the physical distance between us, our familiar routine provides so much comfort. We talk about everything and nothing—Emma's latest antics, his work projects, and the ever present hum of anticipation for our next visit in a few days. But first, I have to get through my last class before spring break, leaving my weekend wide open for my trip to see Peter and my week completely free to spend with Emma.

This class has quickly become one of my favorites, mostly because it addresses topics that affect my day to day life even without being an actual counselor yet. It focuses on family and relationship dynamics and teaches skills we will need in order to provide marriage and family counseling after graduation. I've related to every topic we've covered so far this semester, and it seems today will be no different.

The projector begins to lightly hum as Dr. Evans pulls her presentation onto the screen. Dr. Evans is one of my favorite professors, though you wouldn't know it at first glance. She always has her hair pulled tightly into a slick pony tail at the base of her neck, not a single hair out of place. Today she's wearing a gray and white pinstriped pantsuit accented with a simple pearl necklace. Despite her prim and proper appearance, her classes are interesting and relatable. She's even been known to drop the occasional curse word. She cares about her work, and it shows not only in the way she carries herself but also in the way she teaches each of her courses.

Today's focus is Dr. Gottman—a marriage and relationship researcher who has formulated a way to predict, with startling accuracy, if a marriage will fail. I am instantly hooked, yet simultaneously unprepared for Dr. Evans to take a deep dive into something I know all too well.

Dr. Evans clicks to the next slide, and I have to stifle a chuckle. The Four Horsemen of the Apocalypse. With a name like that, clearly this isn't going to be the insight to prevent me from failing another marriage that I expected it to be.

I'm instantly proven wrong when I hear the soft click of Dr. Evans' slideshow remote and the definitions appear on the screen, propelling me into memories I've tried so hard to forget.

Criticism: a simple complaint turned into a personal attack of character. *'You're so lazy,'* Matt would sneer at the sight of a single dish left in the sink. *'Worthless. Emma deserves better than you.'* My fingers tighten around my pen as I try to slow my breathing.

Contempt: mockery, disrespect, name-calling, disgust. Matthew's signature eye-roll flashes in front of my eyes, and I'm bombarded with the names he'd hurl at me, even in front of our daughter.

Defensiveness: deflecting blame, making excuses, playing the victim. A breath hitches in my throat as I remember his frantic voicemail messages after Emma and I left. *'I only threw the cup at you so you'd put my laundry where it belongs next time.'*

I cannot bear to hear the last one. My chair slides back with a screech, and I stumble my way to the door. I need a minute. I need some air. Matthew did all of those things. All of them. No wonder our marriage failed. Once I'm out in front of the building and a light breeze wafts against my cheeks, I slump to the ground and lean against the brick exterior. *Breathe, Nessa. Breathe.*

My eyes dart up at the sound of a door's squeak. Dr. Evans holds her hand out and hoists me up off the ground. "You okay?"

I clear the lump from my throat. "Umm, yeah. I'm okay," I lie.

"You're not the first person to bolt during this lesson, and you won't be last. Everyone is taking a short break, then—"

The truth bursts from my lips before she can even invite me back inside. "I'm not okay. My husband, well almost ex-husband..." I trail off as my voice gets caught in my throat.

"I understand. If you need to leave early and finish this lesson at home, that's okay with me."

"No. No, I'm okay. I think I need to hear this."

"The next section might actually help. Join us again when you're ready." She softly closes the door behind her as she walks back inside, leaving me alone with my thoughts once again.

I spend another minute outside, listening to the birds sing and watching the sun start to dip behind the buildings. My hands are no longer trembling, my breaths are coming at a normal pace, and my heart rate is under control. Time to face this head on.

As I make my way back into the classroom, I realize my chair didn't just slide out with me. It tumbled to the floor in my haste to get out of there. Well, that's embarrassing. Maybe no one noticed, right? That's totally possible.

Nope. They definitely noticed. Every single person is staring at me as I place my chair back in its upright position. I should have left when she gave me the chance. But it's too late now. Dr. Evans is back at her podium ready to address the class.

Turns out, she was right. The second half of Gottman's predicting abilities is much easier for me to stomach. Many couples do last. Most people don't talk to their wives like they're dirt on the bottom of their shoes. Strong, lasting relationships can be built on trust, commitment, respect, and understanding.

My mind instantly pulls up memories of Peter—showing up with my ridiculous coffee order, refusing to have sex before I'm ready, the regret on his face when I flinched at his reaction to the hole Matt put in the wall, and checking on me and Emma when he knows we've had a rough day.

By the end of class, I've completely cleared all thoughts of Matthew from my mind. I will not allow the Four Horsemen to overtake me ever again. There is immense comfort in the power this realization gives me. I made the right choice in leaving, and I'll never make the wrong ones again.

CHAPTER FIFTEEN

PETER

As promised, I went straight to Aunt Deedee's after work the Monday following my last visit with Nessa, and I'm glad I did. Her delivery order was completely put away except for the bulk package of water bottles. She was unable to drag it inside, leaving it to sit on her porch all night long.

Not to mention, I promised her a breakdown of my weekend. Though she's been like a mom to me for many years, talking to her doesn't quite feel like talking to your mom about a crush. Deedee has perfectly mastered the balance between a loving mother and an interested friend who's always got your back. Most importantly, she's not afraid to put me in my place if I deserve it.

I carried her package of water bottles in and loaded them into the fridge before sitting with her on the couch, fresh lemonade in hand. I give her all the juicy details, leaving out the steamy stuff, including the sensual way Nessa licked the cream cheese from my fingers and our near hook-up on the couch. That's an image Deedee would prefer to live the rest of her life without.

As I neared the end of my play-by-play, I reached the part I most needed Deedee's guidance on. The sight of the hole in

Nessa's wall, courtesy of Matthew, still makes me want to kill him. Nessa has opened up about their relationship quite a bit, and I should have known raising my voice might trigger her. The anger I felt towards him instantly flooded me, and I blurted my thoughts without even thinking. I explain all of this as my aunt listens intently to every word.

"Oh, honey. You made a mistake. But it sounds like you've gotten so many other things right. Don't dwell on your one mess up."

"I know. Things are honestly going so well. I just couldn't live with myself if she thought I was just like him after that."

"She doesn't know you at all if she thinks, even for a second, that you'd hurt anyone."

"But I get where she's coming from. She's known me for a month. After all she's been through, that's not long enough to feel completely safe just yet."

"And that right there is exactly why she'll see who you really are, dear. Character shines through, regardless."

It's exactly what I needed to hear, even more so, I know she wouldn't have said it if she didn't wholeheartedly believe it to be true.

A few days away from our next visit, I'm back at Deedee's house—this time for a cooking lesson. I was worried that I'd ruined things with Nessa, but I'm much more confident that I didn't after the last couple weeks. Nothing has changed; we still talk everyday, and she seems genuinely excited for this weekend.

I offered to book her a hotel room near my place, but she opted to stay with me instead. Now all that's left to do is learn to cook the meal I plan to have ready when she arrives.

Okay, that's not *all* that's left to do, but it's at the top of my list. I still need to go grocery shopping, finish all the laundry so we have fresh sheets and clean towels, and decide what we'll do while she's here. Right now, though, I've chosen not to think about my growing to-do list and instead, fully focus on Aunt Deedee's lesson.

After the dish is prepped and in the oven, the alarm on my phone sounds, alerting me that it's time for my weekly car chat with Nessa. Every week after she finishes up her classes for the night, she connects me to the speaker in her car, and we talk while she drives home. It's an extra twenty minutes each week that we get to have a conversation without distractions, and it's quickly becoming my favorite twenty minutes of the week.

"How long does this need to bake?"

"Forty-five minutes at three hundred and fifty degrees."

"Perfect. I'm going to go sit on your porch swing and call Nessa." She already knows all about our car chats, so it's likely she was expecting this.

"Alright, dear."

I feel bad stepping outside during our visit, but her tone coupled with the smile on her face says that she isn't bothered by it. Hell, she actually looks quite pleased as she tops off my glass of lemonade before shooing me out the front door.

I've spent many hours on this front porch swing. It was one of my favorite places to go when I needed a break from reality growing up. The hardest days of my entire life happened right before I moved in here at sixteen. My dad had just died, leaving my brother and I with only each other. I often spent hours out here with my thoughts while watching kids ride their bikes, listening to the birds sing, and finally allowing myself to cry.

I settle into the groove I've created in the cushion after all these years, and tap Nessa's contact in my phone. She answers on the second ring, her familiar soft, sweet voice against my ear.

"How was class?" I ask after I hear her finally settle into the car.

"Class was... a lot."

"Oh no. I thought you liked this one?"

"Oh, I do. It was just heavy. That's all."

After gentle prodding on my part, she tells me all about the Four Horsemen and how she fled the room. I want nothing more than to hold her in this moment and to punch the guy who caused her so much pain.

"After receiving Matt's response to my petition for divorce this morning, I just couldn't hold it together while she explained him to a tee."

Her reaction to my raised voice makes even more sense after hearing her choke out the words to describe what she learned in class tonight, but my attention is caught on something else. Divorce papers? Since neither her or Nora had mentioned it, I assumed she was already divorced.

"What did the paperwork say?"

"Basically, he's contesting everything—the divorce, my proposed parenting plan, child support. Everything. I knew better than to expect this to be easy. I just…" Her voice cracks before finishing, "I just wish that, for once, he'd do the right thing for Emma."

I hate this guy with every fiber of my being. "I guess I thought you were already divorced." I know this is not the part I should be focusing on right now, but I can't help it.

"Ah. You've uncovered yet another piece of my baggage. It wasn't a secret or anything. I assumed Rob told you. Our marriage has been over for years, and we've been separated for more than a year. Filing for divorce just isn't cheap, you know? Do you hate me?"

"I could never." My head is spinning at this new revelation, but I'm hyper vigilant to the fact that it won't take much for her to lump me in with the Four Horsemen if I over react. I just need some time to think this through.

The rest of our conversation is uneventful, and before I know it, she's saying goodbye. Though I know Aunt Deedee would be the perfect person to talk to about this, I need to get my thoughts in order first. I have so many questions pinging around my brain like it's a pinball machine. She's married. Married!

I know it's not like that, exactly, but Matthew still being her husband literally makes me sick to my stomach. Would I have turned down the blind date if I had known she wasn't divorced yet? Maybe it took her so long to file because she didn't really want the divorce in the first place. That doesn't fit with the Nessa I know, but my mind is all over the place right now. I need some time to process this new information before bringing it up with anyone—Nessa and Deedee included. Decision made, I clear my head and rejoin Deedee for dinner.

The next two days drag by, my anticipation increasing with every second that passes. I've spent a lot of time dwelling on the news that Nessa is still married. The thought alone is enough to make my stomach turn, but I've decided to talk with Nora about it the next time I see her. She knows Nessa and her intentions so well. Despite her loyalty to her friend, I know she'll be honest with me if I have anything to worry about. Letting the worry go for now, a sudden sense of peace envelops me. Starting right now, I won't let this dampen the weekend I have planned. My to-do list is complete, dinner is in the oven, and she should be here any minute now.

A light tap at the door comes just as I'm pulling the bubbling lasagna from the oven. Still wearing my 'Kiss the Chef' apron and an oven mitt on one hand, I open the front door and take Nessa's bright pink overnight bag from her hands.

She eyes my apron and immediately follows its command, firmly pressing her lips to mine. "Something smells delicious. I thought you couldn't cook."

"I said I *don't* cook, not that I *can't* cook. But to be fair, Deedee showed me how to do this a few days ago."

"It looks amazing! Do I get to meet the infamous Aunt Deedee while I'm here?"

"I told her we'd come by if you were up for it."

"Yes! I need to meet the woman behind the cinnamon rolls. Plus, I bet she's got some embarrassing baby pictures of you lying around."

"I knew I should have hidden those." I don't care at all if she sees embarrassing pictures of me growing up, but I may snatch them before she can tomorrow, just for fun.

As we settle onto the couch with our plates, I'm instantly alert to how much of a bachelor pad this place is. The living room and kitchen are basically one room separated only by the thin trimming that follows the edge where carpet becomes linoleum. The living area is completely bare besides a small couch, recliner, end table, and the TV mounted to the wall. The kitchen only has the necessities that came with the apartment aside from the few utensils and dinnerware that fit in one singular cabinet. Until now, I've never had a need for a dining room table. Completely unfazed, she settles in beside me, turning with her legs tucked beneath her to face me.

"I never got the chance to finish telling you about class last night."

"Oh," is all I manage to say through a heaping bite. A heavy topic with potential to make her cry wasn't how I'd hoped to start our short time together, but she seems eager to tell me, and I'm not about to give her another reason to think she can't talk to me about anything.

"So the first part sucked, obviously, but after I went back in, she got to the good part."

Okay, this doesn't sound quite so bad after all.

"I won't bore you with all the jargon, but basically he didn't just identify relationships that are destined to fail. He's identified ones that will thrive. People who show genuine care for their partner, communicate when there's a conflict, and have twenty positive interactions to every one negative interaction are likely to have strong, stable relationships. Wanna know why that's good news?"

"I think I have a pretty good idea, but yes. I do want to know."

"The first half of class, she described people like Matthew, but the second half of class…" she pauses and I don't know if it's for effect or to muster up the courage to finish the rest of her sentence. "The second half of class, the good half, she described… *you.*"

Her proclamation leaves me speechless. Aunt Deedee was right: character shines through. Remind me to never doubt Deedee again. When I still can't come up with a worthy response, I softly brush her hair out of her face and cup her cheeks in my hands. I pull her toward me, gently pressing my lips to hers. She responds with frantic kisses before climbing into my lap. She wraps her arms tightly around my neck; her desire evident as she stares longingly into my eyes.

"Peter, I…" her voice comes out in a strained whisper, but is cut short by the buzzing of her phone.

I need to hear the rest of that sentence. Peter, I what? Missed you? Need a minute? Want you right now? Please, I beg you, finish that sentence.

She doesn't. Instead, she looks down to see 'Jackass' trying to FaceTime her.

"His contact name is 'Jackass' in your phone?"

"I know. I'm a terrible person. I promise as soon as Emma starts to read, I'll change it, but for now it makes me feel just a tiny bit better."

"No judgment here. It's fitting. I like it! What's my name in your phone?"

"I'm not telling." She mimes zipping her lips shut.

"Oh, come on. Now I have to know."

"Stop it. I need to compose myself so I can tell Emma goodnight." She laughs as she turns to guard her phone screen like my contact name is CIA level top-secret. Now I really do need to know.

"Fine, but I will see it eventually. I won't give up until I know."

I'm determined to see what she has my number saved as before she can see what Nora saved her number as in my phone.

"While you call her back, I'm going to take a cold shower. I need one after *that*." I wink just in case she was unsure which part of the last couple minutes I'm referring to, and it has nothing to do with her phone. "Just kidding. Kind of," I add with a grin. "I want to change into something more comfortable so I'm going to shower real quick."

I lift her off of me and set her gently back down onto the couch before kissing her forehead and heading into the bathroom so she can have a few minutes alone to talk with Emma.

Mid shampoo, steam enveloping the small space, I hear the door to the bathroom squeak open, and my head jerks towards the sound.

"Mind if I join you?"

She's kidding, right? I nearly blinded myself with shampoo trying to make sure I really heard her walking in here just now. Dude, speak before she thinks you're going to say no. Words. Now.

"Absolutely. Wait, no. Did you ask if I mind? I don't mind." I'm stammering. "Please pretend that didn't come out as a jumbled mess and definitely join me."

The sound of her clothes landing on the bathroom tile does more to me than I care to admit. Thank fuck that soap didn't blind me. A breath hitches in my throat as she pulls the curtain back and steps in. I'd be lying if I said I haven't thought about this moment so many times the past several weeks, but Nessa crashing my shower is somehow even sexier than any scenario I could have imagined.

My fingers intertwine with hers as I pull her body against mine. The feel of her nipples hardening against my chest as her fingers trail lightly down my back has me instantly yearning for more. "Holy fuck, Nessa."

"Mmm," she moans in response before kissing and nibbling her way down my neck.

I cup her ass with both hands and press her firmly against the wall, and her arousal now glides against my shaft. Her legs lift off the ground and wrap around me, possessively gripping my hips and pulling me towards her. As I take her erect nipple in my mouth, she grinds against me with a soft groan of pleasure.

Pinning her arms above her head, I worship her mouth while exploring her body with my free hand. Her head lulls back as she moans my name, and I can't take it anymore. I'm enjoying the hell out of this, but I refuse to let the first time I have sex with Nessa be in this shower. Caressing and kissing her entire body before finally taking her fully deserves time and space that this shower just can't provide.

I wrap my arms around her back, her legs tightening around me, and carry her straight to my bed. There's no time to towel off, and her wet body glistens as I lay her on her back and step between her legs. I kiss and lick my way across her breasts and down her stomach as her back arches off the bed in pleasure. Taking my time exploring every inch of exposed skin, she squirms as my tongue finally finds the sensitive spot between her legs. Her loud pants of my name as she comes against my mouth sends a surge of desire through me. My length throbs as I slide a condom on and finally glide inside of her.

Afterward, we lay entwined with one another, her head on my chest with one leg draped over me, as our breathing steadies and the world stops spinning. As our conversation fades and she slowly drifts off to sleep in my arms, I feel like the luckiest man in the entire world. Despite my reservations about her divorce not being final, the challenges of being long-distance, and the worry that she might change her mind at any second and rip my heart into a million pieces, there's no going back for me now. I'm in. I am all in.

CHAPTER SIXTEEN

NESSA

After finally putting Nora's rubber empire to good use last night, Peter and I lay intertwined for hours, just talking, his arm underneath me and my head on his shoulder. I must have eventually drifted off that way because I'm in that exact same position as the sun peeks into his bedroom. I'd normally sneak out for a run while he sleeps, but I don't know the area well enough, giving me the perfect excuse to stay right where I am: content and comfortable in his arms.

Peter's bedroom is almost exactly as I had pictured it; there's a king-size bed pushed into the corner, a small sleek dresser, and a desk covered in computer and gaming gear. Despite the blackout curtains keeping the room cloaked in darkness even late into the morning, I can just make out the only piece of decor in the room —a faded black picture frame with a photo of a man, woman, and two young boys.

Judging by the rich brown eyes and the grin I've grown to love, the youngest boy must be Peter. As I lightly rub my fingers down his chest, I realize where I've seen the two adults in the picture. Turning over ever so gently so I don't wake him, I roll to get a better look at the tattoo on his arm, and there they are: both of his parents exactly as they are in the frame with their birth and death dates just beneath them.

He hasn't talked much about his parents aside from telling me he'd lost them as a teenager. Him having a tribute to them on his bicep is the most *Peter* thing I've ever seen. It's touching and absolutely beautiful. They may not have gotten the chance to see the man he became, but I have no doubt they'd be proud.

As I roll back to my new favorite spot, he starts to stir beneath me. "Good morning, beautiful," he lets out in a sleep-filled whisper as he softly kisses me.

I instantly realize that there were more important things to do with the few minutes I had before he woke up. He did not just kiss me before I brushed my teeth. Eck. How mortifying. I'm now certain he can read minds, because before I can extricate myself from his arms and dart to the bathroom, he pulls me back to him, his kiss lingering this time.

"Don't worry about it, Ness. I didn't get to wake up with you in my arms last time, and I'm not ready for it to end just yet."

Though that definitely helped, I'm still a bit self conscious. Nonetheless, I curl into him and nuzzle my head up next to his. His arm instinctively tightens around me as he lets out a contented sigh. "I'm giving myself five more minutes of bliss before I'm forcing myself up. I've got plans for us today."

"Good thing we have enough condoms to supply a small village." I wink.

He cackles. "That is not what I meant, but good to know. I'll add you to the list of things I need to do today." He winks back and plants a small kiss to the tip of my nose.

More like ten minutes later, he finally stretches and pulls us both out of bed. Without knowing our plans for the day, I slip on a pair of ripped leggings and a 'Coffee, Coffee, Coffee' top. It's cute enough to look like I put some effort in but comfy enough for whatever the day has in store. After brushing my teeth and quickly taming the lion's mane that is my hair in the mornings, I join Peter, who was effortlessly ready in two minutes flat, and we make our way down the stairs of his apartment building.

A few minutes later, we pull into a cute little coffee shop that looks to be run out of an old home. Cobblestones cover the front of the building with a small sign that reads 'The Bean' just above a delicate row of rose bushes not quite starting to bud.

"Alex's wife recommended this place. She actually gave me a couple options, so we can try another tomorrow."

Though I'm certain no coffee shop could live up to The Daily Grind, the fact that he asked Alex, his work partner, to ask his wife for recommendations makes my heart skip a beat. After quickly browsing the menu, I decide not to ruin the barista's day by trying to replicate my go-to order, instead choosing an iced cupcake latte.

As we wait for our danishes and my coffee, my back pressed into his chest and his hands softly gripping my waist, I can't help but hear Dr. Evans's lecture in my head. Peter couldn't get more perfect; he's the literal embodiment of everything the good half of class had to offer.

On our way to wherever we're going, his hand never leaves my thigh except to steal bites of my cherry danish or to feed me bites of his cream cheese one. The classic yellow Mizzou button-up he chose this morning begins to make perfect sense as we pull into a familiar parking garage, and nostalgia instantly hits me.

"Since you didn't get your run in this morning, I thought we could take a little walk down memory lane."

It's early spring, and the weather has been absolutely perfect all week. Today is no exception. The sun is shining bright, trees are just starting to fill with leaves, and although there are no students to be seen, we've passed countless squirrels enjoying their own spring break. This campus holds thousands of wonderful memories for me, and I relish every opportunity to come back here.

"We need to show Emma this one day," I say as we walk hand in hand into the center of campus.

I didn't mean to insinuate that we'd be bringing her here together soon, but the idea that Peter may be a central part of our lives before we know it sounds less and less terrifying with each passing day. For me, he already is a central part of my life despite my efforts not to fully let him into my heart.

His fingers never leave mine as we spend hours strolling through the deserted campus telling stories of our time here, reminiscing on parties and homecomings, and wishing we'd had the chance to do it all together. I had the absolute time of my life here, but Peter by my side would have made it ten times better.

As we make our way back to the car, he makes a sharp right turn pulling me with him. "I can't believe we almost forgot," he says as the giant Truman the Tiger statue comes into view.

He grabs my hips, hoisting me up onto Truman's back before using the statue's tail to climb up behind me. I don't know a single Mizzou alum who didn't drunkenly climb up here nearly every single weekend for the entire four years here. Every late night football game, frat party, or friend get-together ended with my friends and I squishing ourselves together atop Truman's back. Despite having done this countless times before, this is not as easy as it was back then, and no doubt made harder by the lack of liquid courage coursing through my veins.

I kick both feet to one side and begin to slide my way down the statue as he reaches up to catch me. The gentle way he wraps his arms around me as I jump, providing safety and stability, has me, once again, envisioning him in our future. I can't help but picture him lifting Emma up here every year before a homecoming game or us helping her move into her dorm freshman year. I never thought I'd trust a man fully ever again, but Peter as an integral part of my future is starting to feel possible. It's starting to feel right.

"Ready to meet Aunt Deedee?" he asks as we make our way through the empty parking garage and into his car.

"Not going to lie. It's a little daunting, but I'm ready."

"It'll be just fine, promise. What's daunting about it?"

"I can't win her over with catnip."

He chuckles. "Just compliment her cinnamon rolls. It's basically the same thing. She already likes you. I'm happy, and that's all she really cares about."

My heartbeat quickens as we pull into her driveway. Matt didn't let me meet his family for several months after we started dating, giving every excuse he could think of. I'd embarrass him. I'm too much or not enough. They wouldn't like me. Knowing what I know now, that should have been a warning for me, but instead, it's a reminder that I deserve better.

You deserve better. You both do. My dad's words play in my head as we step into Deedee's house, and a warm, sweet grandmotherly scent envelops me. Unlike Peter's sparsely decorated apartment, Deedee's house is full of color and character. There are picture frames lining nearly every wall, crocheted blankets of various colors draped over the back of the couch and each chair, and plants hanging in multiple corners of the room. While Peter's house looks like no one even lives there, Deedee's is lived in, inviting, and just a tad eccentric in the best possible way.

"Peter, dear. I wasn't sure you were still coming." She wraps him in a tight hug before turning and wrapping her arms around me too. She's wearing a knee length floral dress with a light cardigan over the top. Though she's small, she doesn't feel at all frail as I return her hug with a tight squeeze. "And you must be Nessa. I've heard so much about you. All good, of course."

"Your cinnamon rolls are to die for," I blurt. Why can't she be a cat? Catnip feels like cheating when I have to make actual, real sentences.

"Hers are even better than ours." He heroically saves me from blurting anything else, but I'm hyperfocused on what he said. *Ours*. Not his, but *ours*.

"How has your visit been so far, dear?"

It takes me a moment to realize she's talking to me, and once again, my ability to form sentences leaves me.

"Oh," I say. It's a simple question. *Get it together, Nessa*. "It's been wonderful. Peter found the perfect coffee shop, and we spent our afternoon strolling through campus. We both went to Mizzou about the same time without knowing it, and it's still one of my favorite places."

"Oh that's lovely. Peter's father went there, too, and the campus is beautiful especially in the springtime. I must say, the party scene worried me for Peter so soon after his dad's passing, but of course, he managed it well. And look at him now." She beams across the room to where Peter and I are now sitting, obvious pride in her eyes.

"After Mom died, Dad started drinking pretty heavily. He'd always been a drinker, but it really escalated after that. He did not handle losing her well. Four years of drowning his sorrow was all it took for his liver to fail him," Peter clarifies.

"Ah, yes. That's why I was worried about Pete when he went off to college. So many opportunities to drink there. It doesn't get its reputation as a party school for nothing." She presses her palm lovingly to his cheek as she walks past us to the kitchen.

"That's why you're always Nora's designated driver."

"Yeah, it is. I saw how much my dad's drinking affected us kids and even Aunt Deedee, and my mom's other sister, Kathy. I'm not willing to risk addiction and hurt them even further. It's just not worth it."

My heart swoons as he explains his reasoning; he chooses not to drink, not for his own wellbeing, but for the people he loves. I squeeze his knee, a silent reminder that I'm listening, as Aunt Deedee comes back into the living room with a tray topped with glasses of lemonade and freshly baked cookies.

"Peter was just telling me you have some pictures he'd just love for me to see." I flash him a mischievous grin.

"Oh, what a good idea. I'll be right back."

As Deedee leaves the room, Peter grabs my phone off the couch and holds it up in triumph. "You get to see embarrassing baby pictures, and I get to see what pops up on your phone when I call."

I don't say anything as he opens up the text messaging app on my phone. 'Jackass' was a no-brainer, but the perfect contact name for Peter took some thought. Nora helpfully suggested adding an eggplant emoji, and I'm not ashamed to admit it was a contender.

"I was definitely expecting a dick reference."

My head tips back as I let out an open-mouthed cackle. Nora's reputation precedes her. "Sorry to disappoint. Nora did suggest that, though."

"This is even better."

At first, his contact name was just 'Peter,' but the more I got to know him, the more that just didn't fit. It's his name, I know, but it needed something... more. *Petey <3* feels right. His relationship with Daisy melts my heart, and as soon as I pictured Emma learning his nickname, I knew I had to use it.

As Deedee re-enters the living room, her arms full of dusty photo albums, he turns his phone screen towards me. Our text thread is open on the screen with 'The One' at the top. I'm certain Nora is behind the name choice, but my body does not care. Butterflies take flight, and it takes every ounce of willpower inside of me not to mount him right here.

Oblivious to the unspoken conversation Peter and I are having, Deedee starts flipping through the pages of her old photo albums. She narrates each and every page, pointing out Peter, his parents, and his older brother, Andrew, as well as his many cousins. He doesn't seem at all bothered to share these memories with me like he pretended to be yesterday, and I'm learning so much about him from her stories. Deedee is doubled over with laughter as she tells my personal favorite: the time three-year-old Peter ran down her street in pursuit of the ice cream truck wearing nothing but Ninja Turtle underwear.

After several albums full of tiny Peter—his babies will be gorgeous in case you were wondering—he flips open a dark green album with pictures from his teenage years. There are several of Peter and Andrew at both of their graduations, prom pictures of him and Rob both dressed to the nines, and a few pictures with Aunt Deedee and all the cousins.

A picture falls to the ground, and as I reach to pick it up, I see Peter and Rob, probably about sixteen or seventeen, smiling proudly at the camera. They're each laying in a twin-sized bed covered in Spider-Man sheets and pressed into the corner of the wall, their heads mere feet from each other.

"Where is this?" I hold the picture out for them to see.

"It's here. Those beds are probably in the exact same spot with those same sheets on them." Peter looks toward Deedee for confirmation.

"You're right, dear. They are."

"Rob had his own bed here? I actually know almost nothing about your friendship except he probably ran with you for that ice cream truck wearing matching undies."

"Now that you mention it, I think he did. Let me see if I can find a picture." She begins grabbing for albums we haven't looked through yet and quickly flips through them.

"We lived next door to each other when we were really little, probably about Emma's age. He didn't have the best home life, so he stayed with us a lot. When my dad died and I moved in here, he moved in too. He was starting to make some pretty bad choices, but Deedee making sure we both went to school everyday and finished our homework helped."

"Oh, wow. I did not know any of that about him. He was so good with Daisy at first, but now, he spends so much time in his game room and almost no time with his family. I feel a little bit bad about not liking him very much now."

I haven't told Peter much about my feelings towards Rob. I know they're good friends, and it feels wrong to talk negatively about him regardless of how I feel. I know I'd be upset if Peter talked badly about Nora, so I try to give him the same courtesy. Hearing about Rob's homelife does help me sympathize with him though. Maybe he just doesn't know how to be a good dad.

"He's had a hard life, that's for sure. But that is absolutely no excuse for not being the man I know he can be. He has an ear full coming the next time he calls. Daisy is such a sweet little girl, and he better be treating them right."

"Leave it to Deedee. She'll have him back in line in no time."

"That's right. And don't you forget it." Although she winks at me as she says it, I know she's completely serious.

"Look, I found it!" She turns the album around, revealing a picture of both boys standing in the street in matching undies, popsicles now in hand.

By the time we've looked through all of the photo albums, I have a stack of pictures Deedee insists I should take home. The stack encompasses most of Peter's life from newborn baby pictures-—his mom and dad snuggled together in the hospital bed—and school picture day photos throughout the years to high school baseball games and a few more recent ones of Deedee and him together. There aren't many decorations in my home, mostly just necessities, but there are pictures all over the place. Most of them are pictures of Emma, but I can't wait to add these new ones to the mix.

Aunt Deedee insists we stay for dinner then loads our arms full of leftovers as well as enough cookies to last until our next visit. I'm not sad about it, and I know Emma won't be either.

After hugging me goodbye, she wraps her arms around Peter and leans in to whisper in his ear.

"You found a good one, Peter. I approve." Something tells me she said it loud enough for me to hear on purpose; the thought, and her words, bring a smile to my face. I'm not too embarrassing to meet family, after all. I was just meeting the wrong family.

CHAPTER SEVENTEEN

NESSA

The next morning, we try another coffee shop, and this time we bring breakfast sandwiches back to his place to relax before I have to head home. I'm dreading my drive home for so many reasons. I'm obviously excited to have Emma back where she belongs, but ending my weekends with Peter is getting increasingly difficult.

I'm able to mostly drown out the worries of my everyday life when I'm with him. I've barely thought about Matt, the impending custody battle, or even how I'm going to continue paying my lawyer if he truly does drag this all out. I took out the largest student loan available to me at the start of the semester and used every left over cent to put a retainer down for my lawyer, but that retainer will not last much longer. I know every single one of these worries will hit me as soon as I'm alone with my thoughts for my two hour trek home.

After spending the early afternoon snuggled together on the couch, I begrudgingly gather my things, kiss Peter goodbye, and force myself to leave. The two week countdown already begins in my head. Though I know it's only been a couple months, the two weeks between visits is starting to take a toll. Our nearly constant communication during the weeks we're apart definitely helps, but soon, I know that won't be enough anymore.

I was hopeful that long distance might actually be perfect for my first relationship as a single mom. It allows me to fully focus on Emma with minimal distractions when she's with me while simultaneously keeping me busy when she's away. The more my heart opens up to him, the more unrealistic our distance becomes. These thoughts instantly dampen the elated mood I've been in since the moment I pulled into his parking lot two days ago. Knowing I'll need Nora as soon as I get home, I type out a quick message asking her to come over and drown out all my thoughts with 2000's pop the rest of the way home.

Nora and Daisy are waiting for me when I get home a few minutes before Matthew is due to arrive with Emma. Having them with me instantly eases my tension, and it's an added bonus that their car in the driveway alerts Matt to be on his best behavior. He rings the doorbell instead of flinging the door open and leaves without a single word. Before he can even drop her bag to the ground, Emma squeals and jumps into my arms.

In an effort to get out the door quickly, Nora and I throw some dinosaur-shaped chicken nuggets into the air fryer and cut up an apple for the girls. We have our best conversations when the girls are distracted, so this super easy, no fuss dinner will have to do. I need to get all my worries out into the open with the person who understands me the most, so off to the trail we go. I promise myself I'll serve a vegetable for Emma's bedtime snack, throw a couple applesauce pouches into the diaper bag, and load everything we might need into the car.

Daisy and Emma both love this trail—the one Peter and I went to a few weeks ago. We always do a lap or two, stopping to see all the animals along the way, then let them play in the small creek if the weather is hot or throw rocks into it when the weather is not. Once we're parked, I pull Emma's umbrella stroller from the trunk and let Daisy buckle her in. This stroller has seen better days—there are crumbs in all its crevices and a chocolate stain on the seat—but it's lightweight and too convenient to get rid of. Most importantly, it's small enough that Daisy can push it, meaning she'll run Emma just far enough ahead of us to allow for an unfiltered conversation with my best friend.

After tossing the emergency snacks underneath the stroller, in case either of them gets antsy, we set off up the hill. Daisy instantly takes off with Emma's stroller leaving Nora and I alone. This is our go-to when we want to have an adult conversation, and it works every single time.

"Don't get too far ahead," Nora calls out to Daisy before turning to me, a look of concern in her eyes. When I don't say anything, she adds, "I like Peter but I'm not afraid to hide a body if I have to. What happened?"

I snort laugh despite the familiar burning in my eyes telling me I might cry before I even get any words out. "He's perfect, Nor. Put down the shovel."

"Then what's the matter?"

"It's not him at all. It's just… everything." Without warning, the words come spilling out of me. "Only seeing him every two weeks is so much harder than I anticipated. I've been thinking about the right time to introduce him to Emma, but it feels fast and scary. I was sure my destiny involved a house full of cats, not falling for someone who's clearly too good for me."

"Woah. Take a breath. Let's take this one step at a time." She lightly bumps my shoulder, bringing my eyes up to hers instead of on my shoes. "Every other weekend is temporary if you want it to be."

"How? Matt would blow a freaking gasket if I brought another man into her life. Not to mention the judgment I'll get from everyone for not waiting six years before letting her meet anyone new."

"First of all, Matt can fuck off. Second, no one is going to judge you. And if they do, I'll tell them to fuck off too. Every single choice you've made since she took her first breath was with her in mind. If you choose to let her meet Peter, I trust that her best interest is still your top priority. You get to live a fulfilling life even as a mom. That's basically the whole point." She sucks in the first deep breath she's taken since she started her spiel.

"I can't do it. Not yet."

"My point is you get to choose. Not Matt, not nosy Ms. Garcia, not some stuck up mom at playgroup. *You.*"

The burning sensation finally starts to clear from my eyes as I take in her words. Nora always knows exactly what to say, but not in a 'just what I want to hear' type of way. She means every word of it. I knew this little outing was exactly what I needed today.

The girls are leaning into a chain link fence completely captivated by the sheep when we catch up to them. Emma is clapping and squealing with glee as three sheep saunter over to where we're standing. The sheep are equally captivated by the loud 'baa' sounds both of the girls are making. Once the sheep are bored of us and turn to leave, Daisy grabs Emma's stroller and races towards the cows.

"Let's get one more thing straight," Nora adds as soon as the kids are out of earshot. "He is not too good for you. His life is not as messy as yours is right now, sure. I get that, but you're a freaking badass, Nessa."

Hello, hot stinging tears. "Thanks," I barely choke out.

"Look at me. I mean it. He's incredibly lucky to have you in his life too. You're an amazing friend, a great listener, a kick ass mom, and you deserve to get to be a good partner."

I'm full on crying now. Ugly, snotty crying. "You have to say that. You're biased," I say through gasps for air.

"That's bullshit and you know it."

I manage a laugh between sobs as I lean my head into her shoulder. "I freaking love you."

"Love you too. Now, tell me what else is bothering you before we jump to the good stuff."

"How'd you know there's more?"

"I'm psychic. Go on."

"Matt's lawyer sent their response to my divorce papers."

"If you say he didn't immediately sign them, I'm getting the shovel back out."

"Of course he didn't. What fun would that be? His life isn't worth living if he's not making someone miserable."

"That son of a bitch. What did the papers say?" She went from loving to protective in two seconds flat, her crossed arms and a scowl firmly in place.

"He's contesting everything. He wants 50/50 custody."

She scoffs, cutting me off. "He has got to be joking. He's seen her three times in the past year. That will not happen."

"My lawyer isn't as sure, but it gets worse."

"The fucking nerve of this guy." She's taking the news about as well as I did, though I ended up crying in my closet while Emma was distracted by Ms. Rachel. She's not going to cry, but she's equally pissed off about it.

"He doesn't want to pay child support and is demanding I give him all of Emma's things, claiming I stole them from him."

She lets out a deranged howl. "No way in hell. Your lawyer thinks he'll be granted any of that?"

"He's pretty sure Matt will still have to pay child support and that I won't have to give him any of Emma's stuff. He's just not sure how the custody piece will play out. Custody is different now. 50/50 is the norm."

"I get that, but Matt is not the norm. He's literal dog crap in human form."

My tears have completely dissolved into laughter now. Remind me not to let her on the stand as a character witness; she can't be trusted to not say that exact sentence to the judge. On second thought, she might actually be the perfect person to lay it all out there.

"Okay, enough depressing news. Ready for the good stuff?"

"Ooo, absolutely." She's all smiles now, ready to ride this emotional roller coaster with me no matter where it takes us.

I give her a full play by play, leaving only the most intimate details out while still painting a full, slightly graphic picture.

"Finally!" she screeches, startling the cows and our children.

"I'm not even finished telling you about Friday yet."

"I know. I know. We'll get there. He laughed at my condom box, didn't he?"

"Of course he did. We were able to fully supply a Planned Parenthood and still have plenty left for a lifetime."

She spews the water she was drinking as I say it. "That Planned Parenthood is lucky to have me. At least one of us is finally getting some."

"You and Rob aren't having sex?" My eyebrows knit together. Nora and I are open with each other about anything and everything. Either this development is new, or things have gotten so bad she just wasn't ready to tell me.

"Nope. He refuses to wear condoms now and still doesn't understand why I am not ready to add a baby to our lives right now."

"He'd rather be celibate? That's manipulative, Nor."

"I know. That's why I'm standing my ground." Though she's trying to sound confident, her voice shakes as she says it.

I'm tempted to tell her what I learned while at Aunt Deedee's, but if Rob wanted her to know, he'd tell her himself. Maybe she does already know and just didn't tell me out of respect for his privacy. Either way, it doesn't feel like my place. Before I can change my mind, we've made it to the creek portion of the trail. Daisy is gathering pebbles while Emma screams to be let out of her confinement, which effectively ends our chat for the day.

Somehow, the next month goes by in a blur but simultaneously at snail speed. Peter and I have fallen into a steady rhythm with nonstop communication throughout the weeks and a weekend visit every time Emma is with her dad. Nora set a lot of my worries to rest that day at the trail, aside from my growing frustration that Matt getting 50/50 custody is a very real possibility. He's paid child support on time every month since it was ordered, and has been having weekend visits every other week for several months now without anything bad happening—to Emma at least.

According to my lawyer, this all works in Matt's favor despite Nora and my dad agreeing to speak on my behalf. In a judge's eyes, their testimony will be viewed as biased unless someone outside my circle, like a third party witness or one of Matt's family members, is willing to speak up. I've considered asking Ms. Garcia to testify but she didn't see enough for it to make much of a difference. I've been working myself into a panic since last week when I met with my lawyer about all of this. This weekend, however, I'm determined to relax and have a good time with Peter.

Emma leaves for her dad's tonight, and as soon as he picks her up, I'm driving to a hotel about halfway between Peter's place and mine. Most of the time, he comes to stay with me, but after the stressful week I've had, he booked us a hotel room with a giant jetted tub. Every weekend that I'm with Peter, I feel some of the tension I usually carry dissipate. I have no doubt that our first little trip together will take my mind off the custody shit show, and hopefully, it will rejuvenate my strength; I'm going to need it to get through this.

Though I rarely talk to Ms. Garcia, ever since she witnessed Matthew's outburst, she sits outside every time he's here. Her mere presence has been enough to keep him calm and civil. I'm extremely grateful for her silent intervention, but I also wish he'd give me some way to prove what type of person he is.

After he left the hole in my wall and forcefully pulled Emma from my arms, Peter installed a camera near my front door. It's discreet enough that it isn't noticeable unless you know to look for it but has a perfect view of my front door and driveway. If he is aggressive again, I'll have something to back up my claims that he is not safe. With the ever vigilant Ms. Garcia present, pick-up goes smoothly, and I immediately follow him out of my driveway to the weekend of relaxation that awaits me.

Peter is waiting for me when I pull into the hotel parking lot just over an hour later. As soon as I step out of the car, he raises my arm above my head, spinning me to him like a ballerina, before squeezing me tight. When he finally lets go, he drops a quick kiss to my lips and grabs both of our bags before turning to walk into the hotel.

Despite the fact that the town halfway between us is pretty small, this hotel screams luxury. The peaks at the top are giving castle in London vibes while the area with a fire pit under beautiful string lights says ambiance and comfort.

Our room is no different, beautifully decorated but with comfort and relaxation in mind. Eyeing the giant bed in the middle of the room, I jump up, landing flat on my back with my arms and legs spread out beside me. Holy guacamole. As soon as my back touches the mattress, I immediately sink down into its soft embrace. This must be exactly what heaven feels like.

Peter plops down beside me, landing on a mountain of down feather pillows. I roll toward him, effortlessly gliding across the satin sheets into my favorite little spoon position and continue to take in our room. In the corner sits a jetted tub big enough for both Peter and me, and honestly probably another person or two. Hanging in the closet are two fluffy, soft robes with matching slippers beneath. I've been eagerly awaiting this day, and in a matter of seconds it's already surpassed any expectations I had.

"How about we order some food, and then we can break in that tub?" Peter winks and wiggles his eyebrows before finding a booklet of takeout menus in the bedside table drawer. We cuddle into the mountain of pillows as we browse through the menu options.

"As long as they deliver, I don't care what we get. I am never leaving this room. I live here now."

"Deal, but I do need you to be the one to go down to the lobby to grab our food when they get here."

"I just told you I'm never leaving this room."

He rolls over on top of me, pinning my arms beside my head, then dips down to lightly nibble at my neck. "It'll be worth it. Just trust me on this one."

A bolt of electricity shoots through me at the gentle touch of his lips and teeth to my skin. I want to rip my clothes off right now and not put them back on again until Sunday, but when we get the call that our food is here, I begrudgingly peel myself out of bed and head to the lobby. I'm back in a matter of minutes, and per usual, he was right. Despite the fact that this is already the most luxurious room I've ever laid eyes on, Peter somehow managed to make it even better in the few minutes I was gone.

There are candles lining the edge of the tub, a fresh bouquet of roses in a delicate glass vase sits next to a box of chocolate covered strawberries on the bedside table, and the lights are dimmed down low. He's wearing one of the robes and a pair of slippers from the closet, and I'm willing to bet he has nothing underneath. As I take in my surroundings, he lifts my dress above my head, revealing the lilac, lace thong Nora gave me. He shimmies the thong down and slides my arms into the robe before tying it in front.

"Oh my god." I don't know what I did in a past life to deserve this man, but clearly I've done something right. He deserves more than a moaned 'oh my god,' but it's literally the only sentence I can form right now.

"I don't know how to help with all the custody and divorce shit you're going through. Honestly, my presence is probably making it worse. I just want to help you unwind and feel better."

Though his sentiment is sweet, he couldn't be more wrong. Being able to talk everything through with him is really helping. He's the only thing keeping me sane right now, but if Matthew found out about him, things would definitely get worse, which is why I'm determined to not let that happen until we are officially divorced and have a set parenting plan, preferably one that doesn't give him any more time than he gets now.

"Your presence does not make it worse. You're perfect. Matthew, however, would not agree." I rummage through the take-out bags and hand him his food as we talk.

"He doesn't know about me, then?"

"Hell no. I don't know how he'd react, but I do know it would not be good."

"I couldn't live with myself if he hurt you because of me. Is that what you think would happen?" There's genuine concern in his beautiful brown eyes.

"It's impossible to know what he'll do. Picture the biggest roller coaster in the world. Then set it on fire. That's Matthew. He's full of ups and downs. Sometimes it's fun, other times your stomach feels like it's going to fall out. Eventually, the fire he purposely set will burn it all to the ground, but you never know when that's going to happen, so you're just stuck in limbo waiting for the next drop."

Describing Matthew to people is difficult. When you've never dealt with someone like him, it feels so far-fetched. Why would you let him do that to you? Why didn't you leave immediately? If he really hurt you, he'd be in jail. People are naive unless they've experienced it firsthand. For that reason, I avoid talking about Matthew with people who don't know him. Hell, my own mother sides with him regularly; a fact that I have a hard time getting over.

It took me a while to open up about Matthew to Peter, but I know this won't turn into a stable, lasting relationship if I can't be open and honest with him about every part of my life. More importantly, it gives me an opportunity to see how he responds. If he victim blames or minimizes my feelings, I now know to recognize it for what it is: a red flag.

A year ago, I would have sugar-coated my relationship with Matthew in fear of getting blamed for the way he treated me. This year and a half away from him and countless hours spent with my own therapist coupled with the eye-opening classes I've been taking have shown me that the right person will be empathetic to what I went through, not judgmental. I don't have to hide my past or who I am to find a person to fully love me.

"Do you have to tell him about me? Legally, I mean."

"We don't have an official parenting plan yet, so I guess, no. Keeping a relationship hidden might not look great to a judge, especially if Emma is involved, but maybe the circumstances will make my decision more understandable."

I know judges are just normal people and likely have Emma's best interests in mind. Regardless, I am absolutely petrified. This judge holds my entire world in her hands, and even though having a female judge who is also a mom does make me feel a little better, you just never know. Anything I do from now on can make or break my case and subsequently take away the thing I love most in this world: Emma.

"If you think it's best to leave him in the dark for now, I do too. You know him better than anyone. I trust your judgment."

"That makes one of us. I'm constantly questioning every single decision I make. I'd want to know if Matt had Emma around another woman, so I should be open about us. But I can't. I know that's so hypocritical. I just don't know what I should do."

"I get that. You're damned if you do and damned if you don't. He doesn't sound like the kind of person who would tell you when he's in a new relationship either."

"Exactly. There's no winning right now, and he probably won't tell me." I sigh. "Enough about my drama. I promised myself I'd try not to think about it all weekend."

"Deal. I can do that," he says as he lights the candles, pours bubble bath solution into the tub, and begins running the water.

"There has got to be a rule about not lighting candles in here. What a rebel."

"Rebel is my middle name." He winks.

"Ah, yes. Mr. Two Miles Under the Speed Limit is definitely in the dictionary next to 'rebel,'" I chortle.

"You're rubbing off on me. I just need you to create a distraction if we set the fire alarms off so I can make a clean getaway."

"Oh no. If I go down, you're coming down with me."

"And ruin my squeaky clean reputation? Not a chance."

He slowly unties my robe, letting it land at my feet, as I reach for his and reveal that I was right. Nothing underneath but the beginnings of excitement for what's to come. He lightly brushes a piece of hair out of my face, staring longingly into my eyes, as he grasps my hands, steadying me as I lower myself into the water.

He settles in behind me, his legs on either side of me with my back and head resting against his chest. I'm an extrovert through and through, so silence is often uncomfortable for me. But right now? I'm perfectly content to just feel Peter's presence against me and relax. Talking about Matthew always gets my anxiety going, but Peter's arms holding me tight as the water swirls around us calms me instantly. I close my eyes, taking in the sweet lavender scent of the candles, and burrow into him. He softly peppers the side of my neck and shoulders with kisses, the only parts of me still visible above the bubbles.

The flowers and strawberries combined with the sensual bath and candles is doing more than help me unwind; it's making me want to climb Peter like a tree. It's not unusual for us to want to rip each other's clothes off immediately after our two weeks apart, but this is just... different. I turn and straddle him, my warm opening against his now throbbing member, as I smash my mouth to his, my hunger for him evident.

The calm, relaxing bath from moments ago quickly fades as his hands find my ass, pulling me against him. My hips buck, grinding my slit up and down his shaft, as he takes one of my breasts into his mouth. I toss my head back and let out a loud moan of pleasure, my body now shuddering against his.

"I need you right now." It comes out in a barely audible groan.

"Mmm," is all he gets out before lifting me up and setting me on the edge of the tub. He pushes my knees apart, licking and sucking on my most sensitive areas as he slides his fingers into me. My toes curl, and I dig my fingers into his back as an orgasm overtakes me.

The mirror surrounding us provides the perfect view as he flips me around, bending me over the edge of the tub. With one hand on my hip, he grabs ahold of my ponytail with the other and shoves into me from behind. Thoughts of him losing his balance and pulling us both under water instantly leave my mind when he hits the perfect spot inside of me. Letting go of all my worries from just moments ago, I thrust myself back into him with a clap as his strokes bring us both to climax with a loud moan.

Afterward, tangled together in the satin sheets, the world outside this room and its neverending problems feel impossibly distant. With Peter, even just for this moment, I can finally breathe.

CHAPTER EIGHTEEN

PETER

The sound of the water running, no doubt Nessa brushing her teeth before waking me, draws me out of a very good dream. Despite me telling her numerous times that it's unnecessary, she slips off of my chest and out of my grasp every morning that we're together to brush her teeth and hair before burrowing back into me until I wake up. I truly mean it when I say it's unnecessary, but damn, it is kind of cute.

I keep my eyes shut and extend my arm out to her side of the bed as she crawls back in and snuggles against me, planting a soft kiss to my cheek.

"Good morning, beautiful." The sleep-filled, raspy voice it comes out in is no facade, despite pretending to still be asleep. She hasn't mentioned her little morning routine, so I haven't either. I'm perfectly content letting her slip back into my arms every morning if it means I get to wake up and immediately kiss her while her bare body is pressed against mine.

The knock at the door comes promptly at 9:30 a.m., perfectly timed for Nessa's little routine to be complete. I roll out of bed and slip on a pair of navy blue boxers before retrieving the tray from the hallway. I don't quite understand why Nessa's lawyer thinks Matt has any shot in hell at getting custody of Emma, but I do know that she had a panic attack while hiding in her closet last week. She deserves a rejuvenating weekend full of pampering, and that's exactly what she's going to get.

"What's that?" The smell of coffee has her instantly upright in bed.

"Bagels, fruit, and of course, caffeine." I hand her the tray as I climb in beside her.

"Coffee! Yay! Marry me right now." She meant it as a joke, but judging by her mortified expression, she didn't mean to say it out loud.

"Not exactly the proposal I had in mind. I'll have to think about it." A small smile plays at my lips and her worried expression begins to fade.

I want to break Matthew's nose every time I witness a knee jerk reaction like that one. Though it would be clear to anyone that she wasn't truly proposing, she was scared of the reaction I might have. That instant worry about every little thing doesn't just happen for no reason. Matthew did this to her. I know bits and pieces about how he treated her, but the fact that she's still scared a year and half later tells me it was even worse than she lets on.

She spreads cream cheese onto the bagel and offers me the first bite.

"I slept like a baby last night. Actually, whoever made up that saying clearly didn't have kids. I slept like a *teenager* last night."

"I always sleep well with you in my arms." I know it sounds cheesy, but it's true. I sleep way better curled up with her than I do in my silent apartment with the entire bed to myself.

"Do you really?" She's wearing an expression of true curiosity.

"Honestly, I do. I'd trade my bachelor pad for waking up with you any day." I immediately worry that might have been too much especially after her 'marry me' joke, but she grins ear to ear as soon as I say it.

"I do too. Granted, you don't kick me in the face like my little bed hog does."

"I can if it makes you feel more at home." I damn near pull a muscle trying to get my foot anywhere remotely close to her face.

"Eww." She squeals as she swats my foot away but not before I accidentally knock her bagel out of her hands. After we get the cream cheese off the duvet and our laughter under control, she leans into me and asks, "What are we doing today?"

"It's a surprise, but first I was thinking we could check out the gym here."

Even though I'm always at work by the time she feeds Emma breakfast and gets outside for their morning walk, I've made a habit of shutting my office door and calling her anyway. We only spend about five minutes on the phone before Emma demands attention from the stroller, but it's the perfect opportunity to say good morning before we both get to our busy days. When she's with me, she often slips out for a run after coffee, so I know a little exercise after caffeine is her favorite way to start the day.

"Oh, that's perfect."

After finishing our breakfast, we both slip on some shorts and running shoes then head down to the gym in a little room beside the pool. There's a treadmill, an elliptical, and a stationary bike next to a rack of weights. Cardio isn't my thing, but Nessa's ass in those tight biker shorts makes the treadmill beside her so much more appealing. She hops up onto the elliptical with ease and takes off, while I set a leisurely pace hoping I don't fall off the back of this thing.

"I don't want to think about anything serious today," she says, just slightly out of breath. "So, tell me, what fictional character do you vibe with the most?"

"Hmm." I was not expecting that, and it takes me a minute to think of an answer. "I'm going to go with Spencer Reed. A little geeky but lovable."

"Ooo. I like that answer. The sexy, nerdy guy that saves the day with random knowledge. That fits."

"Is Spencer Reed sexy?" Reed is many things, but I did not know sexy was one of them.

"Definitely. He's no Derek Morgan, but he's got that sexy, nerdy vibe going for him."

"There's no competing with Shemar Moore. Understandable," I say with a laugh. "Who would you be?"

"Lorelai Gilmore." There's not an ounce of hesitation in her voice. "She has a strained relationship with her mom and works really hard to build a strong relationship with her daughter. Her relationship with Rory is often seen as too friendly and not parental, but the idea that some daughters do look up to their moms was inspirational for me. I want Emma to *want* to be around me and to call me when she needs something, even when she's grown."

"That's where you got the cat's name, right? I've never seen that show."

She looks at me in horror. "Cancel our plans. We're binging *Gilmore Girls* as soon as I finish my run."

"How about we binge it after our plans instead? How many seasons are there?"

"There's seven, so I guess it won't hurt to start tonight. It'll take us months anyway."

I know every other weekend is just how it has to be for now, but moments like this make me wish things were different. We could watch any show she wants every single night after Emma is in bed. I could wake up beside her everyday and brew her coffee before heading to work. Picturing myself fully in their lives, instead of on the outside, has me realizing that Deedee is right. It's time for me to find something serious. I can see myself as an everyday part of Nessa and Emma's life, but will she ever see me the same way? And then there's Deedee; I don't know if I can leave her all alone like that.

I'm pulled from my thoughts as Nessa climbs off the machine. She grabs a paper towel and begins wiping the handles, so I follow suit. Even though we're both sweating, I intertwine my fingers with hers as we walk back to the room.

"Put on something comfy," I instruct after our shower.

"I like surprises, but they make it impossible to know what to wear." She holds up two options—a light pink romper with horizontal black stripes and a flowy baby blue dress.

"This one," I say, pointing to the romper. "What you wear isn't important for this part of the day. You're just going to take it off."

She scrunches her eyebrows in confusion as she slides the romper up over her hips.

A few minutes later, we approach the desk at the hotel's spa. "Ohhhh." She draws the word out, my statement about taking her clothes off making sense now. "I thought you were getting kinky on me."

"You didn't seem disappointed last—" I'm a little vanilla, and we both know it, but I can't miss the opportunity to tease her about it. Her face turns bright red as the receptionist walks in, cutting my sentence off, and notices my eyebrow waggle in Nessa's direction. Embarrassing her is too fun, and surprisingly easy.

Once we're checked in, we're led to a dressing room and left to change into the same robes we've been wearing in the room. Nessa hasn't stopped raving about hers since last night. I'm tempted to shove it in my suitcase, reputation be damned. They'll just charge my card double its actual price. And for her, that's worth it.

"I've never gotten a couples massage. I'm excited!" The anticipation is evident in her voice even though she's whispering as we enter the quiet waiting area. The lights are dimmed so low I can barely make out the elated grin on her face. The look she's giving me makes every effort I put into this weekend 100 percent worth it. There's no limit to what I'd do to see that smile.

There are couches lining the walls of the waiting area and a mini fridge with drinks in the corner. I grab a Hershey's Kiss from the bowl on the table in front of us and pop it into my mouth. "I've actually never had a massage at all. I'm convinced it's going to tickle, and I won't be able to relax."

She lets out a soft chortle. "My feet are ticklish, but other than that, it's not bad. They're rejuvenating. I can't believe you've never gotten one before."

Her feet are ticklish– good to know!. Most of the time, changing the subject or saying something funny eases the tension when she's worried about how I might respond like this morning with her marry me comment. I make a mental note to tickle her feet next time in case lighthearted banter doesn't work.

Before I can respond, our names are called and they show us to a room. There are two padded tables side by side in the middle with the heads of the table close enough that we can talk while the technicians move around us.

We strip our robes off and climb onto our respective tables, face down. Her hand instinctively reaches for mine as we settle in.

When the massage therapists leave the room an hour later, I'm nearly asleep on the table. I enjoyed the massage way more than I thought I would. The relaxed, zoned out smile on Nessa's face mixed with the citrus scent and oily glisten of her skin sends a pang of desire through me. I want to scoop her into my arms and march her right back to bed, but that will have to wait.

"Did you like it?" Her question comes out in a relaxed whisper as we both climb off of our tables.

"I did! I wasn't sure about a stranger rubbing all over me, but it was nice."

She laughs. "Well when you put it that way, it does sound creepy."

"Exactly why this was my first massage."

"Have you heard that couples have sex in here after a massage? Now *that* creeps me out. But if I'm being honest, I kind of get it now. You look so sexy naked and oily like that." We've already established that I am not adventurous enough to do anything about my arousal now firmly pressed against her, but hearing that she wants it, too, has me tempted to break all the rules.

I kiss her gently before crushing both of our dreams and sliding the robe back onto her shoulders. "I'll take care of that later, promise, but you've got another appointment first." It wouldn't take much to convince me to reschedule, but rest and relaxation are the whole point of this trip, so I force myself to be patient.

"You mean we?" She has the cutest forehead wrinkle when she's confused.

"Just you. She had me so relaxed that I almost fell asleep. I'm going to take the best nap of my life while you get your nails done."

She beams and the desire to scoop her up instantly returns.

The second my head hit the soft pillows, I was out like a light. I barely register Nessa entering the room until she's in bed, kissing down my bare torso.

"Let me see." My voice is still groggy from sleep as I pull her into a sitting position on top of me ready to gush over her new nails.

"You're too good to me," she whispers as she holds her baby blue nails out for me to admire.

"You deserve it," I whisper back, parting her lips with a soft flick of my tongue. I flip her onto her back, my knees between her legs before I am interrupted by the alarm on my phone. It's almost time for our dinner reservation. "Wear the dress this time."

She groans as I lift myself off of her and pull her up with me. I am once again regretting the timing of my sweet gestures as she slips out of her clothes and pulls the dress that now matches her nails over her head.

"Cancel everything after this. I just want to be here with you," she says with a wink.

"Deal." I'd cancel dinner, too, if she asked. Keeping my hands to myself is the last thing I want to do right now.

We're escorted to our seats as soon as we enter the restaurant. There weren't very many options to choose from in this small town, but I found the perfect little Italian restaurant; it's delicious but low-key according to its reviews. We're seated at a quiet table for two in the back corner, a black cloth draped across it with flowers and two wine glasses in the center. Instead of taking the seat opposite me, Nessa scoots her chair closer, and I instinctively reach for her knee.

"Thank you," I say to the waitress as she fills Nessa's wine glass and sets a plate of bruschetta between us.

"It looks amazing. Thank you so much," Nessa adds before glancing down at her pocket, her phone now buzzing. "Sorry. I just want to make sure it's not Emma."

"You're good. Don't worry about it," I say through a giant bite of crispy bread topped with olive oil and a delicious tomato mixture.

"It's Matthew's mom. I have to get this." She looks panicked as she brings the phone to her ear and answers in a whisper.

I can't quite tell what his mom is saying on the other end of the phone, but I can tell that she's loud and frantic. Nessa's face drains of color and her hands begin to tremble before she slides her chair back and nearly sprints out the door. Though our main course hasn't arrived yet, I toss a couple hundred dollar bills on the table and chase after her. That should more than cover it, but all I care about right now is Nessa.

I find her leaning against my car, her head in her hands audibly sobbing. Pulling her into my arms, I squeeze her against my chest, the phone still pressed to her ear with her shoulder. Through gasps for air, she finally utters, "I'm coming."

As soon as she ends the call, she slides out of my arms and all the way down the side of my car into a heap on the pavement. She takes a deep, shaky breath before standing up and getting into the car.

"We have to go." Her voice still shakes as she shuts the door behind her.

CHAPTER NINETEEN

NESSA

The buzzing in my pocket immediately drops my heart into my stomach. Nora knows I'm with Peter; I sent her pictures of our bubble bath last night. I can't think of a single person who would be calling me right now, so my mind goes straight to the worst-case scenario. A myriad of nightmares flash before my eyes—Emma in a car wreck, with a broken wrist, or having a severe allergic reaction—as I reach into my pocket for the vibrating phone. The last thing I want to do while seated next to Peter at the quaintest restaurant I've ever been in is check my phone, but I won't be able to focus if I don't make sure it isn't Matthew calling to tell me something horrible happened.

"Sorry. I just want to make sure it's not Emma."

"You're good. Don't worry about it," Peter responds in his typical, easy going manner.

"It's Matthew's mom. I have to get this."

Why on Earth is Angie calling me? I haven't seen or spoken to her since I moved out of Matthew's house. I'm sure he has convinced everyone in his life that I am to blame for our divorce and him not seeing Emma for an entire year. Just the sight of her name on my phone screen sends me into panic mode. She would not call unless something important was happening. I can feel my hands starting to tremble as I take a deep breath and answer the call.

"Nessa! I'm so sorry to call you like this. I... I don't know where Matt is."

I can hear Emma screaming in the background. Though Angie isn't quite yelling, she is loud and frantic. My body is fully trembling now. I have to get out here and figure out what's going on. I push my chair back and jog out of the building without saying a word to Peter. I can feel his eyes on me the entire way to the door.

"Is Emma okay?" I don't care where Matt is as long as Emma is safe. There has to be more to the story for her to be calling me like this.

"She's okay. I don't think anything is wrong with her. She's... she's just scared." Angie's voice is a little calmer now, but I can still hear the worry in it.

"Why is she scared? What is going on?" I need answers right now. My legs are shaking, and my breathing is frantic. I let myself fall against Peter's car with a thud, barely able to hold myself up on my own.

"I haven't heard from Matthew all day, so I came over with dinner to see how Emma was doing." She pauses and takes a loud, deep breath. The pause drags on for what feels like hours. For fuck's sake, tell me what is going on. My heart is pounding out of my chest like a cartoon character as I wait for her to speak again.

"Angie, I'm about to have a fucking panic attack. What is going on?" Never in a million years did I think I'd drop an F-bomb while talking to Matt's mom, but I'm barely hanging on right now.

As Angie takes another deep breath, Peter comes bursting through the restaurant doors and pulls me into his arms. His firm touch instantly calms my shaking body as Angie finally lets everything she needs to say come rushing out.

"Matthew isn't here. Emma was in her crib screaming. I could hear her from the driveway when I got out of my car. I don't know how long he's been gone. Her little face, Nessa. She was so red and sweaty from screaming. He won't answer his phone. I don't…"

I can't hear any more of this. Everything around me—Peter, sounds of cars driving by, everything—disappears.

"I'm coming." I manage to get the words out in a clipped bark before ending the call and slinking down onto the pavement. I let out a few more sobs before taking in a deep, steadying breath, standing up, and getting into the car. "We have to go."

Peter gets to his side of the car in record time before pulling out of the parking lot in a hurry, without even putting on his seatbelt.

"Where am I going?" Worry is evident in his voice. I know I need to fill him in on what's happening. I just couldn't waste any more time in that parking lot. Matt lives three hours from me, but luckily only two hours from where we're staying.

"We have to go get Emma. Matthew left her." I type Matt's address into the GPS on my phone and set it where Peter can see it. The tears have finally stopped, and a burning hot rage is taking their place.

"He did what?" Anger drips from every word, but he's making a conscious effort not to yell. Though his voice comes out steady and low, his face is a deep burgundy. Any second now, I expect steam to start shooting out of his ears. "Is he fucking serious? She's a baby!"

Even though she's nearing two, hearing Peter's protectiveness as he refers to her as still a baby warms my heart. He hasn't even met her yet, but he obviously cares more about her wellbeing than Matthew does. I send Angie a text message letting her know I'll be there in two hours before realizing we can't pick her up in Peter's car.

"Shit. We have to turn around." Though I'm no longer

sobbing, I am absolutely furious, and it's affecting my ability to think. All of the bad things that could have happened while she was alone are shooting through my mind at warp speed. Not to mention what this could mean for our custody case. My brain is all over the place, and I'm struggling to keep up. "We have to get my car. We need her car seat."

"Shit." I've never seen him drive a single mile over the speed limit, but he's been going a solid ten miles over since we pulled out of the restaurant parking lot. He slows down just enough to make a sharp U-turn back towards the hotel. His usual calm, cool, and collected demeanor is nowhere to be found as he pulls into the hotel parking lot, quickly whipping into the open space beside my car, his hands white from how tightly he's gripping the steering wheel. "Do you want me to drive?"

Without a word, I toss him my keys and get into the passenger seat of my car. I was not expecting him to ride with me this weekend, but I don't have the time or energy to care that the backseat looks like a tornado passed through a toy store before throwing everything haphazardly into my vehicle. He doesn't seem to notice since his face is a permanent scowl and his eyes are locked on the road ahead. He's quickly shaving minutes off the phone's predicted ETA.

"Thanks for driving. I don't think I could focus on driving safely right now." I almost showed up to pick my toddler up without a carseat. I know I couldn't focus on driving anywhere right now. I don't know what I would have done if Peter wasn't with me when I got her phone call. As usual, he's my knight in shining armor. The only thing getting me through my darkest days.

"Of course, beautiful. I'm going to get us there as quickly as I can. He better not be there when we get there." He is laser focused on the road, effortlessly switching lanes to pass anyone in our way.

"Oh my god." I've been so panicked since Angie called, I

haven't stopped to think any of this through. Peter is with me. The man that no one knows about is headed straight to my ex's house. They cannot meet like this.

A new dread sets in; not only am I showing up to take our daughter home in the middle of his visitation time, but I'm also bringing a new man. My boyfriend? I don't even know if he's my boyfriend, but if Matt sees him, it won't matter who he is. We may both walk away from this with black eyes, or worse.

"What's wrong?" His eyes leave the road for the first time tonight, concern instead of rage now filling his face.

"Matt cannot find out about us like this."

"Oh."

"I'm sorry. It's not you. I just…"

"It's okay, Ness."

"No, let me say it. Please. It's not you. I just need to get through this before pissing him off even more. Can you just stay in the car when we get there? I'll grab her and come right back out."

"I'll wait in the car."

This is a side of Peter I've never seen. I don't know if he's upset with me or just pissed at Matt. I do know, however, that I'm not scared to find out. I know he's angry at Matt, so am I. But more importantly, he listened to me when I told him he scared me after he found out about the hole in my wall. He listened. His eyes have a fury in them, and I have no doubt he's fantasizing about running Matthew over with my car. Regardless, he didn't raise his voice again even though it was warranted. He didn't try to blame me or make my fear seem silly or childish. He listened. At that realization, I lean across the center console, grab his cheek in my hand, and give him a quick kiss.

"Thank you," I murmur in his ear.

I hope those two words convey everything I'm trying to say. Thank you for caring about Emma's wellbeing. For listening to my feelings even when you're the cause of them. For taking me to get her. For being pissed off in my honor. For... everything. The tilted smile on his face reassures me that he understood my full message despite only muttering two little words. He gently squeezes my knee as a small, wordless 'you're welcome.'

We pull into Matthew's driveway sixteen minutes before predicted, something I'm certain he's never done before. The sun has set, darkness fills the air around us, and no one is outside. I breathe a sigh of relief when I realize Matthew's truck is still not here, now confident Peter will go unnoticed. Before the car is even in park, I jump out and bolt into the house without knocking.

"Where is she?" I blurt as I fly through the door.

"Mama!" Emma squeals from her high chair, blueberries smushed to her face. Angie is standing next to her, her hands firmly on her hips. Her short bob, gray barely visible at the roots, is sticking out in every direction as if she's been running her hands through it for hours. Her eyes are bloodshot and puffy, likely a perfect match to mine after all the crying I did on the way here.

"Doodle!" I run to her and scoop her out of the high chair. She plants a wet, slobbery kiss to my cheek, leaving a blueberry smudge behind. "I missed you so much."

I turn to Angie and add, "Do you know how long he's been gone? Was she here all day alone?" The tears I worked so hard to keep in come flowing out again. Anything could have happened to her.

"I don't know. I always call him on days when Emma is with him. I talked to him before bed last night, and everything seemed fine. I called him four times before deciding to pick up a pizza and just stop by."

We're both crying now. Despite the fact that his entire family shunned me when I left him, Angie is a good person. She genuinely cares about Emma and wants her to be happy and safe just as much as I do. I know going against what her son would want by calling me was not an easy choice for her, and I'm eternally grateful she didn't let his potential reaction stop her.

"But she was okay when you got here?" I'm sure Angie is worried about where her son is, but all I care about is making sure my baby is okay.

"She's okay. She was scared and crying, but safe. I can't say for sure how long he'd been gone, but it had to be at least a couple hours. Her diaper was full, and she went straight to the fridge once she calmed down."

"I'm going to kill him." My voice is loud and matter of fact. The rage I was feeling earlier returns with a vengeance. He left our toddler home alone for hours. *Hours!* She was wet and scared and starving. Matt does not deserve to get to be her dad, and there's no way in hell I'm ever letting her come back here. I don't care what my lawyer has to say about it. She will never see him again.

"Here's her backpack. I washed all of her things before packing her bag." Angie ignores my comment, handing me Emma's Minnie Mouse bag before planting a kiss to her cheek.

"Thank y—" I'm interrupted by the front door slamming shut, and I instinctively clutch Emma to my chest.

"Mother!" Matthew bellows before he's even through the entryway. "You called Nessa! Are you fucking kidding me? It will be your fault when I have to go to court for this."

Oh my god. His voice is angry, and I know first hand that nothing will calm him down once he reaches this point. Plus, he obviously saw my car since he knew she called me. Did he see Peter? I have to get out of here. Now.

"Give me my daughter." He's full blown screaming now as he lunges towards me. He grabs a hold of Emma's shirt, and she screams, fistfuls of my shirt tightly grasped in her little hands.

"Get your hands off of her. I hope wherever the hell you were all day was worth it. You will never see her again." I turn and walk straight out the door before he can respond. I hear a loud crash and Angie crying as I charge towards the car.

I jump into the passenger seat, Emma still in my arms. "Go!"

Without hesitation, Peter throws the car in reverse, backs out of the driveway, and then takes off down the street. "Where am I going?"

"Pull over up there." I point to the next road up ahead. "I need to put her in her seat but didn't want him following us or grabbing her from me. He's pissed and unpredictable right now." I can feel my pulse through my chest. My hands are sweating, and my breathing is ragged. Emma has her little face buried in my armpit, her arms grasping my torso with all her might.

She clings to me as I walk to the other side of the car, and I whisper soft reassurances in her ear. "We're safe, baby girl. Mommy's got you."

Once she's safely in her car seat, I breathe an audible sigh of relief. Peter rests his hand on my leg as he drives us towards home. I don't even want to think about how long Emma was in the crib all alone or what she went through while her dad was gone, but clearly this day has exhausted her. Before we're even to the main road, she's fast asleep with her head drooping forward.

"You okay?" Peter whispers as soft snores drift from the backseat.

"I'm okay now that we have her. I've been so worried about her every single weekend that she's been with Matthew, and apparently I had good reason to be. I'm just glad this means I never have to send her to his house again."

"He looked right at your car when he pulled in. I tried to duck down. Do you think he saw me?"

Peter hiding, crouched in the floorboard, to save me from another confrontation with Matthew melts my heart. Disappointment filled his voice when I asked him to stay in the car earlier, but that didn't stop him from doing everything in his power to keep Emma and me safe. Whether he agrees with my decision to keep him hidden from Matt or not, he is steadfastly trustworthy and reliable. Two things Emma and I need right now.

"I don't think so, but I wasn't staying long enough to find out. He was not happy I was there."

"Did he hurt you?" His head jerks in my directions, tears pooling in his eyes.

"No. He just slammed the door and started screaming at his mom for calling me. I ran out the door as fast as I could."

Relief is written all over his face as he sighs and brings my hand to his mouth for a soft kiss.

We ride most of the way home in silence, my head resting on his arm. I can't get my mind to shut off; question after question popping into my head the whole way home.

What if Angie hadn't checked in on them? The house could have caught fire while he was gone. Can I call my lawyer on a Saturday evening? This has to be enough to keep Emma with me, but will I ever truly be free from Matt? Despite all the worries bouncing around in my head, I keep coming back to one thing—what would have happened if Angie hadn't gotten to Emma or called me.

"I was so scared for her, Peter. She could have died."

"She didn't, though. She's safe with us, and now she can stay with you where she belongs."

"She's safe with us," I repeat his words back to him. He said *us*. She's safe with us.

It's nearing midnight when Peter pulls into my driveway. I gingerly unbuckle Emma from her seat and carry her into the house. Lorelai, ever vigilant to my energy, comes racing down the hall as soon as she hears me enter, meowing loudly as she runs.

"It's okay," I whisper to her as she follows me to the crib in my room. I lay Emma down as slowly as I can, worried she'll wake if I'm not careful. She's had one hell of a day and needs to get some rest. Lorelai jumps in swiftly beside her, curling up at her feet. They're both sound asleep in seconds.

Peter is pacing the living room when I come out a few minutes later. "I'm going to see if Rob is still up so he can take me to my car."

He's still talking when I blurt, "You're leaving?"

"Oh. I thought you'd want me to." His face softens as he tilts his head towards my bedroom. He thought I'd want him to leave because Emma is here. Wait. Do I want him to leave now that she's here? Is it okay for the two of them to officially meet now?

"I need you here. Unless you don't want to be." I hadn't expected him to leave, and the thought brings a hot, stinging sensation to my eyes. He was prepared to leave, even after all of this, to respect my wishes about him not meeting Emma until I'm ready. I'm ready if he is.

"You want me to stay?" He pulls me to him when he realizes I'm once again crying.

"I want you to stay."

He drops his phone to the couch, Rob's text thread still pulled up, and kisses my forehead. "Then, I'll stay."

CHAPTER TWENTY

PETER

The savory smell of bacon wakes me as I roll toward Nessa, a long yawn escaping my lips. I stretch out and realize that she isn't beside me... or brushing her teeth. At that, memories of last night come rushing back.

Though Nessa had me drive her to Matt's in a hurry to pick up Emma, I wasn't sure if she'd want me to be here when they woke up. Technically, I met her last night when Nessa jumped into the car with her wrapped tightly in her arms. But does that really count? She could have asked me to go home, and Emma never would have known I exist, but she didn't. She wanted me to stay. To officially meet her little girl.

Wait. Emma is here.

No wonder Nessa isn't beside me. She's been up for who knows how long, frying bacon all by herself with a toddler, and I'm still in bed. The thought has me instantly throwing the covers off and jumping out of bed. I slip on a pair of shorts and make my way to the kitchen in a hurry.

"Good morning, sleepy head." Nessa's sing-song voice instantly brightens my mood. I should have gotten up when they did, but she doesn't seem bothered by it.

"You should have woken me." I yawn and rub the sleep from my eyes.

"It's not even eight yet. I know you need your beauty sleep."

"If Emma is here, wake me. I don't want to sleep in while you're handling everything by yourself." She's always up before me on the weekends, and clearly she knows I prefer to sleep in, but it's different now. I can't, in good conscience, sleep in while she takes care of everything on her own.

"I'm used to it. I do it every day."

"That's not the point. I want…" I'm interrupted by the sound of Nessa giggling, and I have to be missing something. How is that funny? Nessa having to do the work of two people by herself every single day is not funny. But before I can ask the question out loud, a chunk of scrambled egg hits the side of my face with an audible splat.

"Woah, she's got a good arm!" They're both wheezing with laughter as Nessa clears Emma's tray before she can hurl any more food my way. "Remind me to coach her T-ball team in a few years. She's going to be the star."

Nessa's wide grin twinkles in my direction as she washes Emma in the sink. Normally, I try not to make statements that put me firmly in their future. But getting to meet Emma and Nessa wanting me to stay changed something in me. Being here with Emma, with both of them, means she's picturing me in their future too. She wouldn't have let me pick Emma up with her or stay here last night, if she wasn't positive about keeping me around. She's been adamant about not introducing her daughter to anyone unless things were serious, so I know her decision was not made lightly. I had high hopes for this weekend with Nessa. Even though it took an unexpected turn, I wouldn't change it for the world.

Emma's propped on Nessa's hip, fresh out of her sink bath, shyly peeking in my direction. "Can you say hi to Peter?" Nessa points in my direction, and Emma slowly lifts her head off of her mom's shoulder.

"Hiiii." She draws the word out as she waves her arm enthusiastically back and forth.

"Good morning, Emma." I wave back at her. "Did you save any eggs for me?"

They both laugh as Emma points to the eggs still laying at my feet. I grab a paper towel and wipe it up while making a silly face at her. I don't have any experience with kids this small, but the face I'm making—eyes crossed with my tongue sticking straight out—seems to do the trick. Emma immediately starts laughing as she tries to stick her tongue out towards me, rapidly blinking her eyes instead of crossing them.

"After breakfast, we usually take a walk. Want to come with us?" Nessa is giggling, too, her eyes focused on the bright, open-mouthed smile on her daughter's face.

"Absolutely. What do we need?" I have no idea what it takes to get a toddler out the door, but I've been on the phone several times while Nessa is doing it. She's dropped the phone on more than one occasion, her hands too full to keep it in place, so I know it's no easy feat.

"If it's chilly, she'll need a blanket but it's been nice enough lately. She likes to sit in her little car with a snack, and I usually bring a couple toys just in case." I make a checklist in my head as she rattles off everything we need for our short walk around the block.

"Okay, I can grab some toys and a snack while you get her ready." They follow me down the hall, heading straight for the laundry room while I turn into Emma's room. After grabbing five different toy options, having no idea which to choose, I head to the kitchen.

What do one-year-olds snack on? Emma only has two teeth but didn't seem to have any trouble eating eggs and bacon this morning. I decide to wing it, pouring Cheerios into a small bowl and grabbing a yogurt tube from the fridge.

"Ready?" Nessa looks effortlessly beautiful wearing a pair of jean shorts and my Chiefs hoodie, her hair down and messy around her shoulders. Emma, now in a long sleeve pink dress covered in rainbows with her hair in a ponytail that fountains up from the top of her head, is clutching the unicorn from the picture Rob sent me all those months ago. My heart tightens at how far we've come since then.

"I think I'm ready," I say, holding up everything I gathered.

"Not sure how far you think we're walking, but that should do it." She laughs before setting Emma down and taking a few things from my arms.

Once we're outside, Nessa pulls a small, blue kids car that has a handle like a stroller out of the garage. She sets Emma into it, securing the belt around her, and then arranges all the toys at her feet. She was right; I have way too much stuff. Though, Emma doesn't seem to mind. She's already dropped the stuffed unicorn, trading it out for a pretend gaming controller that lights up and sings the alphabet with each push of a button. Her smile is wide as we start off down the street, and I think we may get along just fine.

"I can push her, if you want."

I've spent many nights thinking about how meeting Emma for the first time would go. I hadn't considered that I'd have no idea what to do when the time finally came. Daisy was easy. She came right up to me the first time we met, demanding to be pushed on the swing set in their backyard. We've been buddies ever since. The stakes are so much higher this time. What if Emma doesn't like me? What if I never figure out how to take care of her? With Daisy, I jumped in as the fun uncle and that was that. With Emma, it's so much more complicated.

Nessa steps to the side, handing pushing duties over to me, then loops her arm through mine as we continue down the street.

"How are you doing?" So much has happened in the last twelve hours, and we've barely gotten any time to talk about it.

"I'm okay. Last night was rough, but having both of you with me made it better." She smiles at me before asking, "How about you?"

"I'm perfect."

"Yes you are." She chuckles.

"That too. But I meant finally getting to be with both of you is perfect, even if I am up with the sun."

"Better get used to it. She's an early bird." I'd get used to just about anything for mornings like this. Mornings with them.

"This is a big step. I know you've worried a lot about this. Talk to me."

"I'm okay, really. I've been trying to decide how and when to introduce you to her anyway. I guess we have at least one thing to thank *him* for." She raises her eyebrows in Emma's direction, not wanting to say her dad's name out loud with her present.

"Finally," I chuckle, although there's nothing funny about what he did yesterday, even if it did inadvertently move our relationship forward. "I'm just glad she's okay, and you didn't have to do it all alone this time."

"Me too." She kisses the side of my arm, smiling up at me.

Emma is restless, leaving a Cheerio trail Hansel and Gretel style, by the time we're back in their driveway. "Bub! Mama, bub!" She claps and points as she screams.

I glance at Nessa, who clearly understands exactly what Emma wants. "Bubbles! Sure. We can do that, sweetie."

"Ohhhh." Bub means bubbles. Got it. Emma does a lot of 'talking,' but it comes out in random sounds that make no sense to me. There's more to this than I realized; Nessa wanting to wait until the perfect moment makes more and more sense as the day goes on.

Nessa unbuckles Emma with one hand, reaching for the

bubbles with her other hand. "Here, take her, and I'll blow some bubbles."

"No! Mama!" Emma screams and clutches onto her mom. I appreciate that Nessa is trying to include me, but Emma clearly isn't quite ready.

"It's okay. I'll blow the bubbles while you hold her." I silently remind myself that Nessa is Emma's safe space, especially after the things her own father has put her through. Just like her mom, she's going to need time to open up to me.

Turns out, bubbles are the key to her heart. She squeals and claps as I blow bubble after bubble. She's so wiggly in Nessa's arms that she nearly topples them both over. As soon as Nessa sets her down, she takes off in circles around me, hopping and stabbing her index finger at the bubbles surrounding us. When she falls at my feet, I instinctively reach out to steady her. Instead of crying out for her mom like she did just moments ago, she takes my hand and lets me pull her up. Baby steps.

An entire bottle of bubbles later, we're finally back inside, Emma running full steam ahead up and down the hallway. "So breakfast, walk, playtime. What does the rest of your day consist of?"

"We play, read books, or run errands. Then we have lunch, and she takes a nap. I usually call you while she's sleeping, then do homework or clean up. Since this semester's over, we can relax a bit once she's down."

"She has so much energy. I cannot imagine her being ready for a nap any time soon." Anytime I think she's about to slow down or rest, she gets a second burst of energy and takes off again. I'm getting tired just watching her.

"She's wearing herself out as we speak. She'll run out of steam." As if on cue, Emma comes barreling into the living room, twirls, and then plops directly onto her bottom.

"Do you want to show Peter your ball pit?"

Emma hops up and takes off once again. Nessa and I follow right behind her this time, making it to the doorway of her room just in time to see her belly flop at full speed into the sea of balls. Multi-colored balls shoot up into the air in all directions as she rolls onto her back, giggling and kicking her feet. Nessa threads her fingers through mine and pulls me down onto the colorful rug. Leaning against the wall, our feet intertwined in front of us, I drape my arm around her shoulder. We watch as Emma leaps in and out of the ball pit before she settles onto Nessa's lap with a yawn.

"Let's read one story, and then we'll make some lunch." Nessa pulls a book from the shelf beside her and flips to the first page. Emma rests her head against Nessa's chest, fully captivated by the book in her hands. By the end of the story, Emma is laying across Nessa's lap and rubbing her eyes. I have never in my life witnessed someone go from zooming up and down the hallway to nearly crashed out in a matter of ten minutes.

I am in awe of the effortless way that Nessa handles Emma like it's the most straightforward job in the world. From doing everything one-handed to calming a meltdown in seconds, she's clearly capable of handling life all on her own, which makes the fact that she wants me in it that much sweeter. I've got a lot to learn, but I'm up for the challenge.

Before Emma can fall asleep, Nessa scoops her up and kisses her little nose. "Let's get some lunch."

I lead the way to the kitchen, determined to be useful this time. "What can I do?"

"She's ready for a nap, so I'm thinking we should do something quick and easy." She sets Emma down before grabbing an apple, cucumber, and deli meat from the fridge.

"Okay, I can chop these up. How small do they need to be? Giving her an apple is making my blood pressure spike." She chuckles, but I'm dead serious. I envisioned a one and a half year old eating applesauce and... well... applesauce. I don't know... things that are soft and easy to chew.

"Just cut it into thin strips. She has a couple teeth, but gums are hard. She can chew just fine. Baby led weaning is the new *thing*."

"Baby led what?"

"Baby led weaning. I don't understand the name either, but basically, she eats what I eat. It's made meal time so much easier. Did you see her eat bacon this morning?"

"I did, and I was ready with the Heimlich maneuver." I let out a small chuckle, knowing I sound like a worried first time dad while she's calm, cool, and collected. We've swapped roles, and the glint in her eyes says she's enjoying it.

"She's never choked, but it's good to know just in case. It's different for a toddler, though." She tips Emma upside down and motions quick thrusts to her back.

"I don't think I can do that to her." I've taken classes to learn CPR in the past, but it's been several years since then. I've never had to use it on anyone, let alone a baby, and I'm not so sure I could do it.

"Honestly, it scares me too. Hopefully we never have to." She loads Emma's tray with freshly cut apple and cucumber, a slice of ham, and a cheese stick torn into strips before placing Emma into her high chair. I'm on the edge of my seat, literally. At the first sign of distress, I'll be ready to jump into action. I've completely ignored my own food, but Emma doesn't end up needing anything. She ate almost everything on her plate without any intervention, much to my relief.

Nessa wipes Emma's hands clean before taking her to the bedroom for nap time. I quickly scarf down my lunch then dump our plates and Emma's tray before wiping it clean and replacing it back onto the high chair. By the time I'm finished cleaning up, Nessa emerges from the bedroom.

"She fell asleep so quickly. She must have been exhausted." She slinks down onto the couch looking a little exhausted herself.

"I'm exhausted," I say as I slump down next to her, leaning

my head on her shoulder and pretending to snore. Between getting up hours before I normally would on a Sunday and chasing a toddler around all morning, I'm ready for my own nap.

"Me, too. I didn't get much sleep last night, and she was up early this morning. Next time, we can nap with her, but I think we should talk today."

My heart sinks. 'We should talk' never ends well. I let out a resigned breath. I knew meeting her daughter was a big step, but I thought it was going pretty well. "Alright, what's on your mind?"

"Meeting Emma is a huge step for us. How are you feeling about it?" I was prepared for her to tell me she changed her mind about having me in Emma's life; this talk I can do.

"I'm feeling pretty good. Though, I didn't realize how little I know about kids her age. Daisy and I bonded quickly, but the stakes are higher with Emma. I just don't know what to do with a not even two-year-old."

"You're doing fine. I've been with her since the moment she was born; I'm just used to her. You'll learn her routine and what she likes. She's been through a lot in her short, little life. Just like me, she's going to take some time to warm up to you, but truly, you're doing just fine."

"Time. I can do that. I'm nothing if not patient."

"Truer words have never been spoken," she chortles and lays her head on my lap, her eyes gazing up at mine.

"So, does this mean I get to see you every single weekend, now?" There certainly are silver linings to the roller coaster weekend we've had, and I'm hoping this is one of them.

"Do you want to?" Her eyes are still locked on mine, a look of uncertainty in them.

"Of course I do." Though I haven't mentioned anything to her, I've been ready for this for weeks now. There's no denying it, I'm falling for Nessa, but she's a part of a package deal. Without

Emma, this relationship can only go so far, and I'm ready for us to move forward—all three of us.

"I need to call my lawyer, but nothing he can say will change my mind. I'm not sending her back there. It'll have to be all three of us from now on. Are you sure you're ready for that?"

"I'm ready," I assure her as I lightly brush her hair from her face.

Rob pulls in to get me before Emma wakes from her nap. I hate to leave without saying goodbye, but I know waking her before she's ready would make the rest of the day harder for both of them. She offered to drive me back to the hotel to get our things and my car, but I don't want Emma stuck in her carseat three days in a row after traveling to her dad's Friday night and back with us last night. Plus, I could use some time with my friend. Having been through this years ago with Nora and Daisy, he'll understand exactly how I'm feeling.

At the sound of his car horn in the driveway, I kiss Nessa goodbye and start the countdown until I see her again... this time only five short days away.

"Hey," I say as I drop into the passenger seat of Rob's car. Despite having a seven year old, his car is far from family oriented. Like mine, his backseat is small and cramped, and there's no sign of Daisy anywhere.

"I got you a fountain Pepsi from Casey's for the road." I can't tell you what it is about Casey's fountain soda machine, but it's far superior to any other gas station, something only a true gamer would know.

"Thanks." The first sip burns my throat as it goes down. "Can we make a pitstop before we head out?"

"Sure." He hands me his phone with the GPS function pulled up, and I quickly search for the address we need. A few minutes later, we're pulling into the Barnes and Noble parking lot.

Rob begrudgingly follows me through the store, looking like I'm holding him hostage, as I locate the parenting section of the bookstore. I grab *What to Expect: The Toddler Years* and a book about baby-led weaning before noticing a display of children's books on my way to check out. Recognizing a few that my mom used to read to Andrew and me, I toss them onto my pile and get in line for the registers.

Once we're back in the car, I set the bag of books at my feet. I know I need to talk to Aunt Deedee about all of this, but I also want advice from someone who's experienced it firsthand. My car is only an hour from here, so I'm wasting no time on small talk before diving right in. "How old was Daisy when you first met her?"

"Uh. About Emma's age, probably a little smaller." He runs his hand through his beard as he thinks, something he always does without even realizing.

"I don't know what to do with her. She's so little. I can twirl Daisy and sneak her cookies, no problem. But it's different with Emma. I can't just be the fun uncle who fills her with sugar and then leaves."

"Definitely not the sugar part; Nessa would hate that. Trust me. I tried winning Daisy over with ice cream. It just gave her a belly ache and way too much energy." He chuckles at the memory.

"So, then what do I do?"

"At the risk of sounding like we're in a chick flick, just be you. Love her mom, play with her, show up. That's it."

Just show up. That's it. Honestly, that's surprisingly good advice. I choose to ignore the 'love her mom' portion of his statement, knowing any argument to the contrary would come out sounding forced and untrue. Do I love her mom? I don't know, but I do care deeply for her. Things are still so fresh and complicated without adding 'love' to the mix just yet.

CHAPTER TWENTY-ONE

NESSA

I called my lawyers office promptly at eight on the dot this morning. Though Emma meeting Peter this weekend was a monumental and unexpected step, it also provided a welcome distraction from the chaos. In the midst of all of it, I haven't gotten much sleep. After months of stressing about when and how to introduce my daughter to the man I'm almost certainly falling for, the opportunity all but fell into my lap.

Being a single mom comes with so much pressure and unsolicited advice, making every decision feel like life or death. Unsurprisingly, Peter makes everything easier. Emma is so small she doesn't understand or care about any of it, and Peter jumped in, all hands on deck, immediately. Now that I can let that worry go, I can put all my focus on keeping Matt as far away from all of us as possible.

After scheduling an impromptu meeting with Dylan, my divorce and custody attorney, my dad rushed over to stay with Emma so I could go alone. Though Emma is welcome to come, I don't want to talk about her dad in front of her. She's been through enough without me shit-talking him in her presence. Plus, anything involving a toddler just takes longer. When it comes to billable time with my lawyer, the quicker we can get this meeting over with, the better.

I'm perched on the hardest couch known to mankind, and the coffee in my lap is the only thing keeping my hands from trembling. As much money as I've already had to pay him, you'd think he could afford a more comfortable couch than the one I got for free off Marketplace. Taking in my surroundings, I wait for Dylan to call me back to his office. It's cold and bare in here without a single decoration on the wall. The bleakness feeding the dread is already forming in my gut. A draft from the overhead vent adds to the nervous bounce, bounce, bounce, of my legs. I press a hand firmly to them, settling the jitters, as Dylan finally comes to get me. At least the time I spent in the waiting room isn't billable.

"I'm going to cut straight to the chase," I blurt before either of us is seated.

"Well, good morning to you too." There's a playful grin on his face that, surprisingly, helps break the tension I've been feeling all morning.

"Good morning," I add before spilling every last detail about Emma's weekend with Matt, though I leave Peter completely out of it.

I know Dylan is technically on my side in all of this, but I can't bring myself to mention Peter. In all honesty, I'm afraid he will tell me that having a boyfriend while in the midst of a divorce and custody battle will not look good in the eyes of a judge. But I'm finally happy. I'm slowly building the life Emma and I deserve. Still technically married or not, Peter is perfect for me, and I can already tell he will step up for Emma in any way he can. Dylan can't tell me to break things off with Peter if he doesn't know he exists.

"Angie, Matthew's mother, arrived at Matt's residence and found Emma alone in her crib after an undetermined amount of time. She reported that Emma was in distress, unfed, and unchanged for at least an hour, though she does not know exactly how long she was left unattended." He's jotting notes down onto a legal pad as he relays what I told him back to me. "Would she be willing to testify to that?"

"I don't know. She was pretty upset, and I know she cares about her granddaughter. I just don't know if she'd actually stand up against her own son like that, especially if she risks losing Emma in the process."

"Hmm." He's nibbling on the end of his fancy ballpoint pen that probably cost more than my rent as he considers the best course of action. After a long moment of silence, he finally adds, "I'm going to file a petition for a protective order against Matthew on Emma's behalf. We can try to include you in it as well, however, I do not see a judge approving that. Honestly, the judge may not approve it for Emma, either, solely due to the fact that there's an open custody case in regards to her. Depending on which judge we get, he or she may opt to let family court handle it."

I take a full, deep breath before responding. "I don't know how any of this works. What happens after we file for a protective order? How long will it be in effect if it's approved? Do I have to go to court? Obviously, I'll get full custody now, but…"

"Woah. Slow down. You will have to appear in court so we can prove to the judge that a protective order is justified. Usually, protective orders are granted in twelve month increments, but again, it also depends on the family court's ruling. I'll walk you through each step as we get to it. For now, just focus on Emma, and I'll do the rest."

"Okay. Sorry. This is all so stressful." There are hundreds of other questions floating around in my head, begging to be asked, but he doesn't give me the chance.

"I have another meeting to get to, but I want to clarify one thing first. I never said you will get full custody because of this. There is a strong possibility that a judge will not approve this protective order, forcing us to wait until we can get in front of Judge Steeple, our family courts judge. Even if it is approved, it's highly unlikely you'll be able to keep him away forever."

I don't respond. I can't. Instead, I stare at him in disbelief as I slowly back away from his desk. Dylan has been telling me that Matt is likely to shoot himself in the foot by giving us a way to prove that he is unfit for months. He did exactly that, and it's somehow *still* not enough.

As soon as I round the corner out of his office, I take off in a sprint to my car. The car door slams, jolting the entire vehicle, as tears burst from my eyes. Slumped with my head in my hands, I sob uncontrollably. My breaths come in gasps as I struggle to get enough air in my lungs.

Once my tears finally run dry and I'm able to draw in a full breath, I find my phone, my thumb hovering above Peter's name. I cannot call Peter right now. He has his life in perfect order, from his dream job to his immense bond with Deedee. He's smart, reliable, and trustworthy, which is exactly why I can't dump any more of my crap into his lap.

He didn't run for the hills when he found out I'm still technically married. He didn't budge when I cowered away from him in fear when he raised his voice. He stayed steadfastly by my side, even hiding in the car, when he had to drive me to pick Emma up in the middle of the night. There's only so much drama an introvert like Peter, or anyone for that matter, can take before he realizes I'm not worth the hassle anymore.

Calling him and interrupting his work day so I can cry to him about how hard my life is right now is out of the question. Instead, I wipe my eyes on my sleeves and call Nora.

"Hey. I have to go get a patient in just a minute. Is everything okay?" Nora works in a dentist office that provides free dental care to low income families. I know she's busy and only answering the phone because she's worried about me. I shouldn't have bothered her, either.

"I'm okay. I can call you later." I sniffle as I pull the phone from my ear, ready to end the call.

"I can tell you've been crying, Ness. I can spare a couple minutes. Tell me the 'too long, didn't read' version."

"Dylan is filing for a protective order against Matt for Emma, which is great, but he still doesn't think I'll get what I'm asking for in terms of custody." Tears spring from me like a broken faucet as I quickly fill Nora in on the most important things that Dylan had to say.

"It's enough for a protective order but not enough to win custody? Our justice system is wack. Do you remember what happened with Devon?"

Devon is Daisy's biological father, who has never even met his daughter. Nora learned that he was abusing drugs shortly after finding out she was pregnant. She cut off all contact after he showed up at her first ultrasound appointment strung out. He hadn't slept in days, couldn't walk without holding onto the wall, and nearly knocked the ultrasound screen over. Security escorted him out, and that was that.

"Of course I do." I've gotten my leaky faucet under control again, eager to see where she's going with this.

"He filed for custody after they started garnishing his paychecks for child support. I hired an attorney who also told me it was possible he'd get visitation rights unless he did something to directly endanger Daisy, which is hard to do when you've never even laid eyes on her."

I'm nodding, even though she can't see me. "Yeah. I remember that. But he's still never met her. What's your point?"

"I'm getting there. My lawyer prepared me for the worst but then turned around and got a judge to agree to exactly what I asked for. My point is, just because it's a possibility doesn't make it fact."

The color returns to my knuckles as I loosen my grip on the steering wheel, and I let out a long sigh as she adds, "Focus on what you can control. Get the protective order, keep her safe with you, document everything. It will all work out."

"One step at a time. Focus on what I can control." I repeat it a few more times in my head, forcing it to fully sink in. Focus on what you can control. Just because it's a possibility doesn't make it fact. "Thanks, Nor. Love you."

"Love you! I have to go, but let's go out for dinner tonight. I want to hear all the juicy details from this weekend." She ends the call before I can agree, though she knows we'll be there.

Emma is asleep on my dad's chest when I get home, Lorelai curled up beside them. "She looks so peaceful," I say as I walk through the door.

"I know. She reminds me so much of you. This was your favorite way to sleep for the first three years of your life. Honestly, if you hadn't gotten too tall, you probably would have kept doing it." Nostalgia fills his face as he reminisces, giving Emma a gentle squeeze at the memory.

"I can try to move her so you can get up." I reach out to grab her, and he shoos my hand away.

"Leave her. She's comfortable, and you look upset. Tell me how your meeting went."

My dad and I are very close, so naturally, I tell him almost as much as I tell Nora. I've called him after every weekend with Peter, leaving out all the dirty details—the ones that do make their way into Nora's version of my weekly recap. He was the second person I told when I found out I was pregnant, second only to Nora, and the first person I told when I left Matt. So, he already knows everything that happened this weekend and that Peter finally met Emma. I suck in a deep breath and fill him in on everything that happened during my meeting with Dylan.

"Oh, sweetheart." He pulls me in for a side hug, careful not to disturb Emma. As a dad who would have been heartbroken not to see his children every single day, I know hearing about my attempts to keep Matt away from Emma is hard for him. "I never liked him, but I'm a firm believer that kids need both their parents."

"I know, Dad. I don't want to keep her from him. Okay, I kind of do want to keep her from him. I don't know what to do. She isn't safe with him."

"I know, sweetheart. I know. I'm on your side, always. I just want you to see where your lawyer, and potentially a judge, might be coming from."

"I will never understand if a judge forces me to send her back there after he neglected her. She could have died."

"But she didn't. She's home safe, and it sounds like she'll be here for the foreseeable future. That's good news. Let's focus on that, for now."

We spend the rest of Emma's nap watching *Gilmore Girls* in silence. My dad raised two girls mostly on his own. He is used to watching *Gilmore Girls* with us and can quote it almost as well as my sister and I can. He understood immediately why I named my cat Lorelai, as well as why I feel so close to human Lorelai now that I'm a mom.

When Emma finally wakes, it's almost time for us to head to dinner with Nora.

"Do you want to come with us?" Nora has been my best friend since fifth grade, so she and my dad know each other pretty well. If I wasn't at her house, she was at mine. He often talks about her like she's his third daughter, and she would not mind one bit if he crashed our dinner date.

"Oh, no. You go ahead. Give Nora my love." He kisses my forehead before carrying Emma to the car and buckling her in for me.

"Papa," Emma squeals with her hands outstretched to him as he turns to leave.

"I'll see you in a few days, pumpkin. I love you."

Nora and I decided to take the girls to The Burger Shack for dinner. Their cheese fries are to die for, and we can feed all four of us for pretty cheap. More importantly, we can sit outside watching the girls play cornhole while we wait for our food, giving us the perfect opportunity to chat without interruptions.

"I'm tired of hearing about Matthew. I want to hear all about Emma and Peter meeting. How did it go?" She takes a sip from her straw, tucks her feet underneath her, and turns towards me.

"He's perfect, Nor. Literally, perfect. He is not a morning person, but he got up without me even asking and helped with Emma all day. I'm not used to having extra hands, and I'm definitely not used to getting help without having to beg first."

"I knew it!" She jumps out of her seat, fist in the air, causing everyone else eating outside to stare in our direction.

"Shhh. Simmer down. How long did it take Daisy to open up to Rob?"

"I will not simmer down. This is big news. It took her about a week. She didn't have any trauma around men like Emma does though. Was she scared of him or something?"

"No. I wouldn't say scared. Just a little hesitant, but you're right. The one man she should be able to trust has proven himself untrustworthy. I think she can sense that, even though she's young."

"She definitely can. Kids pick up on that kind of stuff. Peter is the complete opposite of Matt. I have no doubt she'll pick up on that too. So does that mean you're going to let him come see you even when Emma is here?"

"Yeah, I think so. I think we're ready. He did really well with her, and I think it's time. He's coming to stay again this weekend."

"And she'll be here, right?"

"Yeah. Hopefully she'll be here every weekend from now on."

"Ooo, yay! Let's take the kids somewhere fun. I'm excited to see him with her, plus Rob might actually come if Peter does." Nora and I take the girls out together several times per week, but Rob hasn't come with us a single time. I know how much Nora hates doing it all without him, so I hope she's right.

"Yes! Definitely. Maybe we can all go to the zoo or something. I want to go before it gets too hot out. Are things still not going well between you and Rob?"

"Nope. We still aren't having sex. We barely talk. He rarely leaves his game room." This is the worst it's ever gotten for them, and I don't know if having Peter around is enough to convince Rob to do anything.

"I'm sorry, Nor. He'll come around." I hope, but I can't say that part out loud. Not right now. Things are going so well for Peter and me, and I know it's hard for her to hear about me falling in love again as her marriage crumbles in front of her. Now's not the time for hard truths, even if she needs to hear it.

It's nearly Emma's bedtime when we get home from dinner, so we jump right into our nightly routine with a shower, putting on jammies, a book, and then bed. As I'm zipping Emma's footy pajamas with little rubber duckies all over them, I hear the familiar FaceTime ring coming from my phone. I usually call Peter after Emma is asleep, and Matt almost never calls to talk to her between visits. Actually, I haven't heard from him at all since picking Emma up on Saturday night.

Though sticking to our bedtime routine is crucial, curiosity gets the best of me. I jump across the bed, landing flat on my stomach, in order to grab my phone before the call ends. It's Peter.

"Hey. Everything okay? It's early." Emma crawls up onto the bed and sticks her face directly in front of the screen, leaving nothing but her eyeballs visible to Peter.

He chuckles. "Hey, Emma. I was just calling to tell you and Mama good night."

She doesn't budge.

"Can you say 'good night?'" Though I know she can't quite say 'good night' yet, we've been practicing putting two words together, even if they don't come out exactly right.

She presses her nose firmly into my phone screen, still not saying anything.

"That's okay. Mama will tell him good night. Good night, Peter."

"Good night. I'll talk to you in a—" He doesn't get the chance to finish before Emma presses her finger to the big, red circle at the bottom of the screen.

"You little stinker."

She laughs and claps before sliding off the bed. She knows the next part of our routine is to read a bedtime story, and a few moments later she toddles back into the bedroom with three books in her hands.

CHAPTER TWENTY-TWO

NESSA

Dylan filed the petition for a protective order on Monday after I left his office. Unlike family court, which often takes several months or even a year before getting in front of a judge, motions like this one—protections involving children—are seen within forty-eight hours.

The courthouse is quiet yet echo-y. It smells almost exactly like the old library where I do school work in between classes which somehow makes it feel less foreign. The cold bench beneath Dylan and I is doing nothing to help my jittery legs. He's trying to prepare me for my upcoming testimony, but I'm too busy trying not to hurl to focus. He waves his hand in front of my face, finally pulling my attention back to him, just as Matthew walks through the door with the echoing click of Angie's heels right behind him.

Despite the despicable human he is in private, he cleans up nicely. The midwesterner nod he gives Dylan proves his nice guy facade is firmly in place. He's dressed even nicer than he was on our wedding day—wearing a nice pair of khakis, a button-up shirt, and tie, his short hair neatly combed to the side. He's clearly put more effort into impressing Judge Brown than he put into being a husband or a father.

Angie, wearing a long, striped dress that I've seen her wear to church a hundred times, leaves Matt with his lawyer and walks straight towards Dylan and me. "I was hoping Emma would be here." Her voice comes out in a shy whisper as she looks around the courthouse waiting area.

"I'm not bringing my toddler to court. Especially when her 'father'"—I put air quotes around the word—"who abandoned her is here." I'm done sugar coating Matt's behavior for anyone, including his mother.

"I know. I get it. What he did was wrong. I just wanted to see her. That's all." There's genuine remorse in her eyes, and I almost feel bad for being so blunt. Don't worry. I rally quickly, though.

"If you truly understood, you wouldn't be here to defend him. You'd be here to stand up for Emma."

Before she can respond, Dylan cuts in. "Let's go, Nessa. Now is not the time to pick a fight."

He's right, of course. I follow close behind him as he cracks the courtroom door open just enough to peek inside. He nods for me to follow him as I take a few steadying breaths and force Matt and Angie out of my mind. As we enter the courtroom, I begin running through answers to potential questions in my head. Now is not the time to pick fights. It's time to prepare for my most important battle yet, especially now that Matt has someone to back up any claim he makes.

As I make my way toward the judge's stand, I can't help but notice that the courtroom looks exactly like they do in movies. Two large tables, each with a pair of chairs, face the judge's stand. Dylan escorts me to one of them, already pulling papers from his briefcase as Matt's lawyer does the same at the table beside us. The bailiff is standing statue-still beside the judge's chamber door as we file in and take our seats.

Unlike in the movies, we're the only ones in the room. Angie finds a seat at the back instead of right behind Matthew like I'd expected. I'd prepared myself for a room full of people eager to get protective orders today, and the unexpected quiet unnerves me. Though having no one here to watch my testimony gives me a sense of calm, the thought of other moms being here to protect their babies made me feel seen and understood. Now, with the only spectator here in favor of Matt, I've never felt quite so alone.

Once Judge Brown is seated, gavel in hand, she instructs us to do the same. Though I'm wearing a thin, flowy dress that is perfect for summer heat yet classy enough for a courtroom, I'm sweating profusely as nerves fully take over. My legs are bouncing furiously underneath the table. So furiously that Dylan quickly scrawls the words 'chill out' on his legal pad, turning it in my direction.

Chill out. Easy for you to say. Your entire life isn't on the line right now.

Despite comebacks at the ready, I take his advice. Breathe in for five seconds, hold it in for five seconds, breathe out for five seconds. We use this technique in class all the time, and I've been trying to implement it into my life as well. Using the practice myself will make it easier to teach to my clients one day, and even though this breathing technique sounds overly simple, it's effective. My breathing evens out, my heart rate slows, and I wipe my sweaty palms on my dress. I'm ready for whatever lies ahead.

While I'm giving myself a much needed pep talk, Dylan and Matt's lawyer, Judy, are whispering with Judge Brown while standing in front of her bench. Once they return to their respective tables, Dylan motions for me to take the stand.

In for five, hold for five, out for five. In for five, hold for five, out for five. Ready as I'll ever be, I take the stand, raise my right hand, and agree to tell the truth, the whole truth, and nothing but the truth.

Judge Brown greets me before briefly explaining to the room exactly what will happen here today. She'll hear from both Matt and I, as well as any witnesses and allow both attorneys to address anyone on the stand before meeting with both of them privately. Finally, before we leave, she will give her ruling. I take one more calming breath before detailing exactly what happened on Saturday night.

Once I'm finished, Dylan approaches the stand. "Nessa, thank you for explaining why you're seeking a protective order for your daughter today. Is this the first time you've witnessed anger like this from Matthew?"

"No," I respond, staring directly at Dylan. I know this answer is going to piss Matt, and maybe even Angie, off. I cannot bear to look at them while answering. Matt has intimidated me out of telling the truth for years, but his tactics will not work on me today.

"So, this isn't the first time Matt has gotten angry in front of your daughter. Tell me about that."

In for five, hold for five, out for five. I can do this.

"Matt has been aggressive with me for years. Though he's never physically hurt Emma, that I know of, he has been aggressive in front of her." Courage building, I launch into three different scenarios in which Matt threw something at me or slammed the door in my face with Emma in my arms, including the incident with the coffee cup. Dylan asks a few more follow up questions before I'm released from the stand and Matt takes my place.

I did it. I finally let everything Matt has done to me, and how it affects Emma, out into the open. It's out of my hands now.

Matt takes the stand, forcing me to finally look in his direction. His hands appear steady, no sweat stains in sight. He's confident and arrogant as usual, but the scowl he wears when he makes eye contact with me shows that my words hit harder than he's willing to let on. Before addressing Judge Brown, he plasters an innocent smile back on his face, ready to charm his way out of this.

Judy prompts Matt to tell his version of events from Saturday night, and his words come out with rehearsed ease. "Your Honor, I would never risk my daughter's safety, as some people would have you believe." He flicks his head toward my table before continuing. "The insinuation that I would ever put my daughter in danger upsets me deeply."

"I have no doubt you love your daughter. You wouldn't be here if you didn't. Tell us exactly what happened Saturday night," Judy prompts.

"Taking care of an almost two-year-old, all by myself, is hard, you know? But I love every second of it. She's my world."

Gag me. Stop rambling and get to the damn point. I'm not the only one annoyed by his tactic, though. Before his lawyer can ask him the question for a third time, Judge Brown interjects. "Please answer the question, young man."

"Sorry. Sorry. I just want you to know that Nessa has been trying to take Emma from me almost her entire life. This is just her latest ploy to keep me out of Emma's life. She doesn't want what's best for Emma. She wants what's best for Nessa."

At that, Dylan stands abruptly. "Your honor, he's completely avoiding the question."

"I will not ask again. Answer the question." The judges voice is level but firm.

Despite my best effort, a huge smile crosses my face. He's trying to turn the tables in his favor, as usual, but for once, it doesn't seem to be working.

"Sorry. This is just so emotional for me," Matthew adds without a single ounce of emotion reflected in his tone or features. "Saturday night, I fed Emma dinner at about six o'clock. I always make sure to serve her a balanced meal with protein, vegetables, and fruit. She's a growing girl, you know? Then I gave her a bath, brushed her teeth, and read her a story like I always do."

I know that interjecting right now will not help my case,

though I am ready to scream at the absurdity of what he's saying. He's lying through his teeth. But I must remain calm, so I swiftly slide Dylan's notepad in front of me and begin furiously writing my thoughts down for him instead.

> THIS IS ALL BULLSHIT! SHE COMES HOME EVERY SINGLE SUNDAY IN THE SAME OUTFIT WITH HER HAIR STILL IN THE PONYTAIL I PUT IT IN ON FRIDAY. BALANCED HEALTHY MEAL? READ HER A STORY? WHAT A FUCKING JOKE.

Before I can add any more, he slides the notepad back in front of him, nodding in my direction. "We got this," he whispers before turning his attention back to Matt.

"After reading her the story three times, which she insisted"—He gives a charming, completely fake laugh before continuing—"I tucked her into bed. Once she was sound asleep in her crib, I took the monitor outside with me so I could keep an eye on her. My mom must have shown up right after I left. I was still on the property, just taking a little walk after a long day. Next thing I know, Nessa is running out the door with my daughter, threatening to never let me see her again."

My eyes are stinging, tears ready to fall any second now. I swallow the lump in my throat and force the tears to stay in. I refuse to let Matthew see me cry ever again.

Dylan approaches the stand after giving a soft squeeze of reassurance to my shoulder. I can't listen to any more of this bullshit. It's taking every bit of energy I have not to spring up from my seat and demand he tell the truth. Before I can pull my attention back to what's happening, Matt is leaving the stand without me hearing a single question or answer.

It doesn't matter, though. Angie is taking the stand now, and with her corroboration, Judge Brown will believe everything he just said. I'm no longer able to hold my tears in. They come bursting out of me, and I quickly cover my face with my hands.

Turning away from everyone while I get my crying under control, Dylan nudges me with his elbow. "It's not over until it's over. Dry it up. Focus."

I'm beginning to hate this man. He lacks empathy even though he works with parents fighting for their children on a daily basis. He's blunt and to the point, which normally, I like. I'm blunt and to the point. Sometimes, though, kindness goes a long way, and I could really use some right now. Though I know everything Matt just said was a lie, it came out so convincingly that it's unlikely any one will side with me at this point.

I wipe my eyes and take a deep breath, turning my attention to Angie who's now on the stand. She's leaning over and whispering to the judge while looking in my direction. After a brief back and forth, Judge Brown asks both lawyers to join her at the bench. I am full blown panicking as Dylan leaves the table without a single word to me.

Against my better judgment, I glance in Matt's direction. I can't be the only one confused and worried by this. Boy, was I wrong. Matt's shit eating grin is plastered across his face. They are up to something, and it's not going to end well for me.

Dylan and Judy return to their respective tables as Judge Brown announces, "I need both parties to exit the courtroom. Counsel, you may stay. We'll take a five minute recess."

Dylan guides me out into the hall and into a private meeting room. "What's going on? Did we lose?"

"No one wins or loses. But no, we haven't lost. Angie asked to give her testimony without you present."

"Me? Why me? What is going on?"

"I'm not sure, yet, but Matt isn't allowed in the courtroom either. Just wait here. I'll come get you as soon as I know something."

I am fucked. Completely and utterly fucked. If Matt can talk his way out of a protective order after leaving our toddler home alone—scared and hungry—for hours, there's no way I will win full custody. With his mom's corroboration, Dylan's warnings that I may lose half of Emma's life to my abuser feels so very real.

The realization has me huddled in the corner of the room, my knees pulled tight to my chest, tears flowing freely now. Dylan is gone for an eternity. The tears have finally stopped, and I'm laying flat on my back just waiting for the news that will shatter my entire world.

CHAPTER TWENTY-THREE

PETER

Nessa's court appearance to get a protective order for Emma is today. It started over an hour and a half ago, and I still haven't heard from her. I'm doing my best to focus on the video game I've been working on for weeks now, but can't help but glance at my phone every few minutes. The deadline for getting the kinks worked out on this game is next week, but I just can't concentrate. I've died on the first level six times now.

I need to know how court is going so that I can get this done without having to stay here until midnight. The urge to call to check in on her is about to win out when my phone finally buzzes with a text message.

> **NESSA**
> I'm going to lose her. I can't do this. I'm going to lose her.

> **PETER**
> What happened?

> **PETER**
> Call me.

I respond in less than ten seconds as I'm pacing my office, phone in hand. Waiting for a response is excruciatingly painful. How can she send a message like that and then fall off the face of the earth? I knew I should have been there with her. I offered to take off work today and start our weekend early so that I could be there for her court appearance, but she was worried it would do more harm than good. Maybe it would have, but nonetheless, I'm kicking myself for not going anyway.

When I can wait no longer, I gather up my equipment, grab my car keys, and send a quick text to my boss before heading to the parking garage.

PETER
Family emergency. Leaving now. Will work from home today and tomorrow.

JOHN
See you Monday.

John is a man of few words but is extremely easy to work with. He doesn't pry and allows us to work from home any time we need to. When Aunt Kathy died last year, I worked from home for nearly a month so I could be with Aunt Deedee. Though he asks for nothing in return, I know how much he enjoys Deedee's cookies. I bring them to the office Christmas party every year, and John always takes several back to his office with him. I'll bring him some oatmeal raisin on Monday as a thank you, but right now, I have somewhere much more important to be.

About halfway through my drive, Nessa's name appears on my car's screen. I answer on the first ring, panic lacing my voice. "Nessa, what happened?"

"Angie took the stand, but then the judge made us leave. I had to wait in a meeting room while she testified. Matt lied about everything. Literally everything. He told the judge that he was just walking around his property to clear his head after a long day of being the world's best dad." She finally pauses for air, and I jump at the opportunity to tell her exactly how I feel about him.

"That piece of—"

I grip the steering wheel, knuckles white, as she sucks in a quick breath before continuing on, my expletive left hanging in the air. "I just knew she was going to lie for him. She doesn't want to lose her only granddaughter even if that means lying to a judge. I get that, but what he did is just too scary to overlook."

"But she's the one who called you. She was just as upset and angry as we were. Matt's truck was not there. I saw him pull in while you were inside. She even said that her diaper was full and she was starving. There's no way. I should have been there with you." My words come out in a rush. Angie called Nessa when Emma needed her. How could she back track when it matters the most?

"I know. I know. There's more."

"Oh. Sorry. Continue." I can feel my heart pounding through my chest. I should not have let her do this alone. She needed me, and I let her talk me out of being there for her.

"They made Matt and me wait in separate rooms for almost an entire hour. I'll spare you the embarrassing details of how I spent that hour, but Dylan finally came to get me."

Though I need to know what Dylan had to say pronto, I'm momentarily distracted by the thought of Nessa having another panic attack. The day she received Matt's request for 50/50 custody, she hid in her closet until the panic passed. I wasn't able to be there for her then, but I should have been today. "I should have been there, Ness. I could have at least held you while you cried. You shouldn't have had to go through this alone."

"Peter, did you hear me?"

"Shit. No. I'm sorry. What did you say?" Focus. This is a big deal. You can hold her in an hour. Right now, just listen.

"I won! Emma got the protective order. We won." She's squealing and crying all at once.

"Oh my god. Nessa, that's amazing." We're both crying now, and the urge to tell her that I love her hits me all at once. I let out a long-held breath and force myself to save my proclamation for a less intense moment, one where we can be together.

Before I can ask anymore questions, she ends the call so she can tell Nora the news on her way home. I'll have plenty of time to ask questions when I get there, especially with my new four day weekend. My worries set at ease, I turn the music up and jam to oldies for the rest of my drive.

My anticipation builds the closer I get to her house, and as soon as I'm in the driveway, I run to her. I scoop her into my arms, spinning her exactly like I do with Daisy. She wraps her legs around my waist, dipping her head towards mine.

"What are you doing here?" Her mood is lighter than I've ever seen her, an enormous weight lifted off her shoulders.

"I left as soon as I got your text message. You made it sound like it wasn't going well. I've been kicking myself all day for not going with you." She's still wrapped around me, my hands cupped around her ass.

"That's so sweet, but you know you can't come with me. Not until I'm officially divorced. I wanted—needed—you there. But it's something I have to do on my own."

"I know. I just want to be there for you." I press my forehead to hers and plant a soft kiss on her lips.

"You must be Peter." I jump at the unexpected voice and quickly lower her to the ground. A middle-aged man, who has the same bright blue eyes as Nessa, stands in the kitchen doorway, Emma on his hip.

"Hi. Um. Yeah, I'm Peter." I clear my throat, still caught off guard. "You must be the man responsible for how wonderful Nessa is." It's cheesy. I know. But he just walked in on me kissing his daughter and well... squeezing her butt. Something has to make up for that first impression.

"Nice to meet you. I'm Duane, but everyone here calls me Papa."

As I stick my hand out to shake his, Emma bellows her signature drawn out "hiiii" while throwing her arm wildly back and forth.

"Hi, sweet girl," I say as I wave back to her before rustling her hair.

"Nessa was just about to fill me in on Angie's testimony." Emma is still in his arms as he drops himself down onto the couch, eyes focused on his daughter.

"Yes! Okay, I haven't gotten to tell Peter this either. I'm only going to say 'him' and 'her' so sweetpea here doesn't know who I'm talking about." She lightly pinches Emma's cheek as she says 'sweetpea.' "So, she didn't specifically ask for *me* to leave the courtroom. She didn't want *him* to hear her testimony."

"What?" Duane and I both say in unison.

"I know. I know. He had this terrible, mischievous grin on his face like they were in on it together. I texted both of you and Nora because I thought it was over. I thought we lost. He looked so confident like her asking us to leave was just a part of his master plan. Turns out, she told the judge everything. She backed up my story one hundred percent." She's crying now, but finally they're happy tears. I pull her in for a tight hug, not caring this time that her dad is watching.

"She did a crappy job raising her son, but she's doing something right for our little girl." Duane—Papa—pulls Nessa in for a hug, too, with Emma smushed between them.

"So what does this mean?" This is such a monumental moment, but with a lawyer for a brother, I know a protective order isn't permanent, nor is it likely to solve all of our problems when it comes to Matthew.

"The protective order is good for six months. By then, a

family court judge will rule on our divorce and custody case. This isn't forever, but it's a giant leap in the right direction."

"That's such great news. Your body literally looks relieved." And I mean it. It may be the best news I've ever heard, and she really does look like there's not a worry left in the world.

"Oh, I am. I've been carrying this gigantic weight for so long. I feel like I can finally breathe. And on top of the already great start to my day, you're here. Do you have to go home for work tomorrow?"

"Nope. You're stuck with me."

"Yay!" she squeals, and Emma automatically claps in response.

"I will have to get some work done, but for the most part, I'm all yours until Sunday evening."

"Well, I'll get out of everyone's hair," Duane says as he hands Emma to her mom.

"Oh, please stay. Don't leave because of me. Stay for dinner with us. I know Ness is dying for you to give your stamp of approval."

She lets out a small laugh. "Subtle, but it's true. Dad, stay."

"Okay, I'll stay. Just know I'm going to be brutally honest." He's looking directly into my eyes when he says it, and I know means it. Nessa has talked a lot about her dad and the fact that he tried to talk her out of marrying Matt. She blames herself for how things turned out after not listening to his advice, so I know she will take his opinion seriously this time.

"Good," Nessa and I say it at the same time. I can picture myself having this exact conversation with Emma and her future boyfriends and hope that she listens to us the way I know Nessa will listen to him. The scrutiny should make me nervous, but it doesn't. I know Nessa and I are right for each other and am certain Duane will feel it too.

After a Ted Talk worthy rant about the superiority of Coyotes' wings, Duane convinces us to order dinner from there, including their spiciest wing sauce options. Though I enjoy spicy food more than most, I have a feeling my ability to handle the heat—metaphorically and literally—will play a part in his assessment of me.

Once dinner arrives, I load Emma's tray with chicken, fries, and celery all modified the official baby-led weaning way. Nessa grabs plates from the dishwasher, handing one to each of us before settling Emma into her high chair.

"Did you get her food ready?" She's looking back and forth between her dad and me as Duane nods in my direction.

"I did," I say with a small raise of my hand.

"Nice job. You did it exactly how I would have." She's beaming, truly impressed that I got it right.

"Kudos to you. Every time I make Emma's plate, Vanessa comes right up behind me and fixes it. Kids did not eat like this when my girls were small." He gives a playful eye roll in Nessa's direction like this way of feeding a toddler is preposterous.

"Things change, Dad." She returns his playful eye roll, and I chuckle at the use of her childhood nickname that she still uses on herself.

"I know, sweetheart. I'm only teasing. Change is good. When you were young, your mother and I both smoked at the dinner table. Change is necessary. *Yuck.*"

"Uck!" Emma copies her Papa, sticking her tongue out and scrunching her eyes shut just like he did.

"Yuck indeed. I always forget that you and Mom used to smoke." Nessa makes the same face in Emma's direction.

"Do you smoke, Peter?" Time for the interview portion of the evening, I see.

"No, sir. My parents both did, and I always hated it. My brother and I both tried convincing them to stop for years."

"Ah. Good. Do you live near your parents and brother now?" Nessa sets her fork down, ready to interject. As close as she and her dad are, I'm surprised she hasn't told him this already.

"My brother lives in Chicago, and my parents are no longer

with us." I never know how to tell people this. They died? Passed away? What's the easiest way to say this so people don't pity me as soon as I say it? Over a decade later, I still haven't figured it out.

"Oh my. I'm so sorry. What happened?" The look of pity I've become accustomed to seeing is all over his face.

"Dad! You can't just ask that."

"I'm an old man. Back in my day, we—"

Nessa cuts him off. "You're in your fifties, not ninety." We're all laughing. Even Emma, who has two fries shoved into her mouth, is pretending to laugh.

She's not going to choke. She's not going to choke. She's fine. Answer the question.

"It's okay, really. My mom had cancer and passed away when I was twelve. Then, my dad drank his sorrows away and died from liver failure when I was sixteen, which is why I also don't drink."

Apparently satisfied with my answer, he moves on to questions about my job, retirement accounts, and my plans for the future before telling me all about his time as a public schools' superintendent. Though Duane never gives his official review, he hugs all three of us before he leaves. I'll take that as a good sign.

"Hey, Emmy, I could use some help carrying something in from the car." I wave my arm, prompting her to follow me.

She bolts to the front door, grunting as she jumps up and down in an attempt to grasp the doorknob. I lift her up, and we turn it together. A few moments later, we're back inside, my hands full with work equipment as Emma drags a Barnes and Noble bag behind her.

"What's this?" Nessa scoops Emma up, carrying her and the ripped bag to the couch.

"Books my mom used to read to Andrew and me. I thought Emma might like them too." I settle in beside them and open the only book that Emma isn't clutching with all her might. As soon as I begin reading, she nestles her head into Nessa's chest, fully absorbed by the story and its pictures.

After we've read all three books twice, Emma kicks them off the couch before running down the hall. As if books getting kicked into the floor is a normal occurrence, Nessa ignores it, instead laying her head on my shoulder. "How'd you know exactly how to cut her food?"

"I may or may not have picked up a baby-led weaning book the same day I bought these." I point to the books scattered at my feet, and she smiles up at me, reminding me exactly why I'm here. That smile is what dreams are made of—literally, my dreams. I'd do anything to see that smile.

"The fact that you're still single literally blows my mind. There has to be at least one thing wrong with you. What are you hiding?"

"Hmm." I scratch my chin, thinking really hard. "I've been told I snore, and I drive like a grandpa. Oh, and I have the palate of a five-year-old."

"That's it?"

"Afraid so."

Emma comes barreling back into the living room, with a stuffed unicorn and two more books in her hands. With great effort, she climbs up onto the couch, wiggling her way in between us, before handing both books to Nessa. We each read one to her before fixing her a quick bedtime snack. As they start their normal nightly routine, I pick out some pajamas for Emma and lay them out on the bed, ready for Nessa when they get out of the shower.

Despite my worries that being here would throw their bedtime routine out of wack, Emma handles it well, slipping into her pajamas without a fight. While Nessa finishes getting her into bed, I plug in all of my equipment and get to work. I'm determined to get everything done as quickly as possible so I can enjoy the extra time with my girls distraction free.

CHAPTER TWENTY-FOUR

NESSA

After getting Emma all tucked into bed last night, I found Peter on the couch, Lorelai curled into a ball on his lap, lightly purring. Damn, he looks cute with his headset on and a fierce look of determination in his eyes. I admire him from the hallway for a few seconds before plopping down beside him.

Emma and I visit the library at least once a week. We stock up on new books for her and for me before playing in their children's area. While Peter finished up whatever he was working on, I laid my head on his lap next to Lore and opened one of the thrillers I picked out this week. Once he finished, we watched a few episodes of *Gilmore Girls* before crawling into bed for the night. Though I know *Gilmore Girls* might not be his first choice, I think it's growing on him.

This morning, Emma climbed out of her crib—her newest skill—and then crawled directly across Peter's face on her way to wake me up. Despite the ungodly hour, Peter pulled himself out of bed with us after Emma's repeated requests for yogurt forced me to get up. With the ease of a seasoned pro, Peter fills Emma's tray with breakfast and settles her into her high chair while I make myself coffee. I could get used to this, I think as I stir cream and sugar into my cup. I haven't gotten to drink my coffee while it's still hot in nearly two years, which is something I thought I may never get to do again.

"So, what's on the agenda today?" Peter asks as I join them at the table. "I know my showing up early might have thrown things off a bit, but I don't want to mess up her routine."

Though his confidence at meal time is growing, I smile at the way he's perched on the edge of his seat, eyes glued on Emma. "I was planning to go grocery shopping and run a couple errands before you got here tonight. Emma and I can do all of that while you work today, if you need to."

"No way I'm missing out on my first grocery shopping experience with you two. I can keep working while you're getting her down for naps and bedtime. As long as I'm caught up before Monday, it's no big deal."

I can't help the laugh that escapes me. "You think an Aldi trip with a toddler will be fun?"

"I never said fun. I said 'experience.' It'll be something."

Peter and Emma are both laughing now. One of my favorite things about this age is the way Emma forces a laugh whenever anyone around her laughs. Peter seems to enjoy it, too, because as soon as she starts laughing, he laughs even harder.

"It'll be something. That's for sure."

"Do we have time to add in one more stop?"

"Sure. What'd you have in mind?"

"I left in such a hurry yesterday. I didn't stop to grab any of my things. I was thinking we could make a Target run to grab me some clothes and a toothbrush."

"Ooo. You know the way to my heart."

"Ah. You like Target, huh?"

"I'm a basic bitch. What can I say? Of course we love Target." I say it with a dramatic flip to my hair, and Emma immediately copies me.

In an effort to include Peter in the mundane tasks of my

everyday life, I ask him to pick out Emma's outfit for the day. He emerges from Emma's closet with three outfits in hand, holding them all up for her to choose from. She points her finger at a light gray romper with Barney on the front. Peter drops the other two outfits onto the couch and then holds the romper open so I can slide her legs into it and pull it up over her shoulders.

"Is Barney even still a thing? I loved it as a kid. I was hoping she'd pick that one."

"They actually made a new one. She's never seen the version we used to watch. The new Barney is kind of creepy looking, but she loves it." Emma is smiling down at Barney on her outfit, pointing to him every time we say his name.

"I probably still know the songs. Let me think." He places his hand on his chin as he tries to recall the lyrics.

"They changed those too. She may throw eggs at you again if you try to bring the new ones back." I laugh as I say it, but it's true. Though I try not to let her watch too much TV, sometimes I need a few minutes to do the dishes or fold laundry or just breathe. A few weeks ago, I tried distracting her from a meltdown with the 'I love you' song from the original show only to have her cry even harder. She, without a doubt, will notice if he doesn't get it right.

"Noted. How about we watch it tonight so I can learn the right way?" He crouches down to ask Emma as she continues to point at the front of her outfit.

"She'd like that. I'm going to fix her hair real quick, then we're ready. You can put those extra outfits in her backpack." Carrying a backpack around is so much easier than a diaper bag, especially now that she's a little bigger and doesn't require as much stuff. So, we use the same Minnie Mouse backpack that she used to take to Matt's as our everyday bag.

I brush her hair into two space buns on the top of her head and attach two purple bows to match her Barney outfit as Peter loads the backpack. He watches me intently as I buckle Emma into her car seat, pulling the chest clip into place.

Knowing that we'll be buying perishables at Aldi, we decide to hit Target first. Before Emma is even buckled into the cart, she's furiously pointing toward Starbucks and chanting "pop pop, pop pop" which is her way of saying 'cake pop.'

I love Target as much as you'd expect, and I've taught Emma well. She knows we get coffee and a cake pop then browse the Bullseye section while we wait for our order. It's the perfect routine, crafted through trial and error, that allows us to peruse the store with minimal meltdowns.

"This isn't so bad," Peter says as we push the buggy through the one dollar section, Emma leaning out to grab anything within her reach.

"Oh, honey. We're just getting started," I say with amusement. He's never taken a toddler shopping, and it shows. "Plus, it's easy to behave at Target. A cake pop shaped like the Target dog would keep even the rowdiest of kids calm. Don't let her fool you, though. We have a limited amount of time to look around before she descends into chaos."

Without a word, Peter takes off in a jog towards the men's clothing section. Emma throws her head back in fit of giggles, her hands straight up in the air like she's on a roller coaster. He swiftly throws a couple pairs of shorts, a few shirts, and a package of boxers into the cart before rushing to the toothbrush aisle.

"Do you need anything before we go?" He's slightly out of breath from his marathon sprint through the store.

"No one *needs* anything from Target; you're supposed to let Target tell you what you need."

"Ah. Clearly I've been doing it all wrong."

Considering he had everything on his list in the cart in less than five minutes, yes, he has been doing it all wrong. "Yes, you have."

"Well, what's speaking to you?"

"Nothing yet, but you've been flying through the store. It all blew by in a blur, plus we haven't gone to the seasonal section."

"I was trying to hurry before she finished that cake pop."

"Pop pop," Emma says, holding the half eaten cake pop into the air.

Peter slows to a normal pace and heads to the back of the store, also known as the best part of the store. Despite his earlier efforts to get out of here quickly, he meanders alongside me as I fill the cart with unnecessary, yet really cute, summer decor and a few fun snacks for Emma. Without a single meltdown, we head back to the car, ready for the more challenging task of the day: grocery shopping.

Finally back at home, groceries all put away, Peter flops onto the couch with a loud sigh. He's laying flat on his back, one arm and one leg dangling over the edge. "The amount of caffeine you consume makes total sense to me now."

"Humbles you real quick, huh?"

Despite the fact that Emma barely made a peep at Target, she wasn't quite as calm while we shopped for groceries. Halfway through our list, she started crying to be let out of the cart. Now that she's walking independently, she wants to walk beside me every chance she gets. Knowing that we'd be there all day if we walked at her pace, Peter and I tried everything we could think of to keep her securely in the cart. Peter belted out songs from the old Barney to no avail. Bribing her with a cookie from the bakery worked ever so briefly, but by the end of it, I carried a flailing Emma to the car while Peter checked out.

"Oh, yeah. No parenting book in the world could have prepared me for that. I will never silently judge a parent in public again."

Though I can't picture him judging anyone, it's the first part that catches my attention. "Did you read a parenting book too?"

"I have zero clue what toddlers do or need. I couldn't just

make you teach me everything; you have enough on your plate. So, yeah. I read the What to Expect book about toddlerhood." His cheeks tinge just the slightest bit pink, as if he's embarrassed that he didn't automatically know exactly what to do.

There are no words that could adequately express the gratitude I'm feeling, so instead, I push him into the cushions so I can climb onto the couch beside him, my body now dangling over the edge. With my arms wrapped around him, I take his face in my hand and plant a kiss on his cheek. Emma climbs up onto me, doing the same to Peter's cheek and then to mine.

After Emma wakes from her nap, Peter puts away his work equipment and turns Barney on the TV. Without hesitation, Emma pulls herself up onto the couch and settles in beside him, her eyes glued to the television. Typically, Emma stands on a chair beside me as I make dinner. She enjoys pouring ingredients into a bowl and helping stir. Without her to help (distract) me, I finish making dinner in record time.

Before I tell them dinner is ready, I stand in the entryway to the living room and take it all in. Emma is laying on her belly intently watching her show while Peter sits beside her, his hand on her back. The sight of them together brings fresh tears to my eyes. This may be the happiest I have ever been. Despite the hell Emma and I have been through in her short little life, we are finally putting the pieces back together.

CHAPTER TWENTY-FIVE

PETER

Nora and Daisy pull into the parking spot next to us as Nessa unbuckles Emma from her seat and I pull the stroller out of her trunk.

"Emma!" Daisy calls as she flings her door open, nearly hitting me, and jumps out of the car. Emma squeals in response, throwing her hands out toward her. After Daisy secures Emma into the stroller, she gives me a high five before pushing the stroller toward the zoo entrance.

"I've been replaced," I say with an exaggerated frown as Nessa, Nora, and I follow the girls to the gate.

"You really have been. She loves you, but she loves Emma more." Nora flashes me an apologetic smile.

"I didn't even get to hear her call you Petey. I've been waiting for that," Nessa says with a frown that matches mine.

After stopping for the obligatory photo shoot with the elephant statue just outside the entrance, the girls run ahead of us once we're inside. Despite the fact that they've both been here 100 times, they stop to look at every single animal with equal enthusiasm.

"Look, Em. This one matches the monkey." Daisy points to

the monkey on Emma's dress and then to the one in the exhibit in front of us. Her dress has all the best zoo animals on it—tigers, bears, monkeys, giraffes—and Daisy has been pointing all of them out to her when we see them.

"What does a monkey say?" Nora asks, crouching beside the stroller.

"Oo oo, ah ah," the girls respond in unison before Nora and Nessa make the noise back at them. Thanks to the routine of animal sounds at every exhibit, I have learned a few new animal noises today.

"Who wants to do the petting zoo?" Nora looks to the girls who are both cheering with delight.

"We can go buy some tokens." Nessa grabs my arm, pulling me with her toward the token machine.

"I'll watch Emma," Daisy calls out as she pushes the stroller into the petting zoo area, Nora right behind her.

"Does Nora seem off to you?" Nessa grabs my arm, lifting it up onto her shoulders before snuggling into my side while we wait for the machine to spit out our tokens.

"Eh. I hadn't noticed, but now that you mention it, yeah. Maybe a little. She hasn't made a single quip the entire time we've been here."

"I know. She's not her usual, unapologetic self. Something is up."

"Maybe she's upset that Rob didn't come," I suggest. Rob and I don't talk about his relationship with Nora very often, but when he drove me to my car last weekend, he mentioned that they'd been fighting more often than not. I'm sure Nessa and Nora are more open with each other than Rob and I are, so I won't mention it. She probably already knows, and if she doesn't, she'd likely tell Nora what he'd said.

When Nora first suggested a blind date with her best friend, I never thought it would get to this point. Turns out, my best friend being married to Nessa's best friend is a little more complicated than I would have expected. I don't want to hold anything back from her, but I also need to be my friend's confidant.

"Yeah, maybe." She looks lost in thought as she scoops the tokens up and turns back towards the petting zoo.

There are several food dispensers scattered around the petting zoo. They look exactly like the little machines with candy, gumballs, or toys that are often at the exit of grocery stores, except these ones are filled with small, brown pellets. Daisy cups her hands under the dispenser as Nessa turns the knob. With pellets in hand, the girls head straight for the goats.

One of the bigger goats shoves its head through the fence, nuzzling its way toward the food in their hands. "Petey!" Daisy yells my name as she darts away from the fence, ducking behind me, Emma right behind her with her arms outstretched to me.

I scoop Emma up into my arms then put one arm around Daisy's shoulders. We slowly inch our way back towards the animals, Daisy's hand outstretched with a few pieces of food in her palm. Now that the bigger goat is distracted at the other end of the fence, baby goats make their way to us, and I grasp Emma's tiny hand in mine. I gingerly hold it open so the littlest goat can get to the food she's holding. She giggles and squeals, jerking her hand away each time the goat licks the pellets out of it. She keeps one hand firmly clasped onto my shirt as she continues feeding with the other until she completely runs out.

After rubbing hand sanitizer into both of their hands, I turn to find Nessa and Nora sitting on a bench near the entrance of the petting zoo, both of their eyes fixed on me.

"She let me hold her," I say as we approach them.

"We saw! I took a really cute picture of you helping them. She's definitely warming up to you."

"Or I was just the closest grown up in sight when she thought that giant goat was going to eat her." I laugh as I say it, though I think Nessa is right. Last weekend, Emma wanted her mom to do everything for her. She didn't seem to mind that I was there, but she was hesitant of me for sure.

She chuckles. "Yeah, that too."

"I'm starving," Nora groans as she stands up from the bench.

"No, Mommy, I'm not hungry yet. I want to ride the train first." Daisy forces her lower lip out in a tremble.

"Rain!" Emma yells. "Rain, Mama. Toot toot."

I smile at the way Emma says 'train' as Nessa laughs, raising her hand into the air to pull the cord for an imaginary train horn. "Toot toot. I can take them to the train while you order for us."

Both girls jump up with excitement. I give Nessa a quick kiss before turning to follow Nora. "I can help."

"I want a cheeseburger," Nessa calls out, nearly in a sprint to keep up with Daisy who's running towards the train entrance with Emma on her hip.

Though Nora really will need help carrying enough food for all five of us, I just wanted a few minutes alone with her. I haven't gotten a moment alone with Nora since I found out that Nessa still has a husband. Despite the fact that Nora will always have Nessa's back, I know she'll be up front and honest with me about it, and originally, I needed that reassurance. So much has happened since then that I'm pretty certain where Nessa's head is at. Regardless, I want to touch base with her about it and make sure she's okay after the morning she seems to be having.

After we've both placed our orders, we grab napkins and plastic forks before heading out onto the patio to find a table. It's the beginning of summer, and the weather is perfect. Between that and the fact that it's Saturday, every table big enough for all of us is already taken. We slide two smaller tables together and sit, waiting for our order number to be called on the overhead speaker.

"Are you doing okay today, Nor?"

"I'm fine. Why?" She knits her eyebrows together with a quizzical frown.

"You just don't seem quite yourself. That's all."

Tears start to pool in her eyes as she says, "I'm not okay, but I thought I was hiding it better."

"We don't have to talk about it if you don't want to. I just wanted to check on you."

I hand her a napkin and she dabs it at her eyes before continuing. "We're not necessarily fighting, but we aren't doing great either. I was hoping that having you here with us would be enough for him to actually do something with Daisy and me. I'm just tired of doing everything alone."

I pull her in for a side hug, unsure of what to say. "He loves you, Nor, and he loves Daisy. I don't know why he shuts himself in his room so often, but I'm confident things will get better."

She wipes her eyes and sniffles. "I guess so. I don't want Daisy to see me crying. She doesn't know anything is wrong, and I'd like to keep it that way."

"You got it. Moving on. I actually wanted to talk to you about something."

"Oh." She instantly perks up, her worries from moments ago quickly overtaken with curiosity. "Well, what is it?"

"Nessa is married." Okay, that didn't come out as nonchalant as I'd hoped. Instead, I blurted it like I've been waiting months to finally talk about it. Though I've successfully pushed it to the back of my mind, waiting for an opportunity to talk to Nora about it, it has still been niggling at me more than I realized.

"I mean, technically. It's just a piece of paper waiting to be signed. She's not *married*, married." Our order numbers are announced, and she stands from her seat to grab our trays.

"Okay... so you think it's no big deal that I'm falling in love with a married woman?"

She stops so abruptly that I collide into her.

"You're what?" She's fully turned around now, looking straight at me, her eyes wide as she blurts her question so loudly every one around us turns to stare.

"You heard me," I say in a whisper. "She's got enough going on without hearing me say I love her for the first time to you instead of her. They could be back any second. Hush."

"Fine. Fine." She pretends to zip her lips closed with her fingers before adding, "She would have been divorced eighteen months ago if it were up to her. Divorces involving children, especially when one party sucks, take time. She cares about you. I'd be willing to bet she's thinking the L word too. Don't let Matt dragging things out stop you from having something great."

We round the corner, both of us carrying a tray full of food, at the same time Nessa and the girls come bounding up the steps. "Over here!" Nora calls as she balances the tray against her stomach so she can wave one hand in the air. "I wouldn't stress over it," she adds in my direction before they make it to us.

As I gently set the tray on the table, careful not to drop anything, my mind is reeling. Nora thinks Nessa loves me. She wants out of her marriage as badly as I want her out of it. Though I knew talking with Nora would help, I don't have time to fully digest this new information before Daisy pulls a chair up beside me, leaning across the table to grab her plate. Emma climbs into Daisy's lap, snatching a piece of fruit off of Daisy's plate and popping the whole thing into her mouth. Nessa smiles in my direction, perfectly content to let the girls steal her spot beside me, before something catches her eye.

"Look." Nessa jabs Nora with her elbow, jerking her head toward the zoo's entrance. Though we've explored a majority of the zoo already, the Watering Hole Café is nestled between the gift shop that you have to pass through to enter and the playground. From our patio table outside the cafe, we can clearly see Rob striding out of the gift shop doors.

"I'll be right back." Nora jumps up, jogging towards him.

"Did you know he was coming?" Nessa dunks two fries into nacho cheese sauce, pretending not to have her eyes glued on Nora and Rob.

"I had a feeling he might show up." I hand Emma a few fries off of my plate; she's eaten almost all of Daisy's.

"You had a feeling? How?" She eyes me suspiciously.

"I sent him a picture of the girls in the butterfly house earlier. He asked how it was going, and I told him Nora seemed upset. He never responded after that, so I wasn't sure if he changed his mind and decided to come or if he just didn't want to talk about it."

"Well, I'm glad he came." She smiles in Nora's direction as she and Rob approach the table.

"Hey," Nessa and I both say simultaneously.

"Daddy!" Daisy seems surprised and delighted to see him, dropping her fork on the table and jumping up to hug him. "Can we go play on the playground? Pleaseeee."

"Play! Play!" Emma chants.

"I can take them," Nessa says as she slides her chair back. "Let's go, girls."

"I'll meet you down there after I order Rob some food." Nora turns to get back in line, leaving Rob and I alone at the table.

"You made it," I say as he pulls out the chair beside me.

"I made it." He sits, staring down at his lap, before adding, "I have to make things right. I just don't know how."

"Daisy is excited you're here too. It's a good start."

"I haven't seen Daisy smile at me like that in years. She saves it for you… and Nessa… and Emma. Just not for me, anymore."

Before I can respond, Nora returns to the table. "I'm glad you're here." She leans down, softly kissing his cheek, before handing him his order number and joining Nessa at the park.

After Rob finishes his lunch, we clear the table and join the four of them at the playground. Despite the tension, Nora and Rob walk hand in hand as we stroll through the rest of the zoo, as do Nessa and I. By the time we're finished, everyone is exhausted, including and especially me. Daisy, complaining that her legs are sore, convinces Rob to give her a piggy back ride to the car, relinquishing stroller duty to me.

Finally back at the car, Emma falls asleep in her seat before we've even made it out of the parking lot. Nessa's bobbing her head to the music, keeping herself awake after a long day, as she drives. In this rare moment of silence, I finally stop to let Nora's words sink in. Does Nessa really love me? Despite our unconventional start, I think I may have finally found my person. Though I've never used the L word with anyone but family, I may soon be ready to let Nessa know exactly how I feel.

CHAPTER TWENTY-SIX

NESSA

Since our zoo trip last month, Emma has really warmed up to Peter. Though she still prefers me most of the time, she lets him hold her, get her dressed, and read to her without a second thought. Before meeting Emma, Peter and I talked on FaceTime after she went to sleep each night. Though we still do that, he now calls before she goes to bed to tell her good night too. Despite the fact that Peter can see up her nose the entire time, she enjoys this new addition to our routine, running to find my phone as soon as it starts to ring.

I cannot believe that Emma's second birthday is next week. I know. I know. Everyone says that, but it's true. It went by in a blur. Peter opted for a three-day weekend so he could come down a day early and help me with party preparation. Despite our best efforts all day, prepping for a party with a two-year-old is no easy feat. We managed to blow up ten balloons only to have four of them pop after Emma belly flopped onto them. Giving up and waiting until bedtime was the only option after hours of having our work immediately undone.

After getting Emma tucked into bed, I emerge from the bedroom to the decadent smell of cupcakes. Peter, who has been hard at work in the kitchen for the nearly forty-five minutes it took to get Emma to sleep, turns towards me, his face and hair lightly dusted with flour. "Second batch is in the oven now."

"What kind did you make? They smell amazing."

"These are strawberry." He holds the tray up for me to see, and I quickly snatch one before he can set it back down. "Chocolate cupcakes will be done soon."

"Mmm." My eyes roll back as I let out a soft moan of delight. "I burnt the shit out of my mouth, but it was so worth it. It doesn't even need frosting. That's how good it is."

"They are really good. You'll never guess who taught me to make them." He raises one to his mouth before deciding it's not actually worth a burnt tongue.

"Aunt Deedee." My guess comes out without hesitation. After the cinnamon rolls, anything this good has to be her doing.

"Actually, no. Andrew did." Andrew is Peter's older brother who I still know very little about. I know he lives in Chicago and works as a lawyer, but that's it.

"I was not going to guess that. You've told me almost nothing about him, plus Deedee is definitely the cook in the family." He pulls the chocolate cupcakes out of the oven as I clean up the dishes he used to make them.

"I don't see him very often now that he lives so far away, but he'll be happy to know you liked his cupcakes. For my thirteenth birthday, the first after Mom died, he stayed up most of the night trying to replicate her recipe. He never did get it quite right, but we've been making these for both our birthdays ever since."

"That is literally the sweetest thing I have ever heard." The thought brings a tear to my eyes. Andrew, who would have been only fifteen at the time, cared enough about his little brother to make his birthday special when their parents couldn't. My heart can't take it.

"It really was. She died about a month before that, and I was sure that no one would even remember my birthday. My dad was really struggling by then, and Andrew was just a typical teenager. The fact that he took the time to do that still makes me smile, even after so many years."

We finish up the cupcakes before filling the living room with balloons—a birthday tradition I started last year—while they cool.

Blowing up balloons makes it difficult to carry on a conversation, and in the silence, I can't stop thinking about Andrew's cupcakes. I'm overwhelmed with emotion as I think about Emma needing people like that in her life. She deserves thoughtful, caring people like Deedee, Andrew, and especially Peter. Though dating again was the most selfish thing I've done in a long time, I can't help but think how even that ended up being good for her. She will grow up surrounded by people who care about her. People who will teach her to be kind and considerate. People who will show her what it feels like to be truly loved. And as her mom, there's nothing in the world that I want more than that.

It's two in the morning before Peter and I finally crawl into bed. "Remind me to thank my dad for all the parties he threw me," I say in a whisper as I snuggle into Peter's chest.

"Seriously, that was so much work. Until tonight, I guess I assumed balloons and cupcakes and decorations and food all just magically appeared. Nope. Turns out, it was my mom busting her ass well into the morning."

"Thanks for busting your ass with me," I say through a yawn.

He yawns in response before adding, "I'll bust my ass for her every year for the rest of my life."

I scooch my way up his body so I can give him the soft, sweet, lingering kiss he deserves after a comment like that. "We are incredibly lucky to have you. I'm going to have to start buying Nora chocolate once a month or something to say thank you."

"I've gotten her flowers twice with a little thank you note attached. If we do too much, it'll go straight to her head." He makes a good point, and we both chuckle before falling fast asleep.

Emma has us up and at it bright and early, as usual. Peter, now apparently used to our schedule, takes her to the kitchen to make breakfast, leaving me in bed for a few extra minutes. Now that Emma is here with us each weekend, my usual routine of sneaking into the bathroom to brush my teeth before Peter wakes has been derailed. Despite my insecurities, I have yet to force myself out of bed even earlier than Emma to brush before he can notice. Those few extra minutes of sleep are way more important than taking care of my awful morning breath. Sorry, babe. With a few extra minutes to wake up today, Peter will get a minty fresh kiss to start the day for the first time in over a month.

Brushed and ready to tackle the day, I hear giggles as I enter the living room. Emma is sprawled out on the floor, furiously kicking the balloons as Peter swats them out of the air and back down towards her.

"Good morning, beautiful." He kisses my forehead and hands me a fresh cup of coffee all while batting balloons down to a giggling Emma.

"All our hard work paid off," I say as I take my first sip. Coffee the way I like it can be a challenge to perfect. Despite him not being a coffee drinker himself, this cup tastes exactly like it does when I make it.

"Only getting five hours of sleep was definitely worth seeing that huge smile. She is in heaven." He smiles down at her before adding, "How's the coffee?"

"Perfect. Who typed the recipe into your notes this time?" I take another sip then give him a mischievous grin.

"I did." He laughs. "How else am I supposed to remember that you like a pound of sugar in there?"

I spew my coffee as a laugh sneaks out of me. Though he said it jokingly, I'd be willing to bet he does have the amount of cream and sugar I like typed into his phone for reference.

"Breakfast is ready. I didn't have the heart to pull her from the balloon pile just yet." We watch her for a few more minutes, his arm wrapped around my side. How did my life go from a raging shit show to… this? I have everything I could ever need right here.

Emma's party isn't until noon, so we have a few hours after breakfast to prepare before everyone arrives. We finish icing the cupcakes, cook the food we prepared last night, and then head to the backyard to set up the bounce house and sprinkler.

With everything now in place, it's time to get myself and Emma ready. I slide a pretty, purple dress with 'Birthday Girl' in sparkly silver letters over her head before retreating to the bedroom to change and tame my hair. I shimmy into a dress the same purple as Emma's then add a few messy curls to my hair.

On my way to the living room, ready to style Emma's hair before the first guests arrive, I stop dead in my tracks. Peter has Emma in his lap and his phone propped against a tissue box. He's looking back and forth between the phone screen and the back of Emma's head with half of her hair in a lopsided ponytail as he gathers the other half into his hands. Once he secures the other pigtail into place, I continue my journey down the hall, noticing the 'Toddler Hairdos for Dads' video on his phone screen.

"Time to do your hair," I call to Emma as I enter the room.

She giggles, pointing up at her hair. "Teety do it!"

"Petey," he corrects, putting emphasis on the P.

"Teety do it." She looks at him with her most serious expression.

"Yeah, Teety. That's what she said," I deadpan as she smiles in my direction. "It looks great," I add just as Daisy flies through the door.

"Happy Birthday!" She squeezes Emma in a big hug, and they both squeal with delight.

"Happy Birthday," Rob and Nora call in unison as they walk through the still open door.

"Where should I put this?" He holds up a bag big enough for Emma to fit inside, and Peter motions for him to follow.

As Peter leads Rob to the present table, I lean in close to Nora and whisper, "He came."

"He came." She's beaming, her smile brighter than I've seen it in a while.

Before I have a chance to prod, party guests start flowing through the door. Our house is pretty small, so even though we didn't invite a lot of people, I'm hoping to keep most of the festivities outside today. We all grab a plate of food before heading to the backyard where the kids immediately forget about lunch in favor of the bounce house. Peter and I grab a couple lawn chairs and set them beside my dad.

"I know it's a little overdue," I say. "But I wanted to thank you for everything you've ever done for me. This party took us days to set up. I had no idea how strenuous a simple birthday party would be."

"You're welcome, sweetheart. Raising the two of you is my greatest accomplishment, and I'd do it all over again in a heartbeat. Even the stressful parts," my dad says before pulling me in for a side hug.

"I had no idea how much effort went into all of this," Peter says. "It's not often that I find myself wanting to talk to my mom these days, but she deserves a thank you."

"She knows, son. Even if you weren't able to tell her before she passed, she knows." Dad pulls Peter in for a quick, comforting hug as he wipes at the tears threatening to fall.

The party goes by in a blur. Daisy, Emma, and a few kids from a mommy and me playgroup we attend play in the bounce house for over an hour before switching to the sprinkler. Reluctant to quit playing, we practically had to drag them inside for cake and presents. As we thanked everyone for coming, Peter held Emma, her head on his shoulder, and before the last person was out the door, she was fast asleep in his arms.

Now that she's tucked into bed for a much needed nap and most of the party debris has been picked up, Peter and I settle in on the couch. "Her party went so well. Thanks for all your help."

"It did. She's a lucky little girl."

"She is, indeed." Despite the various parts of her life that make her decidedly not lucky, there are so many things to be thankful for. All of our friends and family who showed up to celebrate her birthday today. A mom and papa who love her fiercely. And a father figure who stepped up when he didn't have to. The thought brings a smile to my face as I rest my head on his shoulder, my eyes drifting shut with exhaustion.

"Hey, Ness." His voice is soft and low, maybe even hesitant.

"Yeah?" I lift my head off his shoulder just enough to look up at him.

"I love you."

"I... I..." I'm stammering. What is wrong with me? Peter is literally perfect. Hell, he's too good for me. And I do love him. I've known it for weeks now. Come on. Spit it out. Say it.

"It's okay. No pressure. I just wanted you to know." He gently pushes my head back onto his shoulder before planting a kiss to my forehead.

I love you too. I just can't bring myself to say it out loud. I like how things are right now. I don't want anything to change, but I do love him. How could I not? I just need a little more time before I tell him.

CHAPTER TWENTY-SEVEN

PETER

I'm in the attic, sweating profusely after twenty minutes of looking through dusty boxes, when I hear Aunt Deedee call out for me. I stumble down the rickety ladder with the box I've been searching for balanced against my hip.

"I found it," I call out as I reach solid ground.

"Thank you, dear."

"What are you making?" She called me yesterday to ask if I'd come find her box of crochet materials but never told me what it was for.

"I thought I'd make a blanket for Emma. I'm very eager to meet her. It's been too long since we've had tiny handprints on things around here."

I chuckle, though I know she's entirely serious. She'd take sticky handprints and toys strewn about over peace and quiet any day. It's one of the reasons she's been pushing my brother and me, as well as our cousins, to marry as soon as possible.

"She'll love that, but that only gives you a couple days. That's not much time."

"I have nothing better to do, dear. What color would she like?"

"Hmm." I pause a minute to think. "She has this stuffed

unicorn that Nessa got her for her first birthday. She carries it around with her everywhere. How about a rainbow blanket to match its mane?"

"Oh, that sounds lovely."

After realizing she'd need new yarn, we place an order together to be delivered tonight. She's yearning to get started, and I have a few things to prepare before they get here tomorrow. So, I take my dinner to go, leaving Deedee to set up her crochet area and allowing me to get some shopping done before it's time to call Emma.

My apartment is the exact opposite of toddler friendly, so I grab a cart and make my way to the baby aisle. I walk up and down each aisle in search of anything she might need before stocking up on snacks I know she likes. I don't even know what half of the things in my cart are for, but they looked important. I'd rather be over prepared. My cart nearly full to the brim, I make it back to my car just in time to tell Emma goodnight.

The next evening, I'm laying flat on my belly, legs sticking out the back door of my car, trying desperately to find the car seat latch supposedly tucked between the seat and backrest, when Nessa pulls into the spot beside me.

"Teety!" Emma yells as soon as Nessa opens her door.

"What are you doing?" She places her hand on my butt, leaning in to see why I'm laying like this.

"I can't find the latch." I huff, exhausted with the effort.

"What latch?"

"For that," I say, pointing my foot in the direction of the brand new car seat waiting to be installed.

"You bought her a car seat?" I slide myself out of the car just in time to see her wipe a stray tear from her cheek.

"She needs a way to ride with both of us." I scoop Emma up and give Nessa a quick kiss before asking, "What do you think of your new seat? I thought the purple one was cute."

"Urple! Yay!" She wiggles out of my grasp and runs to sit in the car seat still waiting on the pavement.

"It is cute, but it's not going to fit in here."

"What? I got the smallest one they had." I wipe sweat from my brow as I glare at my useless car.

"This car was not meant for babies. I doubt it even has the latch you're looking for."

I sigh, the last thirty minutes wasted, and carry the car seat, Emma and all, into my apartment.

Once inside, Emma takes off, thoroughly exploring every nook and cranny she can find. "Mama! Mama!" she calls from the bedroom.

"I'm coming," Nessa calls back as she follows the sound of Emma's excited voice.

I join them in the bedroom as Emma begins jumping on the toddler bed in the corner of my room. "It's a big girl bed. Do you like it?"

"Arney! Like Arney," she says as she lays down on her new Barney sheets.

"Ooo. A Barney big girl bed. That's so cool!" Nessa kneels down beside her, lifting the Barney comforter up so she can crawl underneath.

"I figured she'd be out of her crib soon enough."

Though the thought of moving in with them has crossed my mind a lot lately, I don't mention that this toddler bed would be perfect for her as we blend our lives together. I can feel that Nessa loves me or at least is falling in love with me, but her inability to say it still stings a little. I'm not ready to bring up the possibility of leaving Aunt Deedee and my dream job or asking her to leave Nora and her dad in order to move here just yet. Both of those options feel impossibly hard, and the thought of her rejecting the idea is too painful.

In an unfamiliar place with a new bed, Emma struggles to fall asleep. It takes over an hour before Nessa emerges from my bedroom and curls up beside me on the couch.

"It's getting late and we have an early morning. Do you want to get some sleep?" I hold the blanket that's on my lap out so she can slide in next to me.

"No," she says with a yawn as she lays her head in my lap. "Are we seeing Deedee tomorrow?"

"Yes. She's really excited to meet Emma. So, I bought a premade iced coffee for you to try, then we can go spend the day with her."

"Premade? Yuck." She sticks her tongue out the way Emma did to Papa a few weeks ago.

"I know. I know. But someone had like five cartons in her cart last night. It can't be that bad if she's stocking enough for the apocalypse."

"Fine, I'll give it a try. I'm not sure why, but I'm a little nervous."

"If you hate it, we'll stop at The Bean before we go to Deedee's."

She chuckles. "No, I'm sure the coffee is fine. I meant about Emma meeting Aunt Deedee."

"Oh, how come? She's been praying for the next generation of kids in the family for years."

"I don't know. What if Deedee doesn't like us? Or Emma breaks something?"

"She already lov—" I stop before the word fully leaves my lips. "She enjoyed meeting you and is happy to have both of you as a part of our family. If she accidentally breaks something, we'll fix it. It's okay. I promise she's excited and fully prepared to have a toddler running about."

She breathes a sigh of relief, and without warning, she's snoring softly. I brush the hair out of her face, enjoying the sight of her sleeping peacefully, her head nuzzled into my leg. After a moment, I gently lift her off the couch and carry her to bed.

The next morning, Emma is perched in my recliner like it's her own personal throne, a bowl of cereal in her lap. She's holding a banana in one hand with her eyes glued to Ms. Rachel on the TV.

"Good morning, sweet girl."

"Hi, Teety." She shakes her head and makes the P sound with a pop of her lips. "Peepy."

We both descend into a fit of giggles as Nessa enters the kitchen, immediately pouring herself the new coffee I bought.

"Closer! Petey," I say each sound slowly, and she beams up at me.

"This is actually pretty good." Nessa holds her cup up then pours herself some more for the road.

As we walk into Aunt Deedee's, Emma buries her face into my chest, her arms wrapped tightly around my neck. Deedee sets a plate of cookies and lemonade on the coffee table as Nessa and I settle onto the couch, Emma's face still buried until I pick up one of the cookies.

"Mmm," she says as Nessa hands her a fresh sugar cookie.

"There's nothing a good cookie can't solve," Aunt Deedee chuckles as she slowly lowers herself into the chair opposite us with a small groan.

We tell her all about the car seat that won't fit into the back seat of my car, and Emma shows off her stuffed unicorn. After Aunt Deedee sufficiently oohs and aahs over Sprinkle, or Pinkle as Emma calls her, she pulls a blanket from beneath her chair and hands it to Emma. In only two days, Deedee handcrafted the perfect unicorn blanket with all the colors of the rainbow zigzagged throughout. Emma immediately wraps the blanket around Sprinkle and begins carrying her around the house like a baby.

Between the blanket and cookies, Emma has lost all of her reservations about Deedee, and the two of them stroll hand in hand out to the backyard. Though Aunt Deedee has a small plot of land but no animals, the farm adjacent to her backyard has every animal imaginable. Deedee, determined to befriend the cows, brings them a snack nearly every day. Today, it's a loaf of pumpernickel bread dangling from Emma's hand as they walk.

Nessa and I follow them outside, but stay back so Deedee can enjoy some bonding time, just the two of them. We stand near the back porch and watch as Emma helps rip the bread into small pieces before letting the cows lick it out of her hands.

"She's having so much fun, but I can see the slobber from here." She shudders as she says the word slobber.

I wrap my arm around her shoulder and kiss her on the forehead before asking, "Feeling better about this visit?"

"One hundred percent. I don't know what I was worried about. Aunt Deedee is great. Of course she would instantly accept Emma as family."

"She accepted you both as family the moment she met you, but it comes at a cost."

"Huh?" She looks up at me, a confused look in her eyes.

"She buys the most annoying Christmas presents. Mom hated it and always made us keep them at Deedee's house."

She snorts a laugh. "I think your mom was onto something. We'll have to have Christmas here so we can conveniently forget to bring her present home."

I spend every Christmas here. Easter and Thanksgiving, too, but the thought of Nessa and Emma here with us brings a wide smile to my face. Aunt Deedee would be thrilled to have them, and I can't think of a better way to celebrate literally any holiday but with them.

Once the entire loaf of bread has been eaten, Emma sneaking a few bites for herself, Deedee and Emma join us on the porch. "Cow, Mama!"

"Did you feed the cows?" Nessa uses the sweet voice she reserves only for Emma.

"Cows!" she bellows again, pointing frantically towards the fence.

"Ah, yes. I see. There's the cows."

Satisfied that Nessa finally understands, Emma claps before taking off in a sprint towards the swing set. Despite the fact that all of Deedee's nieces and nephews are grown with no kids of their own, she refuses to take the old swing set down in hopes it will get used again someday soon. Her face lights up at the prospect of pushing her honorary great niece on the swing, and she follows quickly behind her.

"Nora made me realize something the other day. Did you know that we met at their wedding?"

"We did?" It makes sense that Nessa would have been at Rob and Nora's wedding, but I feel like I would have noticed her.

"Well, maybe 'met' isn't the right word. But we were both there. We could have met a year sooner!"

I'm busy imagining where we'd be if Nora had introduced us at their wedding when something catches my eye. I don't notice the swing set shifting until it's too late. Deedee, who's pushing Emma higher and higher as she squeals with delight, jumps back just in time for the swing set to land in front of her, inches from knocking her to the ground. With the last big push, the swing set that has been here since I was Emma's age snaps on one side where the legs meet the support beam at the top, sending one side of it back towards Deedee. The playset, now with only one set of legs fully attached, is dangling precariously but somehow still mostly upright. Emma, still strapped into the baby swing, lands flat on the ground with a thud.

I drop the glass of lemonade I'm holding and it shatters as I sprint toward Emma. It feels like I'm running in slow motion, though I know this is faster than I've ever run in my life. I swiftly unbuckle her and squeeze her to my chest.

What started as ear piercing wails has subsided to a low whimper as I check every inch of her body for any sign that she's injured. Despite the fact that Nessa is now standing right beside me, frantically checking to make sure she's okay just like I did, Emma clings to my neck with all her might.

Having ensured nothing is broken or bleeding, Emma finally calms. Deedee, who ran to the house for the first aid kit, is back, her hands on her knees as she sucks in deep breaths. "I'm so sorry. I'm so sorry."

"It's okay. It was an accident. She's okay. And you're okay, right?" Nessa asks, finally taking her eyes off Emma long enough to look Deedee over.

"I'm fine, dear. And I'll be calling someone first thing Monday morning to haul this old thing away. I'm so sorry."

"It's totay," Emma assures her, her fists still grasping my shirt.

"Hey, Peter." Emma and I both look towards Nessa as her voice shakes with the words.

"Yeah?"

"I love you so fucking much."

CHAPTER TWENTY-EIGHT
NESSA

We left Peter's house right around Emma's nap time in hopes that she'd sleep the whole drive home. Lucky for me, it worked. I got myself a drive-through coffee, and before she even finished eating her pup cup, she was fast asleep. Yes, I know pup cups are meant for dogs, but I don't care. It saves me from buying a five dollar cake pop every time I want a coffee. Sue me.

Now that she's asleep, I'm alone with my thoughts, and all I can do is replay telling Peter I love him over and over in my mind. I felt like such a bitch not saying it back after Emma's birthday party. I just wasn't ready, even though I knew deep down I was already in love with him. Seeing his protectiveness over Emma changed something in me. He was scared for her. He loves her. And she didn't even want me when she was scared. Seeing her cling to him in a moment that she'd normally want nothing to do with anyone but me solidified the fact that Peter is perfect for both Emma and me. There's no more denying that I am head over heels in love with this man.

It's Tuesday morning, and Emma and I are enjoying our morning walk when my phone starts to buzz. I pull the phone from my pocket, eager to spend just a few minutes talking to Peter before he has to get back to work. My heart drops when I see Dylan's name on my phone screen instead.

"Hello?" I say tentatively, wishing I had let it go to voicemail.

"Hi, Nessa. It's Dylan with Family Justice and—"

"Yeah. I know who it is." I don't mean to sound so gruff, but I can hear my heart pounding in my ears. He'd have sent an email if whatever he's about to say wasn't urgent, and that thought makes me want to barf.

"Alright. Well, I was just calling to inform you that Judy Wright, Matthew's attorney, called this morning."

"Okay…" the word drags as I say it. I swear if he doesn't spit it out, I'm going to scream. I can feel my palms getting sweaty, and keeping my cool in front of Emma is getting increasingly hard with every second that he doesn't tell me what the hell is going on.

"I'll just cut to the chase." Thank fuck. On with it. "We have mediation with Matthew and Judy tomorrow morning at nine o'clock. Since there won't be a judge present, feel free to dress slightly more casual. I'll meet you there fifteen minutes prior to discuss what will happen and devise a plan. See you tomorrow."

Before I can swallow the lump in my throat and respond, I hear the phone click as he ends the call. I have to see Matthew. Tomorrow. I'm not sure when I stopped pushing Emma's stroller, but by the time I realize we're standing still in the middle of the sidewalk, my legs give out. I'm shaking from head to toe and my heart is beating out of my chest like a cartoon.

"Mama, cry. Mama, cry."

"Sorry, sweet girl. I'm okay." I wipe my tears with my sleeve, take a deep, steadying breath, and continue on our walk. Emma is excellent at picking up on my feelings, and I don't want to worry her. With that goal in mind, I push my fears about tomorrow out of my mind. Once she's down for a nap, I'll allow myself to spiral.

As soon as Emma's in bed for her nap, I send my dad a text message asking him to watch Emma while I'm at mediation tomorrow before calling Peter. He recently changed his lunch time to match Emma's nap so he can call me before returning to work. In an effort to avoid a panic attack in front of her, I waited until now to fill anyone in on what's happening.

It all comes spilling out of me at warp speed the second he answers the phone, my voice breaking between sobs. Once I've finally gotten the whole story out and take my first full breath, Peter says, "I wish I could be there with you. Do you have any idea what it's about?"

"That's all Dylan told me. I don't know. I'm hoping Matt is ready to agree and get things over with, but Dylan likely would have told me if that was the case."

"Maybe that's it. Maybe after all the protective order mess, he's ready to have everything settled. It could be that." His voice sounds hopeful.

"It could be, but I doubt it. Matt doesn't let things go that easily."

The next morning as I walk into the old cobblestone office building, I look around for Dylan while simultaneously searching for Matt. I find a spot in the lobby that allows me to see the entrance without leaving my back vulnerable. The last thing my nerves need right now is Matt appearing behind me without warning. After several minutes, Dylan finally walks through the door.

"Morning, Nessa. Sorry I'm late. Follow me." He leads me to a small conference room with a circular table and two chairs. "Have a seat. I'm going to walk you through the process for mediation, then we can come up with our plan of action. We have about ten minutes before we go into the mediator's office."

"Alright," I say as I pull out one of the chairs and take a seat. Dylan does the same across from me.

After a brief explanation about who the mediator is and what her role will be today, Dylan asks what I'm hoping to get out of this meeting.

"I have no idea. I don't even know why we're here. He can't be within a hundred feet of our daughter. Surely he's not stupid enough to expect me to go against the protective order. No way in hell."

"Now, Nessa, keep an open mind. The protective order expires in three months. After that, he'll have every right to see his daughter. Let's at least hear what they have to say."

"I'd rather slide down a banister of razor blades into a pool of alcohol than hear anything that man has to say."

He rolls his eyes, my *Gilmore Girls* reference clearly going over his head, as he slides his chair back and exits the room without responding.

Once we're in the mediation room, the mediator sits at the head of the table as Dylan and I take our place across from Matt, Judy, and Angie. Though Angie truly saved the day at our last hearing, I have a sinking feeling in my gut that I'm not going to like what she has to say today.

"Good morning, everyone. My name is Fiona Dale, but you can just call me Fi. Each of you will get a chance to speak, so please be respectful when the other party is talking. If we need to take a break, just let me know. Matthew, since you're the one who called this meeting, let's start with you."

He clears his throat, his hands folded on the table. I roll my eyes at how fake he's being before he finally speaks. "First off, I want to apologize for everything. I should not have left Emma alone, even for a short time. I'm truly sorry for scaring you."

I don't say anything in response. Though he rarely apologizes,

I can tell this one was forced, and I'm not rewarding his bullshit with a response.

When he realizes I'm not going to speak, he continues. "I really miss her. I can't go the rest of my life without her, and she needs me. I'm her dad. A girl needs her dad."

I scoff, unable to keep my mouth shut any longer. "She could have died, Matthew. Anything could have happened. You didn't care enough to keep her safe, and I'll never trust you with her ever again. There's a protective order in place for a reason."

At that, Angie chimes in. "I agree with you, Nessa. I do. That's why I think visitation should happen at my house. I will be with them one hundred percent of the time, ensuring Emma is never left alone or put in harm's way."

"No."

"What's wrong with that?" Matt asks, his lips pushed out in a pout exactly like Daisy's. It's cute on her but pathetic on him.

"You'll be there. That's what's wrong with that. You can go straight to hell where you belong."

"Let's take a five minute recess." Dylan stands as he pulls at my forearm.

"I'm not agreeing to this shit. I'm not doing it." The words burst out of me before the conference room door shuts ensuring everyone hears me.

"Stop for a second and just listen. Emma's protective order expires in three months, and we'll be in front of a judge for an official ruling the week after that. You have to think long term here."

"These have been the most peaceful three months of Emma's entire life. She's finally in a stable, loving environment. I won't agree to this."

After several minutes of failed attempts at convincing me, Dylan turns to reenter the room. "Their request is reasonable. If you can't see that, I may not be a good fit to continue as your counsel."

My jaw drops. Not figuratively. It literally drops open. Did he just threaten to stop representing me if I don't agree to this? I cannot afford another retainer fee for a new attorney. Though everyone but me is back in the conference room, I need some fresh air, and I have zero fucks to give about keeping them waiting.

I find a bench outside, nestled under a giant oak tree, and take a seat. I want to call Peter, but I know how stressed he is about this meeting. Just like last time, he offered to take the day off to be with me. He wants to help, and I love that, but I have to do this on my own. Matt, Dylan, and Judge Steeple cannot know about Peter until this is all over. Despite his good intentions, him being here would only make things worse.

Deciding not to call Peter, I consider calling Nora instead. Nora is almost always the perfect person to call when I need to vent. Today though, I need solid advice, and I don't know if she can put her hate for Matthew aside to truly understand my options here. So instead, I pick up the phone and call my dad. Though he, like Peter and Nora, hates Matthew, I know he will put his feelings aside to really consider the consequences of every available option, even if I don't want to hear it.

"Hi, sweetheart. Is your meeting over already?"

"No, but I need your help."

"What's going on?" He sounds worried.

I explain Matt's fake apology and Angie's promise to never leave Emma alone with him as well as my lawyer's opinion and his final words before taking his seat at the table without me.

"Your lawyer is an ass, but let's think this through. He may be right."

"What?"

"I know, honey. I wish the protective order was permanent, but with Angie promising to keep her safe, I think a judge may side with them. If you don't agree to this setup, the judge may see it as manipulative and keeping Emma from her father which will not help your case."

"Manipulative? Are you kidding me?" I chose the wrong person to call, my face heating with rage at his choice of words.

"I know that's hard to hear, and frankly, I agree that it's a load of shit. But if we can get it in writing that Angie will be there at all times, I think Emma will be safe. Angie stuck her neck out for her granddaughter when she could have easily sided with her son. That says a lot about who she is and what she's willing to do for Emma."

I hadn't thought of it that way, and his explanation eases my anger. "What if she gets hurt? I'll never forgive myself for letting her go back there if something happens to her."

"I can't promise that nothing will ever happen. She's got a long life ahead of her, she's bound to get hurt every now and then. But if something serious happens again, a judge would have enough to grant you full custody, giving him only supervised visits. What Angie is proposing *is* supervised visits, and saying no to them will come off as selfish. His lawyer will drag you through the mud, making you look vindictive to the judge. You don't want that. You need to be seen as a mom doing everything in her power to give her little girl the best life possible."

"That is what I'm doing." I'm unable to stop the tears from falling as I say it.

" I know you are. As much as I want to tell him to go to hell, I think your only option is to give this a try."

After telling my dad I love him, I end the call. Before heading back inside, I try a couple breathing techniques that I've been practicing with my therapist then rejoin everyone at the table. Reluctantly, I agree to let Angie supervise visits between Emma and Matthew as long as it's written, signed, and notarized that Matthew will not be with Emma alone for any length of time for any reason. As soon as it's over, I rush out the door and straight to my car, unable to look at any of them for a single second longer than I have to.

CHAPTER TWENTY-NINE

PETER

As soon as Nessa hangs up the phone, I flop down into my office chair, nearly knocking it over in the process. I walked the perimeter of my office over and over as she explained that Emma will have to start visiting Matthew again. I want to throw my computer screen out the window then drive to Matt's house and give him a piece of my mind. Knowing I can't do either and that I also am unable to focus right now, I opt to get some fresh air instead.

Without thinking, I pull my phone out and tap my brother's contact information as I exit the elevator.

"Hey, boner. How's it going?" I laugh at his use of my middle school nickname despite the anger coursing through my veins. With a name like mine, all the boys in middle school enjoyed comparing Peter to pecker which eventually escalated to any name used to refer to a penis—woody, dong, peen. You name it and twelve-year-old me got called it. It never bothered me. Honestly, I always found it a little bit funny, and the fact that my thirty-year-old big brother still uses it calms me ever so slightly.

"I need advice."

"Are you in trouble? I can't represent you out of state, but I have friends who can."

I chuckle. "What exactly do you think I might have done to get myself into trouble?"

"Good point. What's up?"

"How much do you know about protective orders and custody?" I know he's a defense attorney, but I'm desperate here.

"I know enough. I've got a client soon. Spit it out."

I give him a quick synopsis of what's going on, making sure to emphasize how horrible Matthew has been to both Nessa and Emma.

"Good lord. What have you gotten yourself mixed up in?"

"You're in a hurry, remember?"

"Fine, but for the record, no one is worth this much trouble."

"They are. Trust me." The words come out in a snarl. I don't have time for this, and I'm starting to question if he really knows what he's talking about.

"Alright. Alright. I believe you. The legal system is notoriously sloppy with domestic violence cases. Hold on. I'm texting Willow. She'll know." Willow has been Andrew's best friend since high school. She followed him to law school, but instead of defending criminals, she represents at-risk youth and their families on the south side of Chicago. I'm not sure why I didn't think to call Willow instead since she'll definitely know what to do.

"Okay." I let out a loud sigh as we wait for Willow's reply.

"She agrees with me. Getting a judge to rule on custody based on domestic violence is going to be tricky. I know it sucks, but her lawyer is right. Her husband will—"

"Ex-husband," I interject, my patience wearing thin.

"Her ex-husband and his attorney will have a hay day in court if she doesn't let him have supervised visits. His mom has proven herself trustworthy to both her and the courts. I hate to be the bearer of bad news, but this is the right choice."

"Fuck!" I yell, my teeth gritted, before adding, "Tell Will thanks for me."

"Sorry for being so blunt. I just don't see how anyone could be worth this much drama, but if you're happy, I'm happy."

"I'm happy. Happier than I've ever been, actually. We don't all have a jaded view on love, like you."

"I'm not jaded. I just saw how hard it was on Dad after Mom died. I've never met anyone worth the possibility of that pain."

Though I was old enough to understand what my dad was going through, Andrew had to step up in a way I never did. My birthday cupcakes weren't the only way Andrew took care of me after Mom died and Dad was too drunk to cook dinner or help with homework or drive me to baseball practice. I don't blame him for choosing not to open himself up to the potential for that kind of hurt, but I wish he'd understand why I don't feel the same way.

With Emma going to Angie's this weekend and seeing her dad for the first time in months, I take a half day Friday so I can see her before she leaves. In the nearly five years I've worked here, I've only used a handful of personal days. I've never had a good enough reason to miss work until now—until Nessa.

Parking my car down the street, out of Angie's view when she arrives, I carry my bag and gaming equipment a block or so before quietly closing the door behind me. I assume Emma is still napping when I don't hear footsteps running down the hall at the sound of the front door's squeak. Peeking into the kitchen, I see Nessa at the sink, headphones in her ears.

I set my stuff down and slide my arms around her waist making her jump at the unexpected touch. "I missed you," I whisper in her ear after she pulls her headphones free.

Turning to face me, her lips linger on mine before she adds, "I missed you, more."

"Not a chance. Does Emma know she's going to Angie's tonight?"

"No. I don't know how to explain it to her. She hasn't seen or heard from her dad in months. I don't even know if she knows who he is anymore."

"I hadn't thought about that. Angie will be with her. Everything will be okay, and if not, I'll be right here with you." I squeeze her hands in reassurance, and she lays her head on my chest, her arms wrapped possessively around my waist.

A smile instantly crosses my face when I see Emma turn the corner into the kitchen, her new rainbow blanket dragging behind her. "Petey!" She comes running towards me as soon as she sees me.

"You did it! Petey. That's right!" I spin her in the air before giving her a tight squeeze. "I missed you."

"Miss ooo." Andrew's cynicism is costing him more than he knows. This right here is worth any obstacle in the world.

An hour later, Emma runs to the door at the sound of a soft knock as I'm hiding in the kitchen, out of sight of the entryway. "Oh, Emma Bear. I missed you so much."

"Hi, Angie." Nessa's voice is bitter as she greets her.

"I will keep her safe. I promise. Even if that means I have to call you again or he loses custody altogether. *She* is my priority." Though I can't see her expression, she sounds sincere. She's done it before, and I'm hopeful she really will do it again if necessary.

"You're going to spend a couple days with Nana, okay? Mommy will miss you so much, but I want you to have the best time."

My heart is screaming at me to go to her when I hear Emma wail as she's carried to the car. I don't realize how tightly I'm gripping the counter until Nessa comes back inside, prying my hands free to wrap them around her.

"I can't do this."

"I don't know if I can either," I admit. "We'll get through it together."

We spend Friday night wallowing in self-pity. We barely leave the couch, down a pint of ice cream each, and cry during parts of the movie that don't even warrant it. By ten o'clock, we're both so exhausted from crying and the long, emotional week that we fall asleep as soon as our heads hit the pillow.

"We had our pity party last night, but today, we have to get out of this house and have some fun." Nessa, eyes still puffy and red from last night's cry fest, puts on her best smile as she pulls me out of bed.

"Deal. I could use some fun today. What did you have in mind?"

"Coffee. Then, I don't know. Nora invited us to their house for dinner, if you want to go."

"That could be fun." Rob and Nora were their normal, outgoing selves at Emma's birthday party. As long as things are still going well, dinner at their house really would be fun.

After a pinky promise that neither of us would think about Emma or Matt for the entire day, we actually had a pretty good time. Nessa picked up her favorite coffee then drove us to a glow in the dark mini golf course. Though I enjoy golf and am decently good at it, Nessa beat me by three strokes, rubbing it in the entire way home.

"I miss her to pieces, but I've also missed time with just you," Nessa says as we walk up Nora's driveway that night.

"I miss her, too, but you're right. Today has been nice." I give her a quick kiss before knocking on the front door only to have Nessa push it open and waltz right in.

"Hey!" Nessa calls as she walks through the living room.

"In here!" Rob and Nora call in unison.

Nessa shoots me a 'did you hear that?' look before heading

into the kitchen. There is a huge taco bar spread out across the counter complete with salt-rimmed glasses and margaritas.

"Damn! This looks delicious," Nessa says as she scoops guacamole onto a chip.

"I helped Daddy make the cwakamoley." Daisy beams up at Rob.

"You should be on Top Chef," Nessa mumbles, her mouth still full.

"Thank you." She curtsies before grabbing her own chip and scooping up some guac.

Daisy sits between Nessa and me as we eat dinner before running off to play with a neighborhood friend, claiming she'll be bored without Emma here. Rob and Nora are laughing and teasing, just like old times. With all the chaos this week, it's nice to just play cards and chat with good friends, not an ounce of tension in the air.

Though we stay at Rob and Nora's until nearly midnight, we're both wide awake when we get home. "Shit! We forgot to call Emma," I blurt as we walk into Nessa's house.

"I didn't forget," she responds. "She was so upset when Angie picked her up. I didn't want seeing me to upset her all over again. Once she's used to this, we can go back to calling her every night."

"I heard her crying when she left. It took every ounce of willpower inside me not to run out there and grab her. It was torture to not comfort her while she was upset."

"It was torture! She's gone through so much in her little life. I feel so guilty."

"It's not your fault, Ness. You did the right thing by leaving him. It will just take time to straighten itself out." I hope I'm right. I don't know if I can handle a lifetime of Matt putting Emma and Nessa through hell. We lay in bed entangled and naked for the first time since the jacuzzi tub, and I fall into the deepest, most contented sleep of my life.

We spend Sunday tangled up on the couch watching movies, playing video games, and just enjoying each other's company. Knowing I have to leave in a couple hours, I don't want to waste a single second.

I pull Nessa onto my lap and grasp her hair in my hand, pulling her toward me for a long, sensual kiss. She runs her fingers through my hair, opening my mouth with the flick of her tongue. Sliding her shirt over her head, I take her nipple into my mouth as I fumble to get her pants down without moving her off of me. Both fully undressed now, she scooches down, kissing down my torso, before taking me into her mouth and letting out a soft moan. Wrapping her arms around my neck, I lift her off the couch to carry her to bed, stopping to press her back against the wall and nibble at her neck and breasts. Her nails dig into my back as her need becomes frantic. Finally to the bedroom, I lay her softly on the bed and take her sweet spot into my mouth, making her climax, before sliding into her with a deep thrust.

As we're drying off after our shower, the doorbell rings. "What time is it?" Nessa gasps, worry evident in her voice.

I turn my phone screen towards her. "Only four fifteen."

There's still forty-five minutes before Emma will be home. Deciding to ignore it, I glide Nessa's towel down her back and spend extra time drying her butt when the doorbell rings again. Twice.

Nessa throws on a T-shirt and shorts, jogging to the door. From the bedroom, I hear her swing the door open ready to let the salesperson down gently.

"Who the fuck is here, Nessa?" The door handle slams into the wall with a bang.

"You're early." Her voice is laced with fear.

"His car is here. Where is he?" his voice booms.

"Hey, sweet girl. It's okay. Come to Mama," Nessa coos in the soft voice she uses only for her daughter as I hear Emma begin to wail.

"Where the hell is he?" The front door slams as I hear footsteps stomping down the hall. Straight for the bedroom where I stand in nothing but a towel.

CHAPTER THIRTY

NESSA

Angie comes sprinting into the house at the sound of my door being slammed. "Matthew! Matthew!" Her voice is loud and frantic, almost a screech.

Completely ignoring her cries, Matthew storms into my bedroom with Emma still in his arms. She's crawling up onto his shoulder, her little arms stretched out to me, in an attempt to get away.

I finally free Emma from her dad's grasp just in time. As soon as she's safely in my arms, Matt raises his fists towards Peter.

"No!" Angie and I yell at the same time as Lorelai lunges for Matt's ankles with an insistent hiss.

Despite my worry for Peter and my need to make sure he's okay, I have to protect Emma from seeing or hearing any more of this. I walk her to the backyard but not before I hear Matthew's fist connect with his target and the ensuing groan from Peter.

In all the commotion, Ms. Garcia appears on her back porch, peering into my backyard. "Is everything okay, dear?"

"No. Can you come play with Emma for just a minute? I need to go back inside, but she has to stay out here."

"Of course." She jogs down her back porch steps and walks through the gate a moment later.

As soon as Ms. Garcia has Emma strapped into a swing, I dash back inside. Angie is pulling at Matt's shirt and arms, trying and failing to lift him off of Peter. Running up beside her, I grab one of his arms and we both pull him back at the same time.

"Get your ass back to the car, right now." Angie's using her strict mom voice as she presses both hands into Matt's chest, propelling him toward the exit.

My focus solely on Peter's swollen and bloody face, I pay them no mind until I hear Matt starting to scream. "You just gave me the perfect reason to take your daughter from you. The judge is going to love the fact that you've been whoring around in front of her. Mark my words. I will get full custody, and you'll never see her again."

Peter, now up and wiping blood from his nose with a wash cloth, starts to respond but is cut off by Matt's continued rant.

"She's married, you piece of shit. You're screwing a married woman. I suggest you leave her alone. I will put you in the hospital next time." His voice bellows down the hall as Angie pushes him out the front door.

"Are you okay?" I ask, sliding in to hug him from behind as he tends to his face in the mirror.

"I'm fine. Did he hurt you? Where's Emma?" At the mention of Emma, his voice raises and he looks around frantically, worried she might have witnessed the beating he just took.

"I took her outside before she could see what he was doing. Ms. Garcia is playing with her for a minute. He didn't hurt me or her. But he got you pretty good."

"I think he might have broken my nose." He turns towards me, my arms still wrapped around him, and envelops me in a hug.

"That does not look good." Though his nose is no longer bleeding, it looks a tad off center, and his eye most certainly will be black tomorrow.

"It doesn't feel so great, either. I'm just glad Emma didn't see it and he didn't hit you. None of what he said is true, by the way. Promise me you know it's not true." Even after getting his nose broken by my ex, he still cares more about Emma and me than he does himself, which makes what I'm about to do that much harder.

The plan was for Peter to leave before five to avoid being here when Matt arrived. Despite the turn of events, Peter now getting to see Emma before he leaves is a welcome change of plans.

Once his face is cleaned up, we go outside to relieve Ms. Garcia from Emma duty. "Petey!" Emma runs to him, her arms outstretched. "Owie. Petey have owie."

"Petey does have an owie," I say as she points to his swollen eye.

"Awe better," she announces after kissing the side of his face like I do for her when she gets an owie.

Peter winces at the pressure before adding, "Thanks, sweet girl. It's all better."

"You probably need to get it checked out. Her boo-boo kisses are pretty magical, but I think you need stitches."

"I'll stop at urgent care before I head home. I'm okay. I just want to spend a few minutes with my girls before I go."

After drawing hopscotch with chalk and turning on Emma's bubble machine, I sit in Peter's passenger seat so we can have a moment to talk without Emma overhearing.

"Hey, Peter."

"Yeah?" This is exactly how he first told me he loved me. The look in his eyes and smile on his face absolutely breaks my heart. This is the last thing I want to do, but I have to put Emma first. No matter what.

"I can't see you anymore."

"What?" His smile instantly drops, a frown taking its place.

"I didn't want him to find out about you until all of the court stuff was behind us for this exact reason. He's going to use this to take Emma from me. She is my top priority. She has to be." My throat burns with the effort to hold in my tears.

"He can't take her away because you moved on, Nessa. That's not how it works. He's just trying to scare you." His voice cracks as he forces the words out.

"Well it worked. I'm scared. I can't lose her. I knew dating while I was still married was a risk, but I didn't think it would come to this. His lawyer is going to make it look like I'm choosing you over her. I cannot let that happen. You're probably right that he won't win full custody, but I can't even risk 50/50. I have to do what's right for Emma. I have to."

"*I'm* right for Emma. *We're* right for Emma. Please, Nessa. We'll get through this together. We always do."

"I can't, Peter. I'm sorry. I love you. This is absolutely crushing me, but I have to put her first. I'm sorry."

Before he can respond, I join Emma in front of her bubble machine, tears pouring down my cheeks. Peter *is* right for me and for Emma, but until custody is decided, I have to focus on her, no matter the sacrifice.

CHAPTER THIRTY-ONE

PETER

Pulling out of Nessa's driveway, knowing I'll never be back, is an absolute gut punch. One that hurts far worse than the real punches I just took to the face. Wiping my eyes on my shirt sleeve, I stumble into the nearest urgent care. My nose and eye sting pretty badly, and the fresh tears only make it worse. Though I know I need to get my face looked at, it's the last thing I care to do right now.

Nearly an hour later, I return to my car, two stitches above my right eye and a bandage covering my nose. The time I spent waiting for the doctor gave me time to process what just happened and decide what I should do, if anything. I have never been a confrontational person nor have I ever given or received a punch. I've never found myself in that position, but the fact that my body chose freeze over fight or flight makes me feel so damn guilty. I should have hit him back and at the very least, defended Nessa. I failed her in the moment, but it very well may help my case now. Despite Nessa breaking my heart, I have an important stop to make before I make the long drive home for the last time.

In hindsight, it might have been better to stop by the police station before having a doctor reset my broken nose and clean my face up. It certainly looked worse beforehand. Hopefully the stitches and bandage will be enough proof to press charges against Matthew. I'm not about to let him off the hook for what he just did, in front of his daughter no less.

I know Nessa only ended things because she doesn't want anything to jeopardize custody of Emma, rather than truly not wanting to be with me anymore. Regardless, it hurts like hell. Maybe pressing charges against Matthew for assault while his daughter watched will give Nessa a fighting chance when he tries to use me against her. Whether or not I'm with Nessa, Emma deserves to be, and giving Nessa's lawyer proof to show the judge is the least I can do for her. Once again, the right thing fucking sucks sometimes.

Officer Lyles takes my statement, warning me that I'll be called to testify if the district attorney pursues charges against him, before taking pictures of my injuries. I want nothing more than to see Matt dragged out of the courtroom in handcuffs, so testifying will not be an issue. The thought alone brings me immense joy in a moment of complete agony.

The three weeks that follow can only be described as pure hell. My eye is various shades of purple for the better half of a week, and my nose still whistles with every breath I take—a constant reminder of the love I lost. I force myself up and out of bed every morning then stay at work until well after the sun sets, allowing myself to fall into bed as soon as I get home. Though this new routine has significantly increased my productivity at work, it's draining me mentally and physically. My current diet is mostly takeout pizza and microwaveable spaghetti, which doesn't help either. That is, when I have the desire to eat at all.

Rob and Nora have both texted me several times but have yet to receive a response in return. What is there to say? Nessa ripped my heart out and stomped on it. Okay, that's a bit of a stretch, but it feels true. They want to know if I'm okay, but they won't like the answer. I am far from okay. Nessa hasn't called or texted a single time since I left, leaving a gaping hole in my heart that will never heal.

My only comfort is knowing that my physical pain ended up being for a good reason. Officer Lyles called yesterday to inform me that Matt has been arrested and will appear in court in a little over a week. This can only be good news for Nessa and her fast approaching divorce and custody hearing. On top of that, Matt being in jail means he isn't taking Emma for her usual weekend visits, which provides me with a little comfort.

Despite pulling away from everyone I care about, I still visit Deedee once a week, helping her with anything and everything around the house. Now that I'm working sixty hours per week by the time I leave on Friday evenings, I save my visits with Aunt Deedee for Saturday. It makes Sunday, the only day left with nothing to distract me, my least favorite day of the week.

Today happens to be that day. I didn't get out of bed until well past noon, and even then, I had to force myself to stand up. I ate a stale piece of bread with nothing on it and cracked open a can of Mountain Dew before plopping myself down in my recliner. I haven't moved since, despite the fact that the sun is starting to set.

My phone buzzes beside me, pulling my attention away from my fourth movie of the day. I reach for it but feel only the soft fabric of the armrest. Maybe it's beneath me? I have no reason to check my phone; it's been sitting untouched for hours and must have fallen into the crack between the cushion and the armrest. Before I can get to it, it stops buzzing, and I decide it's not worth the effort of fishing it out from underneath the chair. My attention returns to the TV screen.

Moments later, it buzzes again. I sigh, turning the volume up on the television to drown out the sound before realizing that my phone hasn't made this much noise since Nessa broke up with me. That thought lunges me from my seat, knees popping from the sudden movement for the first time in weeks. Despite the pit of despair I've been living in, the thought of Nessa calling to tell me she's changed her mind fills me with hope and anticipation.

Flat on my belly, my arms as far under the recliner as possible, I finally grab hold of my phone. Without taking the time to stand, I tap my phone screen. Two missed calls. From Andrew. A fresh wave of pain envelops me as I flop onto the couch flat on my back with my arms and legs spread wide.

When my phone begins buzzing once again, I swipe to answer it without even looking. "What?" My voice comes out raspy from lack of use.

"Hello to you too." It's Andrew. Again.

"Hi." I don't mean to sound like a pouty toddler, but I know I do.

"Aunt Deedee is worried about you. What's going on?"

"Oh, I'm just busy proving you right."

"For what it's worth, I didn't want to be right." There's sincere empathy in his voice despite the fact that he warned me that a relationship with Nessa could lead to nothing but hurt mere weeks ago.

I've been thinking more and more about what Andrew said the last time we talked. No one is worth the risk of the kind of pain our dad experienced, but he's wrong. Nessa and Emma are worth it, and I'd do it all over again in a heartbeat, but his thought process makes a lot more sense to me now.

I know that my dad losing his wife and the mother to his children is not the same as what I'm going through, but I'd be lying if I said it doesn't feel just as serious. It's the kind of pain that's led me to swear off dating ever again. The two people I belong with don't want me, and I don't want anyone else. So, maybe he was also just a little bit right.

When I don't respond, Andrew adds, "Come see me next

weekend. We'll go out, have some fun, and get your mind off of her. Willow is already helping me plan your visit."

"No, thanks."

"You can't wallow forever. I haven't seen you since Christmas. It's time for a visit. Come hang out with your big brother."

"I do miss you two. I'll think about it." I lie just to get him to stop begging.

I love my brother and Willow and know they'd show me a good time in an effort to help me get over this slump, but I have no desire for Andrew to be my wingman. Casual hookups may work well for him but not for me. There's no way I could have a no strings attached night of fun. Not after experiencing how it feels to love and be loved.

My promise to consider it works as I'd hoped. Andrew changes the subject to my broken nose, offering advice on what to say and do next week when I'm called to the stand to testify. I 'mmhm' and 'got it' in all the right places, but I'm not listening anymore, my thoughts stuck on Emma. On how scared she was the day Matt punched me. On how she's doing since I left. And most importantly, on thoughts of Emma thinking that another man, someone she was growing to think of as a father, abandoning her yet again. That's the thought that sends me back into a spiral. I abruptly end the phone call with Andrew, turn my movie back on, and drown out the world for the rest of the night.

CHAPTER THIRTY-TWO

NESSA

After Peter left, Emma and I played outside until dark in an attempt to distract my brain from thinking about what I'd done. Peter. Sweet, thoughtful, nerdy, funny, loving Peter. He did not deserve the way I treated him especially after taking a beating because of me. Yet I broke his heart anyway, breaking my own in the process.

Matt's words still haunt me, especially because I don't doubt a single word he said. He will do everything in his power to take Emma from me. To hurt me. Even if it hurts his daughter in the process. She's never been at the top of his priority list, and that's more apparent now than ever before.

After showing up to pick Emma up for her weekend visit, two weeks after the incident, and being turned away, he hasn't come by or reached out a single time. Angie, however, has. She's called to apologize at least three times since that day and refused to come with Matt to pick Emma up for her visit, allowing me to shut the door in his face. We agreed to supervised visits, and Angie refusing to supervise is a tiny glimmer of hope in my current sea of despair.

If Angie continues to refuse supervising duty, I may have a

better shot at gaining full custody of Emma. There's a chance they'll appoint someone else to supervise, according to Dylan, but supervised visits will still mean I get full custody with a weekend or two a month of Emma visiting Matt for a few hours each time. That is an arrangement I can live with, one that might just make all of this worth it.

In two months, I'll be divorced with a custody agreement set in stone. Not only am I crossing each day off my calendar—a countdown to my freedom—I'm also counting down to the day that I can call Peter again. I've typed out a hundred different messages before forcing myself to delete them.

He probably hates me, rightfully so, but I've never been loved by someone the way Peter loved me. I'd be doing myself and Emma a disservice if I didn't at least try to reconnect once this whole mess is over with. Exactly fifty-one days until I can try to repair things with the love of my life, as long as everything stays on schedule.

When Emma stopped seeing Matt, she didn't seem to notice, perfectly content with it just being me and her. Despite the fact that she's only known Peter for a few months, she misses him far more than she ever missed Matt. Every time she hears a knock at the door or the signature FaceTime ring coming from my phone, she excitedly yells 'Petey' as she runs to find him with Lorelai right at her heels. It shatters my heart into a million pieces every single time, making me second guess my decision despite knowing it's what I had to do.

Regardless of the intensity of the knock at the door, Emma yells for Peter as she runs to answer it—dropping the crumpled up photo of Peter helping the girls feed the petting zoo animals she's been carrying to the ground in the process. Peter's knock is soft and considerate compared to the loud bang coming from whoever's at my door, a detail Emma hasn't yet noticed. I pick her up, balancing her on my hip, and swing the door open to find a police officer on my doorstep. Unable to speak right away, my thoughts running a mile a minute, I simply stare at him.

"You've been served," he says, handing me a manila envelope before returning to the police car parked in front of my house.

I stand in disbelief, the envelope dangling from my hands, as I watch the cruiser fade out of view. Though my heart nearly stopped at the sight of the officer at my door, it picks back up as I lower Emma to the ground and tear open the envelope. I can only imagine what Matt has up his sleeve this time. If this messes up my countdown to rekindling with Peter, I may puke.

The envelope is in several pieces by the time I work the pages free. With a shaking hand, I flip the paper over to see that I'm being subpoenaed for a court date next week. Our court date isn't until October, seven weeks from now. Despite the legal jargon at the top of the page, I have no idea what court case this is referring to, so I quickly check the time before dialing the number for Dylan's office. They close in six minutes and are out of office on Fridays, so I desperately need to catch him before the weekend.

"I need to speak with Dylan. It's urgent," I blurt the words before the receptionist has a chance to finish saying the name of the law firm, her typical way of answering the phone.

After a short hesitation, no doubt due to my abruptness, she sends my call to Dylan's phone. Though I'm not a superstitious person, I cross my fingers just in case. I will spend the entire weekend worrying if this call goes to voicemail. I'm stressed enough without adding this to my—

"This is Dylan." I have never been more grateful to hear his voice. I quickly relay all the information I have about my subpoena paperwork, knowing that as soon as the clock strikes five, I'll be charged double for this phone call.

He types the case number into his computer, nothing but the tap, tap, tap of his keyboard coming through the phone for a painfully long time. "Ah. This is good news. You're being subpoenaed to testify against Matthew. He's been charged with assault and battery as well as endangerment of a child."

Dylan recites everything he can find about the case, and I feel my body relax with every word. I quickly end the phone call at 4:59 p.m. and immediately sink onto the floor, covering my face with my hands.

Emma hears me sobbing, tears of relief for once, and climbs into my lap. "Mama, totay. It totay, Mama."

Her attempts to comfort me bring a smile to my face. "Let's go, sweetpea. We're going to celebrate."

Though it feels strange to celebrate the fact that my soon to be ex-husband and father to my child is in jail, that's exactly what I intend to do. Not only can he not hurt us from behind bars, it also takes credibility away from him when he tries to drag me through the mud. I send Peter a silent thank you in my head for once again saving the day. Even after shattering his heart into a million pieces, he pressed charges against Matthew, knowing full well it would help me in court. Fingers crossed he still cares this much in fifty-one days.

I immediately send Nora a text message telling her that I have some good news and to meet us at Andy's—the best frozen custard place on the planet. I throw on Peter's hoodie, his smell finally fading from it, and carry Emma to the car. After fastening her into her car seat and then running back inside to grab Sprinkle and her new favorite blanket, we finally pull out of the garage.

As we approach the only stop light between our house and Andy's Frozen Custard, my phone begins to ring. I hit the button to accept the call and it immediately connects to my car.

"Hey, Ness. I just got your message. You're going to beat us there, but we're on our way."

As soon as Emma hears Nora's voice, she begins chanting Daisy's name louder and louder with every passing second.

"No worries. We should be there in…"

Emma dropped Sprinkle in her eagerness to talk to Daisy and is now wailing at the top of her lungs, cutting me off mid-thought. I need the screaming to stop so I can hear Nora and focus on the road. I quickly glance up at the light, still red, then lean into the back seat to locate Sprinkle.

Before I can hand her the stuffed animal and finish telling Nora our ETA, sharp honks pull my attention back to the road. In my efforts to find her unicorn, my foot slipped off the brake pedal, slowly inching us into oncoming traffic.

"Shit!" I scream before Sprinkle flies out of my hand and my head slams into the steering wheel.

CHAPTER THIRTY-THREE

PETER

My attempts at convincing Andrew that a trip to Chicago to see him is not necessary were fruitless. I opened my email this morning to learn that Andrew booked my plane tickets, sending the confirmation email straight to me. I guess I'll be flying out to see him tomorrow and returning late Sunday night.

It's now Thursday, and I'm at Deedee's a few days early to fix one of the wooden steps on her back porch. She tripped last night, falling and requiring an emergency room visit. So, here I am building new steps for her porch instead of working well into the night like I'd planned.

"I guess I'm going to see Andrew tomorrow." Aunt Deedee has been watching me work, handing me any tools I need, and refilling my glass of lemonade every time I take even the smallest sip. I'm sure she already knows all about this trip, but it'll be good to talk to her about it anyway.

"That'll be good, dear. You need a distraction, and spending time with your brother sounds lovely. I made Willow's favorite cookies for you to take with you."

"I guess."

It's not that I don't want to see him. I enjoy visiting him a couple times a year. We watch the Cubs lose, play every video game that I've created since our last visit, and eat spicy chicken wings almost every night. It's a good time, but I know things will be different this time. He seems dead set on convincing me that his single forever way of life is better than the pain I'm still feeling. Maybe he's right, but I'm not ready to face the facts just yet.

"I know you love her, dear, but she did what she thought was right. Until you become a parent, you can't possibly understand the reason she made the decision she made."

Though I wouldn't dare say it, she's wrong. I became a parent four months ago, and I'd do anything for that little girl. But I'd never rip a loving parental figure out of her life. Never. Before I can find the words to explain that to her, my phone rings.

Without needing to look at the screen, I say, "Andrew's calling. Again. I'll be right back."

I slide the answer button on my phone as I close the back door behind me, taking advantage of this interruption to enjoy some cool air before returning to my project.

"Hey. I'm sure whatever you've got planned is fine." He's been calling me all week with various outing options, but I couldn't care less where he drags me to this weekend.

"What? Peter, it's me." A feminine—definitely not Andrew—voice comes through the phone, and despite the familiarity, I have to glance at my phone screen to realize who it is.

"Nora? Is everything okay?" She almost never calls me. She's texted several times a week over the last month to check in on me but never a phone call. Rob has also been texting regularly to check on me, and if one of them needed to call, it would be him not Nora.

"No." She sucks in a deep, shaky breath.

"What's wrong? Is Daisy okay?"

"Daisy's fine. It's Emma and..."

The mere mention of her name sends panic through me.

"What happened? Is she okay? Where is she? Did Matt—" She cuts me off before I can finish my rapid-fire questions.

"They were in a car wreck. They're on their way to the hospital. It's not super serious, but they are hurt." She finishes telling me everything she knows before ending the call so she can head to the hospital.

My first instinct is to drop everything and drive to them right now. But the rational part of my brain says showing up will only make things worse, so I decide to finish Aunt Deedee's steps instead.

"How's Andrew doing? I haven't talked to him at all this week. He's been too busy planning for your visit." She tops off my lemonade before pulling her seat out into the sunshine.

"That actually wasn't Andrew."

"Oh. I thought you said it was. These ears aren't as good as they once were." She gives a soft laugh as she lowers herself into the chair.

I chuckle. "Your ears are just fine. I assumed it was him since he's the only one who calls me anymore. Several times a day, might I add. It was Nora."

"Rob's wife?" My eyes are focused on the nail I'm holding, so I can't see her expression but her voice is full of confusion.

"Yes."

"Does she normally call you? Is everything okay?"

"No, she doesn't. Nessa and Emma were in a wreck. She was just calling to let me know." Though I try to say it with nonchalance, my voice betrays me, cracking as I say their names.

"What? Are they okay? Why are you wasting time talking to me? Get out of here."

"They're okay. I'm not going. She made it very clear that she doesn't want me in their lives anymore."

"That's a crock of shit, and you know it."

Hearing Deedee cuss pulls my attention away from the step, my head spinning to look at her. "It's not. I haven't heard from her since her husband beat the shit out of me. Not a single time. If she cared, even a little bit, her best friend wouldn't be the one checking on me instead of her." Though my hurt and frustration have been palpable from the moment she told me she couldn't see me anymore, I hadn't realized how much her silence was affecting me.

"I know. And that's been painful. I know that too. But if you truly love them, *both of them*, you'll go make sure they're okay."

"I do love them. That's why I can't go." Tears fill my eyes as I defend my decision to the person whose opinion of me matters most.

"She didn't break up with you because she doesn't love you. She broke up with you to ensure Matt had nothing to hold over her head in front of a judge. Now he's in jail with plenty to be held over his head. It's worth considering that she did this to protect *you* from getting hurt again too. That little girl looks up to you, and I'll be disappointed if you let her down."

Her words hit like a punch to the gut. My heart is screaming for me to get in the car right this very second, but my brain is telling me to stop and think this through first. Nora wouldn't have called if she didn't think Nessa would want me to know, and disappointing Aunt Deedee is something I avoid like the plague. On the other hand, I'd never forgive myself if I showed up at the hospital and it upset Nessa even more. Or worse, Matt found out about it and made things even more complicated for her. Before I can talk myself out of it, I grab my keys and jog to the car, leaving Aunt Deedee's steps still in a heap on the grass.

CHAPTER THIRTY-FOUR

NESSA

"Emma!" I scream as our car jolts to a stop.

"Mama," her little voice calls back to me. She's starting to cry, and I can hear the panic in her voice.

I quickly unbuckle myself and climb over the console, between the two front seats, to get to her as fast as possible. She's reaching for me, her breaths coming in and out in short, frequent bursts. "I'm so sorry, sweetie. Are you hurt?"

"I totay," she responds, her voice still a bit shaky.

I unclip her car seat buckles and look her over from head to toe before noticing the pain in my left wrist. In my panic to ensure Emma was okay, I overlooked myself entirely. Not only is my wrist in pain, but blood is trickling down my forehead. My wrist throbs as I lift her out of her seat, the pressure causing excruciating pain to shoot up my arm.

A light rap on the window pulls my focus away from the pain once again, and I climb into the front seat, Emma in my arms, to roll the window down.

"Is everyone okay?" A man, probably about my dad's age, asks as he peers into the car.

"We're okay. My wrist hurts, but my baby is fine. That's all that matters. Are you hurt?"

"We're fine. I was able to slow down quite a bit before hitting you. My wife saw your 'Baby On Board' sticker on the back windshield, so I rushed over to make sure no one was hurt while she called 911. An ambulance should be here shortly." Though I just caused him to get into an accident, his worry about our safety, instead of being upset or angry, allows me to calm myself down.

We pull our cars into a nearby parking lot and exchange insurance information while we wait for the police and first responders to arrive. Though Emma qualifies for insurance through the state, I will be uninsured until I graduate with my counseling degree and find a job with good enough benefits. I cannot afford an ambulance ride, and since neither of us are badly hurt, I'm going to have to decline treatment for myself when they arrive.

A few minutes later, I hear sirens in the distance as two police cars and an ambulance approach and pull into the lot beside us. A female police officer, whose name badge says Hodges, takes my statement while one of her partners talks with the older couple that hit us.

I explain that my foot must have slipped off the brake pedal, causing us to roll into the intersection while the light was still red. Fred, the driver of the other vehicle, approaches as we're assessing the damage to my car. Though the impact was hard enough to jolt our car through the intersection, there's not much damage besides a large dent and a bent front tire.

"Officer, I just want to say that there's no need to escalate things, legally, I mean. We're not hurt, and we'll file with our insurance to get any needed repairs done. We don't want to press charges," Fred, who's looking over the damage with us now, says to both officers, and relief floods me immediately.

There's no denying that this accident was my fault, and I am eternally grateful that Fred and his wife aren't looking to get me into any trouble because of it. Though Matthew has made our custody case a little easier for me with his latest outburst, I know an at-fault car wreck with my daughter in the car will not look good.

While the first responders look Emma over, Officer Hodges walks over with a yellow piece of paper in her hands. Shit. Apparently Fred's little speech didn't help me after all. Now I'll have to replace my car and Emma's car seat all while dealing with the ramifications of yet another legal battle. I should have left Sprinkle on the floor. Answering Nora's question was not important enough to risk all of this.

Oh my god, Nora! I completely forgot that Nora was on the phone when we got hit. Nora heard all of it and is no doubt freaking out right now. Before I can return to the car to frantically search for my phone and assure Nora that we're okay, Hodges makes it to us, her hand outstretched with the yellow paper extended towards me.

"Mr. Banks is adamant that he doesn't want to get a young mom into trouble when no one was hurt. I can't ignore the incident completely, but he certainly saved you from a complicated case."

I look the ticket over before responding. "Thank you. I really appreciate that." There's a lump in my throat as I start to tell her everything that's going on in my life right now. Divorce, custody, an abusive ex who beat the crap out of the love of my life, but the first responder spares her the unnecessary details when he hands Emma over to me.

"Everything looks okay besides a small cut on her leg. I'd still like to take her in just to be sure. Plus, your wrist needs to be looked at."

I take Emma from him as I explain that I can't accept the ambulance ride to the hospital. Though Emma's ambulance ride will be covered by insurance, mine will leave me with a hefty bill I won't be able to pay.

"Ma'am, you both need to be seen. I can't force you to come with us, but it's strongly advised."

"I'll drive us." But even I know that's not a viable option. Emma's car seat needs to be replaced, and the driver's side front tire is bent. My car isn't going anywhere without a tow truck.

Reluctantly, I grab my phone and purse from my car and load Emma into the back of the ambulance before calling Nora. I relay the events of the wreck, assuring her that we're both okay, then tell her which hospital we're headed to.

By the time we make it to the hospital, they've checked both of our vitals three separate times, stabilized my wrist in a splint, and cleaned up the wound on my forehead. Once inside, they settle us into a room in the pediatric unit of the emergency department. Emma is snuggled into my lap on the hospital bed, Sprinkle in her arms and her rainbow blanket spread across her legs, when I hear Nora's frantic voice from out in the hallway.

"Which room? Where are they?" Her voice is a high-pitched whine as she tries to figure out which curtain we're behind.

I poke my head through the small curtain providing us a little privacy and wave toward Nora and Daisy. Daisy runs straight to the bed, looking Emma over exactly like I did, before settling in next to her.

"How's your arm?" Nora grabs it, turning it every which way.

I grimace and pull it out of her grasp. "They're pretty sure it's broken. We're waiting for an X-ray."

"But that's it? Nothing else is wrong?" She gives me an apologetic look as I rub my wrist with my other hand.

"I think that's it." I point to the cut on my forehead before adding, "I hit my head on the steering wheel, but other than that, we're okay. Emma was shaken up, obviously, but she's fine. I've never been so thankful for car seat laws in my entire life."

Despite the fact that Emma is two and can technically face

forward in her car seat, I've held off turning her around until she's a little bigger. I have no doubt that this precaution is the reason she walked away nearly untouched today.

After what feels like hours, a man and woman in scrubs, enter the room with a wheelchair. Despite my insistence that I can walk, they each take one of my arms and lower me into the chair. Due to radiation from the X-ray machine, Emma can't come with me. After everything we've been through, I'm most comfortable when Emma is right beside me, or at least in eye sight, but I know she's in good hands with Nora and Daisy.

It takes about twenty minutes to wheel me to the X-ray room, take the necessary pictures, and wheel me back to Emma. Nora shoots me a look I can't read as one of the nurses slides the curtain aside, revealing exactly what the look was about.

Peter is in Emma's hospital bed, her and Daisy on either side of him with Sprinkle propped up in his lap. His eyes flick up from the page he's reading as I'm wheeled into the room.

"Peter? How did… what are…" I can't get the words out. Peter was the last person I expected to see right now. I'm so caught off guard that I don't even notice my dad in the corner of the room, diligently reading over both of our charts.

"I just needed to know that you're both okay." He looks from me to Nora then to my dad, a look of trepidation on his face.

CHAPTER THIRTY-FIVE

PETER

Sending a quick message to Nora asking which hospital they were taken to, I throw my car into drive and speed off towards them, speed limit be damned. My thoughts are racing throughout the entire two hour drive. What if Nessa doesn't want me there? What if I'm too late and they're already home, or worse, something major went wrong before I could get there? I promise myself I'll see how they're doing and then be on my way. The last thing I want to do is make things worse for Nessa or myself. I'm already not coping well, so another rejection may push me over the edge.

Though I managed to calm myself down and focus on the road, as soon as the hospital comes into view, my heart rate speeds back up again. With all the possibilities running through my head, I forgot where Nora told me to go. I pull her message up, standing in the middle of the entryway, when a nurse greets me.

"Where are you headed?" Her voice is soft and gentle as she gently places a comforting hand on my shoulder.

After telling her where I'm trying to go, she escorts me to the pediatric wing of the emergency department. She knocks on the wall before sliding the curtain open revealing Emma, Nora, Daisy, and Duane, but no Nessa.

"Petey!" Daisy and Emma notice me at the same time and excitedly call my name as one.

"Peter." Duane looks at me with surprise. "It's nice to see you."

"Umm. Sooo," Nora starts and then stops.

All four of us, Emma included, look at her with anticipation. When she still doesn't finish her thought, I scrunch my eyebrows together and add, "Yes?"

"Nessa doesn't know you're coming." She says it so quickly, like one giant, run-on word before turning her attention to a random sign on the wall. Duane looks at her with a shake of his head like he's completely used to her antics.

I should leave. Right now. But instead, I ask, "Where is she? Are we going to get in trouble for having so many people in her room?"

"Getting an X-ray. She's been gone about fifteen minutes or so. She should be back any minute, I hope. Leave it to you to be worried about breaking the rules. Daisy and I can leave if anyone says anything. It's fine."

Emma flings her legs over the side of the bed, stretching her toes out towards the ground.

"Hold on, sweet girl. I'm coming." There are cords shooting out of various machines in every direction, and I'm still not sure if Emma is hurt. Instead of letting her run to me, I scoop her up and settle onto the bed with her before choosing a book off the shelf.

Duane untangles the cords that got wrapped around her little feet and tucks them behind the bed. This hospital bed was definitely not designed for this many people, so I pull Emma into my lap, Sprinkle propped up beside her, and scoot over to give Daisy space to squeeze in beside us.

A few pages into the book, the curtain slides open again.

Nessa's jaw is on the floor as she's wheeled into the room, her eyes locked on me. "Peter? How did... what are..."

"I just needed to know that you're both okay." I can feel my heart rate accelerate as I wait for her to say something, the anticipation too much to bear.

"I'm... we're..." Tears are welling up in her eyes as she struggles to make a full sentence. She's staring a hole through Nora as she uses one hand to push herself up from the wheelchair.

Nora, completely unfazed by Nessa's glare, gives a shrug while mouthing "oops" in my direction. Nessa is now standing beside the bed, inches from me. It takes everything in me not to reach for, but then she reaches for me.

Gently placing her hand on my cheek, she pulls me toward her, dropping her lips to mine with a force and intensity I've never seen from her. The tension in my body dissipates before I realize what's happening and pull back.

"We'll give you a minute," Nora says, grabbing Daisy's hand and leading her out into the waiting room.

Duane follows closely behind, Emma now in his arms. "I love you, sweetheart. Let us know if you need anything."

Once they're out of the room, I quickly add, "I'm sorry for just showing up. I should have known Nora wouldn't tell you."

"I'm glad she didn't."

"You are?" Shock is evident in my voice. I scoot to the edge of the bed and pat the spot next to me, inviting her to sit.

She slides in beside me, and I physically feel the loss when she doesn't lean against me.

"I'd have told her not to call you if she asked, and she knew it. But if she'd mentioned it beforehand, you wouldn't be here. So, yeah. I'm glad she didn't."

Whether or not I'm glad is still up for debate, but I'd be lying if I said I wasn't relieved as hell to finally be this close to both of them again. Unable to stomach the thought of her not wanting me to stay, I steer clear of the topic I most want to address. Settling instead for small talk.

"It looks like Emma is doing okay. How's your arm?"

"Emma, somehow, is completely unscathed. Well, she has a scrape on her leg where a toy hit her when it flew across the backseat, but that's it."

Relief instantly floods me. Nora told me she thought Emma was fine, but I couldn't help but fear the worst. Though I lost them both weeks ago, the possibility of them being taken from me for good was too much to stomach. My voice cracks when I finally manage to speak. "I was so worried. The thought of losing either of you... I can't even think about it."

She leans against my chest. Finally! Wrapping my arms around her shoulders, she leans her head against me, tears forming in both of our eyes. "We're okay. We're both okay."

"I missed you so much." I can't keep the words in any longer, no matter the consequence.

She's full on sobbing now. "We missed you so much. Emma misses you way more than I expected her to. She's so small. I thought she'd get over it quickly, but she thinks everyone who knocks on our door is you. She's been carrying your picture around everywhere she goes."

Hot, stinging tears flow from my eyes as she says it. I was convinced that Emma would forget me. After only knowing me for three short months, it wouldn't take much to erase me from her memory completely. The thought of her looking for me while I was gone brings me so much happiness but so much sadness at the same time. I hate that she probably felt abandoned by me, but knowing she misses me fills the void I've been living with for nearly a month now.

Just as I'm about to tell her how much I love her, a nurse and doctor walk into the room. The nurse pulls the X-rays out of a folder she's holding, handing them to the doctor.

"Looks like you broke your wrist in two places. We'll get you all fixed up, but you'll need to check in with your primary care provider sometime next week." The doctor points to the tiny squiggles on the pictures of Nessa's bones.

We're both silent as the doctor wraps Nessa's arm up and places it in a neon pink cast. As soon as they slide the curtain closed, I can't hold my words in any longer. "So, what now? Do you want me to leave?"

She looks at me, tears filling her eyes. "I never want you to leave again. I just want to do what's best for Emma."

As if on cue, Emma bolts back into the room with Nora and Daisy close behind. She runs straight for me, tugging at my shorts until I pick her up. If there is a God, he or she is certainly looking out for me in this moment. "I think we are best for Emma. We can figure everything else out as we go. I love this little girl and she loves me. I can't keep living life without either of you."

Nessa wraps her arms around my neck, Emma squished between us. When she finally pulls away, her cast thumps the side of my head making Emma absolutely crack up and easing the tears that have been falling from both of us.

"I need to figure out how I'm going to get us home, then we can talk all of this through." She signs a mountain of paperwork then begins gathering up all of Emma's things. Nora and Daisy take everything out of Nessa's arms, offering to carry it for her while she gets the hang of living life with a cast.

"I can get us home," I say as we all finally make our way towards the exit. "Did Duane leave? Should we let him know we're done here?"

"He left a few minutes before we came back in the room. He said to text him when everyone is home safely."

Completely ignoring Nora's comment, Nessa adds, "She has to have a car seat. I'm going to have to see if I can find an Uber or something that can get us home."

"I can get us home," I repeat as we walk through the parking lot.

"She has to have a—" she stops mid-sentence as I open the trunk of my car and load her stuff into it. "What's this?"

"This would be a car," Nora chides, a smirk on her lips.

"No shit. But whose?"

"It's mine. I needed something that could fit a car seat. It was time to trade in my car anyway." I scoop Emma up and place her into her new purple car seat before helping Nessa into the car. Her cast is on her left, non-dominant hand, but I buckle her in nonetheless.

"You bought a new car? I broke your heart and you still bought a new car for Emma?" Though we'd both stopped crying before leaving the hospital room, fresh tears are rolling down her cheeks.

"To be fair, I'd already picked it out before that day. It's been a constant reminder of you and her, but I was hopeful you'd come around. Well, Deedee was hopeful. I just do what she says." I let out a chuckle as I pull out of the emergency department parking lot, headed towards the one place I thought I'd never step foot in again.

CHAPTER THIRTY-SIX

NESSA

Emma is absolutely giddy in her purple car seat in Petey's new car. When we're quiet for too long, she calls out for him, no doubt checking that he didn't leave again. The guilt I feel at this realization is too much to handle.

Though I thought I was doing the right thing for Emma and our custody battle, I'm worried that I actually made things worse for her. I wanted to be able to tell the judge that I broke things off in order to focus on my daughter, but it may end up looking like Matt's argument—namecalling and belittlement—actually holds some weight. And in the process, I, once again, proved to Emma that dads don't stay. They can't be trusted or relied upon.

Peter has proven time and time again that he *can* be relied upon. He bought a car for Emma right after I ripped his heart out, for fuck's sake. From the second he met her, every single choice he's made has been for her. He's been more of a father to her in a few short months than Matthew will ever be. If that's not worth fighting for, nothing is.

I realize I've been too quiet, preoccupied with regret, when we pull into my driveway and Peter hesitates. "Everything okay?" I ask as I unbuckle my seatbelt.

"Yeah. I... we just never decided what now. Do you want me to come in with you?" He looks so sweet and so fragile as he asks.

"Sorry. I forget I had this conversation in my head." We both let out a soft chuckle despite the tension before I say it all out loud this time. "I made a huge mistake. I need you. Emma needs you. I'll do anything to get you back."

"*Anything?*" The ear-to-ear smile on his face fills me with relief.

He had every reason in the world to not show up tonight, but that's not Peter. Despite that, he still has every reason in the world not to take me back, to not to risk getting his heart broken all over again. I've been counting down the days until I could hear his voice just one more time all while fearing that he wouldn't be able to forgive me. His smile assures me I had it all wrong.

I'm crossing in front of the car, on my way to get Emma out, when Peter grabs my arm and pulls me to him. I wrap my arms tightly around his neck, careful not to knock him out with my cast this time, and squeeze him tight, taking in his scent as I do. I missed that smell. His hoodie loses his scent more and more every day. I missed him. Far more than I realized.

My hand being partly covered in my cast makes it difficult to undo Emma's buckle, but after insisting I don't need help, I finally wiggle it free. He won't be here everyday to help me, so I'm going to have to relearn how to do all of this on my own.

Though it's past Emma's bedtime when we get home, she struggles to fall asleep, insisting that Peter be in the room, and my heart aches for her. I want to tie Peter up and never let him leave. Not in a kinky way, though that doesn't sound half bad either. I just want to prove to Emma that she should be able to rely on men. She *can* rely on Peter.

Once she's finally asleep and all tucked into her crib, Peter and I get comfy on the couch knowing we have an important,and lengthy, conversation ahead of us. Though Lorelai usually snuggles in with Emma at bedtime, she no doubt senses that I need her emotional support right now. With her curled up in my lap, one of her front paws stretched out to rest on Peter's leg, we finally have the conversation we should have had weeks ago.

"You bought a new car for us. I can't get over that." I'm sitting criss-cross applesauce turned to the side so I can face him.

"You're wearing my hoodie."

"Every single day. I have all the pictures Deedee gave me hanging up too. We missed you."

"I missed you both so much. I needed something Emma could ride in, and I'm glad I did. Remind me never to question Aunt Deedee ever again. She never lost faith even when all my hope was gone."

"Done. I knew I loved her." Thoughts of Aunt Deedee rooting for us fills me with hope and happiness.

"It's mutual. Have you heard about Matt?" He turns to face me now, too, the mention of Matt making him furrow his brows.

"Getting arrested?"

"Yep. I have to testify against him next week." He looks pleased while simultaneously hesitant.

"I do too. We were on our way to celebrate with Nora when we wrecked tonight."

"Oh, good. Well, not good. But you know what I mean. I wasn't sure if you'd want me to press charges or not. I was worried you'd think I was overstepping."

"I don't know what I would have said if you'd asked beforehand, but I'm glad you did it. This can only strengthen my case. And, I think it's enough to make any remarks about you and me seem vindictive rather than an actual concern for Emma."

His eyes brighten, a small smile forming on his lips. "So, does that mean you can put me out of my misery?"

Knowing that Emma and I haven't been the only ones miserable fills me with guilt while also making me smile. He missed us just as much as we missed him. Wordlessly, I climb onto his lap, straddling him, as I attempt to cup his face in my hands. I settle for just my right hand, resting my heavy cast on his shoulder, as he grasps my cheeks and pulls me in for a kiss.

After several minutes, he attempts to catch his breath before adding, "I'm going to take that as a yes."

"As Nora would say, Matt can fuck off."

He laughs, a genuine, hearty laugh, and it's the most beautiful sound I've ever heard. We spend several hours tangled together, catching up on everything we missed during our time apart. I tell him all about Angie refusing to supervise visits for Matt and how Dylan thinks that will help when we go to court. He tells me about his brother's attempts to pull him out of his funk and how he's burning himself out at work before texting Andrew to cancel his visit.

The next three days are absolute bliss. Emma pulls Peter out of bed first thing each morning instead of me. They make breakfast and pour me a cup of coffee while I enjoy a few minutes to wake up before starting my day. Though I love a good cup of freshly brewed coffee, I've been drinking the premade iced coffee in a carton that Peter picked out for me the last time we went to his place. It's surprisingly delicious, but that's not what led me to stockpile it like we're in for a long, lonely winter. It reminds me of him, of our visit with Deedee, and telling him I love him for the first time. It made me feel like he was with us when he couldn't be.

After breakfast, we take Emma on our morning walk before spending each day together as a family, at last. We play outside with chalk and bubbles, take turns pushing Emma on the swings in our backyard—though she begs for Peter most of the time—and read countless books. At night, we split bedtime duties and then spend hours just being together.

By Sunday, the day we have to say goodbye again, we're fully immersed in our routine and none of us are ready for it to end. I worry that Emma won't understand that he isn't leaving for good this time. We try explaining that he'll call each night and we'll see him in five days, to no avail.

As Peter and I say our goodbyes, tears in both our eyes, Emma wails, begging him not to go. "I can't leave her like this," he says, one foot still outside his car.

"It's only for five days, this time. We can do it." I sound more sure than I am, for Emma's sake.

"Come with me." His eyes instantly brighten at the suggestion.

"What?" I was not expecting that.

"Come with me," he repeats.

"For the week?" Classes don't start for two more weeks, so until then, I guess we technically could go with him.

"For good. I never want to say goodbye to either of you again."

"We can't come for good. As much as I'd love that, classes start soon. I only have one more year until I graduate. I can't quit now. Not to mention, Nora and my dad. I don't know if I could leave them."

Though he looks disappointed, he hides it well. "For the week, then."

Renewed energy coursing through me, we pack up a week's worth of stuff for Emma and me and load it into Peter's trunk. Emma's tears instantly dry when he buckles her into her purple car seat, settling Sprinkle onto her lap and covering them both with her rainbow blanket. Though next week's goodbye may be even harder after a full week together, I plan to enjoy every second of it. We have a month of missed time to make up for.

CHAPTER THIRTY-SEVEN

PETER

Though I was disappointed when Nessa turned down my offer to move in with me, I never could have let her drop out of grad school after all the hard work she's put in. I just couldn't bear to leave them again. Leaving them in bed when I leave for work each morning has been hard enough, though coming home to them after a long day makes it worth it.

Matthew's court date is quickly approaching. They've been staying with me for three days now. Though we've visited Deedee nearly every day since they've been here, I really need to talk to her before we leave again in two days. With a private conversation in mind, I leave Emma and Nessa to play on the new swing set I assembled and join Deedee in the kitchen.

"What can I help with?" I wash my hands at the sink before slipping an apron over my head. I couldn't care less if my clothes get dirty, but an apron is required when cooking with Aunt Deedee.

"Chop these, dear." She hands me carrots, celery, and an onion as I dig a cutting board out from underneath the oven.

"I want to run something by you." My voice is hesitant. This isn't ideal, but being away from Nessa and Emma is no longer bearable.

After four torturous weeks and finally having them back in my life for good, I cannot go back to only seeing them on the weekends.

"I'll be fine, dear." She has always been able to read me like an open book. Today is no exception, apparently.

"You don't even know what I was going to say."

She side-eyes me as she sautés chicken on the stove. "You want to move in with Nessa."

"Okay. So, you do know what I was going to say. We'll visit often, and if something needs to be fixed and I can't get here, I'll send someone out to do it. I hate not being near you, but—"

She doesn't let me finish before jumping in. "But you've finally found happiness. You deserve it, Peter. I am a grown woman. I can manage without you. I can mobile order now, remember? I promise I'll be okay."

It's not exactly what I was planning to say, but close enough. I wrap my arms around her, careful not to touch her with my hands now covered in onion. I know she can manage without me, I just like being close to her if she needs anything. I mean it when I say we'll visit as often as possible.

On Friday, Emma wakes us before my alarm goes off, giving us plenty of time to get ready before we head to court. Showing up together is a huge statement, one we've discussed at length for days now. Nonetheless, Nessa is nervous about the fallout. Surely he's not stupid enough to lash out at us while we're inside the courthouse, so I'm hoping to get inside before he spots us. He'll, no doubt, be furious at the mere sight of us together.

Because of our tiny built-in alarm clock, we're out the door early enough to stop for coffee, a necessary treat for Nessa on a day like today. Halfway through the drive, Emma gets antsy, crying to be let out of her confinement. Despite our attempts to appease her, nothing helps until I play nursery rhymes through my car's speakers. After nearly an hour of "The Wheels on the Bus" on repeat, we pull up in front of Duane's house.

He's waiting for us on the front porch, cup of black coffee in hand. His house is old, like Deedee's, but with none of the eclectic charm. Unlike Deedee's, there are no decorations in the front yard, but everything from the way the lawn is cut to the handprints in the concrete from when Nessa was small screams 'Duane.' His front porch spans the entire width of the house with a table and patio furniture on one side and a plastic kid's table on the other. When Emma sees him, she runs to him, immediately jumping into his arms.

"Oof," he says as Emma barrels into him. "Papa made pancakes. Are you hungry?"

"She ate a few hours ago, but I'm sure she'll eat again. She loves your Mickey Mouse pancakes." She gives her dad a quick hug before he turns to carry Emma inside.

"My pancakes are good luck. Something good always happens to me when I make her these for breakfast. I love you, Vanessa. You've got this."

A small smile plays at her lips at the sound of her nickname. God, I've missed that smile.

We pull into the courthouse fifteen minutes early. I can see Nessa's hands trembling as she reaches for the door handle, so I take her hands in mine and give them a gentle squeeze. "I'll be right beside you the entire time. We've got this."

She lets out a long sigh before pushing her door open. "I don't see his truck. Let's get inside before he gets here."

"I still can't believe they let him out of jail right before the court date," I say in a huff. The justice system has continually let Nessa down. This is just one more example of how sloppy, as Andrew put it, courts can be when it comes to domestic violence, and frankly, it pisses me off. I grab Nessa's hand and we hurry inside before Matt shows up.

We're seated inside the courtroom, directly behind the district attorney's bench when Matthew and Angie walk in. "I can't decide if I'm happy to see Angie or not," Nessa whispers as Matt's lawyer leads him to their table.

"I'm going to give her the benefit of the doubt until she shows me I shouldn't." Though it's entirely possible she doesn't want to see her son get into trouble today, she's done the right thing thus far. I can only hope she'll do it again.

"You're nicer than me. I'm still holding a grudge from years ago. She knew Matt was hurting me and said nothing, but you're right. She's definitely redeemed herself lately."

I squeeze her to me and kiss her forehead. Before I can respond, the bailiff tells everyone to rise and the judge enters the room. The district attorney states the charges as assault and battery and endangerment of a child. After he gives the judge a rundown of what happened, I'm called to the stand and sworn in. I give a full play-by-play of that day, minus the fact that I was in nothing but a towel, still wet from a post-sex shower. Part of me wants to mention it, just to rile Matt up before he takes the stand, but it's not worth the risk of making my testimony less credible.

Nessa is called to the stand after me, giving her version of events that includes her going out back with Emma so she wouldn't have to watch his attack on me.

When Matthew is finally called to the stand, nerves that had dissipated after our own testimonies come flooding back. Nessa's knee keeps bouncing into mine, and I can hear her sharp intake of breath every few seconds. I place my hand on her knee, weighing it down, and give a squeeze of reassurance before turning my attention back to Matthew.

His lawyer prompts him to tell his version of events from that night, and my ears instantly perk up like a dog on the prowl. Though I'm certain he's about to spew nothing but bullshit, I want to hear every word.

"Your honor, they're blowing this way out of proportion. Yes, I lost my temper, and for that, I am sorry. But I can't just let her whore around in front of my daughter, you know? What will that teach her? That it's okay to sleep around even when you're still married?"

Nessa's grip on my hand tightens as his lawyer approaches him. Though she's whispering to him quiet enough that I can't hear what she's saying, it's clear she's reprimanding him for what he just said. A few moments later, she backs away from the stand and again prompts him to tell the judge exactly what happened.

"Sorry, Your Honor. I'm just very worked up about all of this. Look, they even came in together today. Obviously he didn't learn his lesson."

"I thought you said he's charismatic when he needs to be?" I lean toward Nessa to whisper in her ear. Though I'm glad his testimony is not going well, I expected him to be charming and convincing.

"He usually is. Angie is the only reason the judge sided with me last time. He had a sob story ready to go," she whispers back to me.

"Us being here together really got to him." Though I don't know if that's true or not, the thought makes me smile. I'm not usually a vindictive person, but knowing that Nessa and I together continues to piss him off gives me immense pleasure.

Once Matthew is done shooting himself in the foot, Angie is called to the stand. Though I'm fairly confident that she'll be open and honest about what happened that day, after his testimony, it won't matter. There's no coming back from that.

As I'd hoped, Angie's version of events matches mine and Nessa's. As soon as closing statements are given, the judge gives his ruling. Maybe it always happens that quickly, but I like to think this was just an easy verdict after Matthew spent his entire time on stand incriminating himself.

As we approach Duane's house, my fist raised towards the door, Nessa walks in without knocking. After calling out for them a couple times, we head to the backyard, pausing in the doorway when we spot them. Emma is on a pink trike, Duane bent over behind her pushing her back and forth on the patio as she giggles and cheers.

Nessa snaps a picture with her phone before sliding the back door open and walking out onto the patio. "That cannot be comfortable for you." She chuckles as he places both hands on his lower back to stand up.

"I'm going to be feeling that for a week." He chuckles. "But she was having so much fun. I couldn't *not* push her." I swap places with him, allowing him to chat with Nessa about court while I push Emma back and forth on the trike.

"So, tell me. How did it go?"

"It went better than I expected. He was not happy to see Peter and me together, and I think that threw him off. He went on this big rant about me being a whore and Peter deserving what he got."

"The judge found him guilty, then?" I'm focused on keeping the trike upright, so I can't see his expression, but his satisfaction is apparent in his voice.

"On the assault and battery charge, yes. He found him not guilty of child endangerment because I took her outside, and she didn't get hurt. Six months in jail is still a win in my book."

Though they're still talking about Matt, I'm no longer listening. Instead of walking her back and forth, I'm sprinting and making vroom sounds as we go. She's giggling at the top of her lungs, and I don't want to miss a second of it. I'm happy there are finally consequences for Matthew's behavior, but I'd much rather concentrate on Emma right now. Now that I've finally got my little girl back, nothing else matters quite as much.

Though I'm completely out of breath and a cramp is forming in my side, I keep running back and forth until she's finally ready to stop. The whole time, I'm thinking about how to ask Nessa what she thinks about me moving closer to—or better yet, in with—her.

After Deedee gave her blessing the other night, I ran outside to tell her but chickened out. I wanted to ask her right away, but with court looming over us, I knew it was best to wait. Now, I'm just worried that she might say no. It's totally understandable that she may still want to wait until she's divorced or until we've been together for longer. After losing the last month with them, I'm ready to be with them every single day. I just hope she's ready too.

CHAPTER THIRTY-EIGHT

NESSA

Today's the day! The day we officially become a household of three, and my heart has been racing with anticipation ever since Emma woke us up this morning. After Matt's court hearing last week, Peter asked what I thought about him moving closer to us even though I'm still dealing with all the divorce chaos. Without skipping a beat, I asked if he'd rather move in than find a new place here, and he said yes!

Relief immediately flooded his face before he lifted Emma into the air, spinning her above his head just like he does with Daisy. Seeing them celebrate together solidified the choice in my mind. Peter is what's best for Emma. He always has been and always will be.

Though I left Matt nearly two years ago, I've spent a vast majority of that time still playing right into his hands. Between everything I'm learning in my counseling classes, countless hours with my own counselor, and having to learn some lessons the hard way, I've grown so much in myself in that time. Not only is my self-confidence finally back, but I no longer care about Matthew's threats. I have no doubt that he will continue to do everything he can to make my life hell. I just no longer care what he thinks. Taking the power to make me miserable away from him, I have a renewed sense of control over my life and my own happiness.

After my phone call with Dylan about being subpoenaed for Matt's hearing, I finally told him all about Peter and I, down to the last detail. I want him to be prepared if Matt does try to bring it up in court. Dylan knows when we first started dating, when he met Emma for the first time, and all about Matt's attack and subsequent legal troubles. At first, he was weary of the idea, afraid that it wouldn't look good in court, just like I was. But after learning about Matthew's rant during his testimony, he agreed that it shouldn't hurt my case. Like Peter has said since the start, we're in this together. It just took me a little longer to realize it.

My tiny little house, furnished solely with Marketplace finds, feels like a home now more than ever. We sold my too small bed and mismatched couches, replacing them with Peter's much nicer, matching furniture that doesn't yet have jelly smudges on the cushions. We've stored Emma's crib in the attic where it will wait for the little Nessa and Peter's to come—hopefully sooner rather than later. In its place sits the toddler bed from Peter's house, Barney comforter and all. Most importantly, we now get Peter full time.

After the court hearing last week, we stayed the weekend at our house, cleaning out space in the closet for Peter and deciding which furniture would stay before going back to his place for one last visit. My classes start back up on Monday, so I spent my last week of summer break packing up Peter's house and visiting Deedee as often as possible. Though she's only two hours away, I know Peter is worried about leaving her. Not seeing her every week will be a huge adjustment for him. Emma and I moving to Peter's just wasn't a viable option. Nonetheless, I feel so guilty that he's leaving his beloved aunt behind.

As I carefully unload the last few boxes with my one good

hand, Peter calls out to me from our bedroom. I walk in to find them both in Emma's bed, fully under the covers, soft giggles emanating from both of them.

"Where did Emma go? I thought I heard her laughing in here." I pretend to search all around the room, lifting blankets and peeking into dresser drawers, until she finally pops out.

"Boo!" she yells as she pops up like a spring and he throws the comforter off the bed.

"There you are! I thought I lost you!" I feign relief with the back of my hand to my forehead.

She giggles before hiding under the covers and popping out again and again.

"Welcome home," I say as I show Peter where I put all of his belongings. This was easily the most effortless move in the history of moving. Besides his bed, couch, and recliner, he only had four boxes worth of stuff plus a suitcase with all his clothes. We fit everything into his car in one trip and had everything put away the same day.

After a blissful weekend, our first as a family unit, this next week is a busy one. Today is the first day of my second to last semester of grad school. That's a mouthful, but an exciting one. After the three classes I'm taking this fall, I will complete an internship in the spring before graduation in May. After months of thought, I've decided to intern in a school setting, allowing me to become a school counselor once I graduate. Though I originally wanted to be a counselor in the community setting, this will allow me to have summers and school breaks off with Emma once she heads to kindergarten.

I'm not the only one embarking on a new journey this week. When he initially mentioned moving here, I was hesitant to agree because I knew it meant him leaving a job he loves, but of course, Peter had a plan. He'd already talked to his boss about working from home a majority of the time. Though he will have to be in the office a few days a month, he now gets to work from the comfort of our bedroom more often than not. With Emma and I banned from the bedroom during working hours, we've had to find ways to occupy ourselves without disturbing him. No small task with a toddler in tow.

In an attempt to keep Emma from bothering him while he works today, we went with Papa to find me a new car. We finally found the perfect one: a minivan with plenty of storage for Emma's things and room to expand our family. After filling out all of the paperwork, including my dad putting a down payment and co-signing on a loan, we're finally ready to leave. We purchased a new car seat before heading here, and I'm buckling it into the seat behind the driver's side when my phone rings.

"My phone is in my purse. Can you grab it?" I call to my dad as I finally hear the click of the latch tucked underneath the seat back.

"Sure, honey." I hear him rustling through my purse before he finally pulls it out.

I quickly swipe to answer before it goes to voicemail. "Hello?"

"Hi, Nessa. It's Dylan." He keeps talking, but I'm not listening. This cannot be happening again. Not right as everything is falling back into place. I can hear my heartbeat in my ears as my throat tightens in an attempt to hold back the tears.

"Hello? Nessa, are you there?"

"Sorry. I'm here." I take a deep breath and brace myself for the hit.

"Did you hear what I said?"

"No, sorry. Say it again, please." Or don't. I'd rather live in my little bubble of peace for just a little bit longer.

"Matthew's lawyer called. They want to settle."

I let out a loud, ear piercing scream. "Oh my god. Oh my god."

In my celebration, I dropped my phone and probably scared every single person at this dealership, but I couldn't care less. I have my daughter, the love of my life, and Matthew's lawyer wants to settle. *Settle!*

My hands shaking, I bring the phone back to my ear as Dylan finishes giving me the details of our new mediation appointment. Next week, I will finally have all of this behind me. I'm trying not to get my hopes up, but Matthew's lawyer wanting to settle has got to be a good sign.

I quickly fire off a text to Peter with the good news before hugging my dad goodbye and pulling out of the parking lot. I can't help but cry happy tears as I drive home to Peter in my new-to-me minivan with our sweet daughter safely buckled into her new car seat. After a long, hard battle, I can finally see the light at the end of the tunnel—something I thought I'd go a lifetime without seeing again.

Emma and I walk through the front door to the smell of Deedee's famous cinnamon rolls in the oven, no doubt Peter's way of celebrating the good news. Emma calls for him and he scoops her out of my arms before planting a long, tender kiss to my lips. If you'd have asked me two years ago what my life would look like right now, I'd never have guessed... *this*. Though the road here was tumultuous, I'd do it again in a heartbeat for Peter. For Emma. For us.

EPILOGUE
PETER

18 months later

Tomorrow is the two year anniversary of my blind date with Nessa. It's also the day I finally get to make her my wife. I hear hustle and bustle out in the hallway, no doubt our wedding planner making sure everything is perfect for the big day tomorrow. The rehearsal dinner is set to start any minute now. Andrew and Willow flew in a few days ago so he could perform all of his best man duties. Andrew, Rob, and my cousin, Steve, are in the groom's suite with me, waiting to be called out for rehearsal when a small knock comes at the door.

"Daddy!" Emma's little voice calls out.

She's three and a half now and has been calling me daddy instead of Petey for the last year or so. Nessa and I both agreed that she could call me whichever name she wants, especially now that Matthew is out of the picture for good.

When Nessa showed up at mediation after his lawyer decided to settle, he offered to sign his rights away as long as Nessa agreed to let Angie remain in her life. After the way Angie handled everything, saying yes to the last thing he'd ever ask of us was easy. Emma now stays with Angie one weekend per month and is home with us the rest of the time.

"Hey, sweet girl. Where's Mommy?" I ask as I open the door. Emma and Daisy are our flower girl team, and they're supposed to be with Nessa and Nora getting ready for tonight's practice run.

"In her room. I bored."

She looks adorable in a pretty purple dress, her hair tucked neatly behind her ears. Though it's not the dress she'll be wearing tomorrow, it is the same color as the bridesmaids dresses and compliments the daisy in her hair perfectly.

"I know just the thing to cure your boredom. I need some help," I say as I carry her to where I was sitting.

Since we aren't wearing our tuxes tonight, we've all been ready for rehearsal for the last thirty minutes. Instead of drinking like my groomsmen are, I'm putting the finishing touches on a wedding present for Nessa. In order to avoid seeing her before she walks down the aisle, she'll be staying here with her friends tonight. Since they'll be getting ready here while I get ready at home, I'll sneak this bag onto her pillow after dinner for her to find once I'm gone.

Emma sits in my lap, dutifully stuffing tissue paper into the bag as I attempt to arrange what's inside as best I can. My job is made a little more difficult now that there's enough tissue paper for a lifetime in the way, but I'm managing.

We finish up just as the wedding planner pokes her head into our room. "Has anyone seen the littlest flower girl? We're ready to do a couple practice run-throughs but can't find her anywhere."

"I here." Emma giggles as she slides off of my lap and runs out the door.

Rehearsal goes by without a hitch, and even Emma nails it on the first try. Before we sit down for the rehearsal dinner, I sneak off to plant my present in Nessa's room. As I turn to rejoin everyone at the festivities, I see Nessa and Emma watching me from the doorway.

"You little narc." I laugh as Emma points to me with an apologetic look.

"She definitely ratted you out." They're both laughing as Nessa snatches her present off the bed.

"Hey! You're not supposed to open that until tonight."

She sticks her tongue out at me as she and Emma rip the tissue paper from the bag and begin pulling everything out. They're now surrounded by the bag's contents, Nessa beginning to cry as Emma tears open one of the chocolate truffles.

"This is too much," she says with a sniffle. She's clutching a light gray onesie to her chest with one hand on her belly.

"Did you read it?"

She chuckles through a hiccup. "'Gilmore in training.' I love it. If only little bean here would actually let me drink some coffee."

A few weeks ago, after Nessa's wedding dress fitting revealed her dress to be a little tight around the middle, she decided to take a pregnancy test. As soon as the two pink lines appeared, I immediately began researching baby essentials online and stumbled across this onesie with a Luke's Diner coffee mug on the front. Though the mere thought of coffee makes her nauseous, she's nearing the end of the first trimester and hoping the coffee hiatus will end as she enters the second trimester.

She holds the onesie up towards Emma. "Look, sweet girl. This is for the baby in mommy's belly."

Emma shoves the chocolate into her mouth before placing her hand on Nessa's belly. Though it's far too early for us to feel anything, I've been resting my hand on her belly every night, Emma right there with me. Nessa gives me a quick kiss before loading her two most craved items—chocolate and Cheetos—back into the bag along with a Polaroid camera for instant memories of our special day and a handwritten note detailing how happy the three of them have already made me. Hand in hand, we rejoin the celebration with our family and friends on this last night before we become an official family.

The next morning, my groomsmen and I make it back to our venue a few hours before wedding time. Ashley, our wedding planner, has taken care of everything. With not much left for me to do, I take a stroll through the flower garden and then down toward the waterfall that will be the backdrop of our ceremony. Passing Andrew and Willow on my way, I see Duane and Deedee admiring the waterfall as I approach.

"Congratulations, dear. You deserve it." Aunt Deedee wraps me in a hug before kissing my cheek. "I wish your mother was here to see this. She'd be so proud of you."

I wipe a stray tear from my eye as Duane takes his turn to hug me. "Welcome to the family, Son. We're glad to have you."

As the three of us walk back toward the venue, Deedee nudges me with her elbow. "Look, dear."

I turn towards the flower garden just in time to see Andrew tuck a curly, brown lock of hair out of Willow's face. I can only hope that one day he sees that some people really are worth the risk. With his philosophy on love, he may never experience heartbreak, but he'll never know the power of holding the love of his life in his arms either.

As the ceremony is about to begin, I stand beside my brother, waiting for my soulmate to walk down the aisle. I can't help but reminisce about the journey we took to get here. I'm pulled from memories of our first date as "Bridal Chorus" begins to play. Tears fill my eyes as I see my daughter making her way towards me on the best day of my life, flowers falling all around her. A breath catches in my throat as Nessa enters the room, her arm intertwined with Duane's.

When they reach me, he gives her a quick kiss on her cheek before hugging me again and taking his seat.

"You look absolutely breathtaking," I whisper in her ear as she takes her place beside me, both of us turning to face the officiant.

With her hand in mine, I feel like the luckiest man in the world. Despite the wild journey we took to get here, having my one true love and our two beautiful children by my side makes every last bump in the road worth it—and I have Nora and her meddling to thank for all of it.

AUNT DEEDEE'S GOOEY CINNAMON ROLLS

Ingredients
   Dough
   - 1 cup warm milk
   - 1 packet of instant yeast
   - 2 large eggs (room temp preferred)
   - 1/3 cup of salted butter (melted)
   - 1/2 cup of granulated sugar
   - 1 teaspoon of salt
   - 4 1/2 cups of all purpose flour

Filling
   - 1/2 cup of salted butter (almost melted)
   - 1 cup of brown sugar
   - 2 tablespoons of cinnamon
   - 1/2 cup of heavy cream (to pour over baking rolls)

Cream Cheese Frosting
   - 1 block of cream cheese
   - 1 cup of powdered sugar (sifted)
   - 1 teaspoon of vanilla

AUNT DEEDEE'S GOOEY CINNAMON ROLLS

Instructions

Prep dough

1. Pour warm milk over yeast and mix
2. Add eggs, butter, and sugar. Mix.
3. Add salt and 4 cups of flour. Mix until combined and let sit for 5 minutes.
4. Beat dough for about 5 minutes until smooth (add the extra 1/2 cup of flour if needed). Dough should be sticking to sides of bowl but slightly firm.
5. Put dough in oiled or buttered large bowl to proof. Turn oven on to lowest setting and then turn it off once it reaches temperature. Place a pan or bowl of hot water on the bottom rack of the oven to provide moisture.
6. Once oven is heated and turned off, proof for about 40 minutes or until doubled in size.

While dough proofs, prepare cinnamon filling.

7. Partially melt butter then add brown sugar and cinnamon. Mix.

Time to roll!

8. Once proofed, turn the dough out onto a floured surface and then dust the top with flour.
9. Roll out to about 24x15 sized rectangle then add the cinnamon filling to the top and spread to the edges.
10. Starting on one of the longer sides, tightly roll the dough to form a long tube shape.
11. Cut into 12 even rolls and place into a deep 9x12 pan.
12. Preheat oven to 375 degrees while roll proofs for another 20-30 minutes.*
13. Bake at 375 for 25 minutes stopping halfway through to pour warmed heavy cream over the top.

AUNT DEEDEE'S GOOEY CINNAMON ROLLS

Prepare cream cheese icing.

14. Add cream cheese, sifted powdered sugar, and vanilla to a bowl and mix until smooth.

15. Allow rolls to partially cool then spread cream cheese icing over the top!

16. Enjoy and pretend Aunt Deedee is giving you unsolicited (but totally necessary) advice!

* Option to slow proof in the fridge overnight and bake in the morning. Bake time may differ for cold rolls.

Aunt Deedee is one of my favorite side characters, and I couldn't *not* give you all her famous cinnamon roll recipe. But, there was just one problem: I can't bake to save my life! So, I presented my dilemma to my fellow book babes of Instagram. After sifting my way through the various recipes submitted, I finally landed on this one.

These cinnamon rolls are delicious and perfect for an afternoon with the sassy, caring, always-right Aunt Deedee. What makes them even more special is the fact that they come from another indie author! Courtney Bowlin, author of Green Witch, was once a pastry chef who loved putting her own twist on classic recipes, and that's exactly how these rolls were born! Courtney often sold these to local coffee shops—even decorating them with green, purple, and yellow sprinkles for Mardi Gras!

I hope you'll join us in re-creating Aunt Deedee's cinnamon rolls for the ones you love.

ACKNOWLEDGMENTS

At the beginning of 2025, I had no idea that I was even going to try to get this story out there. The fact that you're holding it in your hand right now means my village rallied behind me and made it happen! Pen would never have hit paper if my sister, Emily, hadn't encouraged me to take the leap. None of this would have begun if it weren't for you. Thanks for knowing when to push.

Publishing a book was so much more work than I ever could have imagined. I spent countless hours holed up in a library study room, writing plot ideas on the shower wall in kid's bath Crayons so I wouldn't forget, and editing (and then editing some more). The behind the scenes was equally as important. It would have taken fifteen years to publish anything if it weren't for a supportive partner at home encouraging me and holding down the fort. To my happily ever after, thank you so much for believing in me.

I also want to thank my family for all their love and support (like buying this even though it's his least favorite genre. Thanks, Dad!). Thank you so much to the entire indie author community and all the beautiful bookstagram souls I've become great friends with. Thank you to my beta readers, my wonderful editors, Melissa McGovern and Kristen Hamilton, and Aubrey Labitigan for the beautiful cover and art work.

Last, but certainly not least, THANK YOU to each and every one of you. It means so much to me that I got to share this story with you. I appreciate you more than you know. Thank you, from the bottom of my heart.

ABOUT THE AUTHOR

Nikki Witt was born and raised in southwest Missouri, where she lives with her partner and their three kids. A lifelong lover of *Gilmore Girls*, iced coffee, and emotionally rich stories, she rekindled her passion for writing while taking time away from her career as a school counselor to be home with her young children.

Nikki's passion for healing, emotional growth, and wholehearted love are woven throughout her work. Her stories explore what it means to rebuild after trauma, choose love again, and do the hard work of becoming whole. When she's not writing, she can be found chasing kids, sipping coffee, and running.

If you enjoyed this story, follow my journey on Instagram: @nikkiwittauthor. Books two and three in this series coming in 2026!

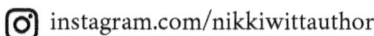 instagram.com/nikkiwittauthor

www.ingramcontent.com/pod-product-compliance
Lightning Source LLC
LaVergne TN
LVHW040042080526
838202LV00045B/3449